WINDWALKER

A NOVEL OF BEDLAM

SABRINA FLYNN

Windwalker

a novel of Bedlam

SABRINA FLYNN

WINDWALKER is a work of fiction. Names, characters, places, and incidents are either the product of the author's overactive imagination or are chimerical delusions of a tired mind. Any resemblance to actual persons, living or dead, events, or locales is entirely due to the reader's wild imagination (that's you).

Published by Ink & Sea Publishing
www.sabrinaflynn.com

ISBN 978-1-955207-16-4
eBook ISBN 978-1-955207-17-1

Cover Art by MerryBookRound
www.merrybookround.com

to Vivien's hair, Sherman

1. DEATH

Bad things happen all the time. For a rat like me, there's a mucky rainbow of bad. There's the foot stuck in the mud kind, the cold and hungry kind, and the shadows that roam the pea soup. Worse is the bad I don't know about—the kind that gets stuck in your throat. This was one of those. It was the day I died.

2. THE RAT

BEFORE

THE BAD THAT DAY WAS A MAN: TWO LEGS, A LARGE GUT, AND A face covered by a plague mask. He stank like me, of river muck.

My respirator, little more than a tin can filled with moss, came undone. Foul air filled my lungs. I scrambled to retrieve it, even as I threw myself away from his grubby hands. His bulk came full out of the pea soup, and he loomed over me. A hand locked on my ankle. I kicked. But runt that I was, a child with no age, I only made him laugh.

The man plucked me into the air, and that's when I felt the eel clamp around my stick-like limb. *Slurp*. It was a faint sound, but to my ears it sounded as loud as the thunder overhead.

"Got another!" The voice came grating from the mask, like scraping rocks.

I fought, of course. Teeth, nails, a flurry of limbs. I was a two-headed cat with seven toes. It bothered the man enough that he pressed a hand to his belt. The eel delivered a shock. It jolted over my skin like the pricks of a thousand needles, leaving me convulsing in his hand.

Mud swayed below me. I was a limp fish. I smelled piss—my own. It wasn't flowing down my leg—that would be too civil, dignified even. Upside down as I was, it dripped in my face.

"It's a rat," the catcher said. If I was a rat, he was a rock. A big, dumb one. He stomped through the river muck, squelching and sucking his way towards the embankment wall. And I had been so close to escaping.

The Rock snapped my cobbled respirator back over my nose and mouth. I sucked in a breath. This far down the river Styx the fog was toxic. My lungs felt tight, but not from the fog —that poison had wormed its way into my blood the day I was birthed. This was the tightness that fear brought. I wanted to twist, turn, anything, but my muscles had a grudge against my body. There wasn't much I could do but perfect my fish imitation.

The man squelched up to a cart pulled by a hunched figure in a cloak. With a swing, I was tossed into the cart, which was full of other unfortunate rats. My kith were as wide-eyed as me, mirrors to my pounding heart. We were the fools who were snatched and never came back.

I closed my eyes and imagined my legs, ankles, and toes.

Move, I ordered.

If the big toe, or even the little, ever obeyed, I'll never know. A tarp was tossed over us, and the cart lurched forward. Bells jangled insanely, a warning crushed by fog and thrown out only in pieces to fellow travelers. I was done in. And I had no coin for the Ferryman.

But enough maudlin talk. Back to my death.

3. THE FALL

I HEARD IT BEFORE I EVER SAW IT, BEING UNDER A TARP AS I was. It sounded like a market, gathered at what was likely a crossroads. Hawkers were crying themselves hoarse, steam hissed from somewhere close, and there were all sorts of shouts—from grunts, and prigs, and growling mutts. All the denizens of the Below.

The tarp was ripped away, and I blinked against sudden light. The fog was alive with lights. Leeries had lit up the crossroads till it glowed. I tried to twitch, but the eel had me tight.

Rock and his lackeys dragged us rats from the cart, and dropped us to land as we might. *Plop*. Muck cushioned my fall against stone. Cobblestones. This wasn't just any crossroads market. This was *the* market.

The Bazaar.

But what other destination would there be for a cartload of rats? I didn't really know. Being a rat, the realm of my knowledge was slim, but I had heard rumors, whispers in the dim, which made the likes of me keep clear of any road with stone underfoot.

I would've spat in the name of Luck, but there was the matter of the eel. Right. I turned my eyes from the brightness, and concentrated inward, to that starving, empty pit I called a gut. A muscle twitched. I'd flexed my stomach! But before I could triumph overly much, a catcher grabbed my ankle and dragged me across the square.

I was privy to a great deal of muck on that brief journey. And feet. Muck's the only word for it. It's a stew of swampy mud, rubbish, and shit simmering under a thousand feet. It clings to everything. The denizens of the Below are born from muck, and we go right back into it when we die. Our bones give it a grisly texture.

The other rats and me were thrown into a cage. A rusty metal door clanged shut, and the eel released its paralyzing grip, but not its hold. I could move again.

I grabbed a bar and hauled myself to my feet. My head hit the top of the cage, and I hunched down. The cage was half my height, which wasn't very high at all.

Muck-caked boots stomped by as I blinked against the light. Figures came out of the fog draped head to toe in various clothing: hooded cloaks, longcoats, mud slickers, even a few with armor that hissed and steamed with every step. And respirators. Not makeshift respirators like mine, but the real deal. The natty kind with designs, even a few with gold inlays. And goggles that weren't pieced together from broken bits. There was money here.

If the buyers glanced our way, I didn't know—I stared awestruck at a stone monolith. Limited life that I'd had, I'd heard they were called towers once upon a time. But I'd never seen one so big. It dominated the fogline. A maze of iron pipes twisted around its foundation before climbing upwards. Leeries had lit lamps all along its base, but even without those lights, the pipes were eerily visible. Sickly-green lichen glowed faintly on the iron, giving me the impression of a great stone body with its guts turned inside out.

I pressed my cheek to the bars, and rolled my eye, trying to get a better view. As a rule, we rats stayed as far away from towers as we did from stone underfoot. Both were bad luck.

A crier was hawking his wares from a nearby stage. "Good breeding stock! Clear eyes. Teeth intact! Scared witless!"

"Ten coils!" a man's voice answered.

Chains rattled nearby. And food. Scents of curry and meat called to my stomach, which growled a hearty response.

A fellow rat in the corner of our cage was crying. We were all caked with muck and wearing dumpy respirators; the only thing visible was our eyes. Red. That's where we got our names. Rats, the four-legged kind, have red eyes and so did we. We were the lowest of the low in the Below. We weren't even boys or girls, just rats—an ungendered mass of unwanted vermin.

I was staring at my fellow rat, wondering where they got the energy to cry, when a hush fell over the area. A wake of silence heralded something more, as the air went cold.

I pressed my face back to the bars.

A figure strode out of the fog. It was covered head to toe in a red, tattered shroud, and it moved like a ghost through the fog. Round black eyes, no nose, no mouth, long curving fingers with tendrils of mist dripping from the tips. The wraith-like figure held a chain, and at the end of the chain was a thin man who was squirming and struggling against his restraints. The prisoner's respirator had come loose, and he was gasping for air, unable to scream. His glowing eyes were puffy from abuse and I was sure there was blood mingling with the muck that smeared his face.

We rats shrank back, and the others in the market gave the shrouded figure a wide berth, scrambling to get out of its way.

Some even hid their faces from the thing. It was long minutes before anyone moved. But as soon as the air warmed and the ground thawed, the bazaar went back into high swing. I didn't have time to wonder what that thin man had done, where he was headed, or what the shrouded thing was. My own situation was dire enough.

"We be at the Bazaar," a rat by my side whispered. Again, red eyes, muck-covered face, and matted hair. Nothing to distinguish one wretch from the next. I wagered I looked the same.

"Am I looking dumb?" I asked.

"Dumb as dumb. We're all in for getting snatched."

I couldn't argue. "How do we fly?" A small rat was gnawing at an iron bar with their teeth. That, I was sure, was not going to work. But I gave them Luck's blessing for trying all the same.

I turned to my eel. It was latched tight, but not secreting its shocking poison. I touched it. Cool and malleable. Dormant, for now.

"Don't," my fellow rat said. This one had large red eyes, the pupils barely visible.

"We dead if we don't." I got a fistful of muck from the ground and smeared it all over the eel. Then pushed, trying to slip it off my bony ankle. It buzzed. Then shocked. I landed on my back and stared at the fog tickling the giant monolith. A man laughed, then lifted his mask to spit down at me.

And so I was.

Plenty of rats had gotten snatched in my short life. It was a daily grind. I never thought I'd be one of them, though. Quick and smart, I'd always managed to slip through the Catchers' fingers. But this was not my day. Luck had run clean out. I'd been distracted, watching the fog swirl of all things. It was hypnotic-like, and the sight had awakened a small flutter of beauty in my wretched heart.

Stunned as I was again, I lay for a time watching the fog swirl just as it had done earlier. What moved it, I wondered? Where was the fog going? Was it alive? Did it breathe?

The eel went dormant. My fingers twitched and I stirred, but didn't get far. I was busy being entranced. I reached out, touching the space between bars, as if I could grasp the fog in my hand and hold it tight.

A leerie towering over us on stilts walked to our cage, his fire sputtering in its globe. He lifted his soot-covered goggles and squinted down at us. The fellow had beautiful blue eyes. It was more color than I had ever seen in my muck-filled life.

"Not a clear-eyed one in the bunch," he said with a cluck of his tongue. "You won't get a coil for this lot."

"They're *rats*," Rock grated. "Bound for the Sweepers. I'll give you one for a jot."

"They're not even worth a half snip." Blue Eyes snapped down his goggles and moved on.

Sweepers. My heart wanted to burst from its cage. The other rats started clawing at the muck, trying to burrow under the bars, but there was metal underneath too. A Sweeper. *No, no, no,* my mind screamed.

Sweepers were every rat's worst nightmare, and let me tell you, we had some colorful ones. We didn't know what they did to rats. But we'd *heard* of the horrors they inflicted on our kind.

Rock attached a thick hook to our cage. The hook was attached to a chain that disappeared in the fogline. Rock slammed his billy club against the chain, and the cage jerked. With a sucking '*pop*' it broke free from the muck, leaving us clinging to the bars. As the ground fell away, the cage swung with the panic of rats moving from one side to the other. I stayed where I was. No use wasting energy.

"Get off!" I hollered at a rat, shoving them away. "No use is this." But they had lost their wits long before they had been trapped in this cage.

People below laughed and pointed, as the swinging cage was brought closer to the tower. Leeries on stilts raised their fire globes on long poles, illuminating slick pipes and stone. Other leeries waited far above, perched on the guts of the tower, their lights bobbing in the gray.

I looked up at the chain attached to our cage, wondering what was holding us above ground. As we rose into the air, the fog thinned and I spotted more leerie lights bobbing above. The chain was attached to a metal skeleton that resembled an upraised arm—a crane used for lifting heavy loads.

Rock touched his belt, and my eel started humming. I braced for another shock, but none came. Instead it lit up bright, a glowing blue band of light around my ankle. The other rats fell still, and their eyes grew wide, as they whispered of the mark of death. Not a one of us knew what a mark of death looked like, but this was as good as any other in our pathetic lives.

"Now they be dropping us lot," a rat whispered in terror.

"No use catching us. What for we be dying in this cage?" I asked boldly.

"Sweepers be eating us," the rat argued.

I swatted their head. "What meat we got, muck-brain?"

To my surprise, my logic held. My kith calmed enough to still the cage from swinging back and forth.

Little did I know that Sweepers didn't have use for logic.

The crane turned to the right and our cage swung with it, then it was dropped. We all screamed as the chain rattled. But the gory end I imagined didn't come. The cage jerked to a stop just above the ground. I peered down through the cage bars. We were centered over a circle of pitch black ichor, and the air had turned acrid and bitter.

"What the muck?" I muttered. We were destined to find out. A leerie stepped forward and touched his fire stick to the circle below us. Flames roiled across the pool of pitch. Cheering and wagering applauded our terror as heat licked our bare feet.

A ring of figures watched us through the flames. Sweepers with tall hats and fine coats—rough men who made their fortune off rats and strays.

"If you lot want to live," Rock shouted. "*Climb!*"

Instinctively, I tightened my hold on the bars. One side of the cage swung open. My side. I tumbled out, and a wide-eyed rat fell right after me. I reached out to them. For a moment their hand found mine, but then another rat fell on top of us, breaking our precarious bond. I was nearly ripped away, but I had a death grip on the cage with two of my fingers.

I watched in horror as the wide-eyed rat fell into the flames. The child's screams spurred the onlookers on. The other rats weren't as foolish as my heroic self. They saved themselves, flooding out of the cage and climbing onto its top. One by one they started clawing their way up the chain towards the crane. The flames climbed too.

My respirator came loose and fell into the fire below. Acrid smoke clogged my throat and burned my eyes; I was choking on poisonous air. I held what breath I had left, and flung my other hand towards the cage door.

The cage lurched this way and that, until it was swinging over the circle of fire. Muck this, I thought, watching my kith clawing at each other's heels. The cage had momentum now, swinging like a great bell, back and forth over the tar pit as I climbed.

With fire licking my toes, I scurried up on top of the cage.

A rat on the chain lost their grip and thudded into the flaming pit of sludge. They landed just on the edge of the pit, sending a wave of flames splattering at the audience below.

I squeezed my eyes shut, glad for the cheers that drowned out their dying screams, as I clung to the top of the cage. I reached out my hand to touch the quivering chain. The metal was heating fast. And it was clogged with a line of rats, clawing their way over their kith, towards the safety of the crane. Another rat fell, and another. The fourth fallen rat decided me. I crawled to the edge of the cage, and shifted my weight with each swing, trying to add momentum.

"Climb!" Rock bellowed. He looked directly at me, his hand hovering over his belt. If he activated my eel, I'd be roasted alive.

On the upward swing of the cage, I leapt. Flame, heat, momentum. I flew through the air and landed at the outside edge of the pit. The audience stood stunned, and I bolted at them. But it was a solid wall of brutes. A hand shoved me back and a foot kicked me towards the burning pit. Fleeing the barrage of feet and fists, I scurried for the monolithic tower. There was only one way out. Up.

Not the brightest escape, I know. But it was all I had. And it was my choice. I'd take that over the Sweepers' deadly game in a heartbeat.

I stopped at the base of the tower, in front of the maze of pipes. I didn't dare look up. The lichen was slick, so I braced my back against one wall of it and my feet against another, then started to climb the twisting guts of the thing, shimmying up at a treacherous speed as a catcher came lunging for me. I slipped his grip and kept climbing. The eel on my ankle glowed in the fog, giving off a little bubble of light. I passed a leerie, who cheered me on, then another, who tipped his cloth cap. But soon the great lichen-covered pipes gave out, and there was nothing but stone.

The last leerie standing on the piping chuckled, his light bobbing in the dim. Below, I could see a group of Sweepers, their necks craned back to watch me, while the others in the audience wagered on how far I'd get climbing.

I could see my kith now—the ones who had made it to the top of the chain. Sweepers waiting at the top had corralled the victorious rats into another prison.

"There's a secret to those eels," said the leerie with a wink. "They have a range."

I didn't pause. I didn't think. I didn't thank him. I jammed my fingers in a stone crevice, and I started to climb the naked tower, with no mind to where I was going. Only up. Up, up, up, my body screamed.

Despite the slick stones and with barely a purchase, I climbed along a vertical crack, shimmying along, jamming one small fist after another into a long, jagged line that snaked on the stone like an electric current. It was my path to freedom.

Before I knew it, the last leerie had disappeared, swallowed by fog. The Sweepers and fire, and all the gawkers were gone too. It was only me in a great sea of roiling fog. But the pea soup that I knew had changed. Greenish air had turned to silver, and I breathed easier—a great breath of the stuff. It filled my lungs, my heart and body, and gave me a needed boost.

I climbed higher, oblivious to all else.

But my path to freedom came to its end. The crevice led to a jutting ledge, like the rim of a cup. I slapped a hand onto this surehold and hauled my shaking self upwards. But the flat stone only seemed to stoke my fear as I stood all atremble on a two inch ledge. The crack had ended. The stone above was smooth and unmarked. How high did the monolith rise?

I put my back to smooth stone and edged around the ledge, my toes curling over the lip. As I rounded a corner, my fingers quested for a handhold.

The mist—for I could not call it pea soup at this height—swirled, and a touch caressed my cheek. It was playful and fleeting, and I wanted more of it.

The air around me brightened and light seared my eyes.

I squeezed my eyes shut, but savored the air's touch. Had I ever felt the like of it before? Not in the stagnant underbelly of the Below. It called to me like home.

The darkness behind my lids was red, the light was so bright. I had never even dreamed of its like. Bracing myself, I opened my eyes, and squinted through the silver mists. An orb hung high above like a giant leerie's light bobbing in the sky. I reached out a tentative hand, fingers trembling. For that brief moment, I touched the sun. Then a shock electrified my body. The eel's bite turned me to stone, and I fell.

AFTER

"THAT'S MUCKING IMPOSSIBLE, RED. NO ONE SURVIVES A FALL from that height!"

Red's not my real name; it's a nickname. Unimaginative if you ask me, but no one ever does. It's a name given me after my miraculous rebirth, you see. Not one I had from the Before.

"It's a true story, Mick." I traced an X over my chest. "I swear it on the Four Elements."

"*Five* elements," he corrected. "MUCK."

The pub erupted with laughter.

"How'd you survive?" a patron called out.

"Luck his sweet self snatched me from the Ferryman's grip," I crooned. "I fell right into a hay wagon. And here I stand to enjoy a pint with my best mates." I bowed with a sweep of arm and a cheeky grin.

Another round of laughter rippled through the pub. They took it for an embellished story, a tall tale of the best sort. But truth can be stranger than fiction. And far more dangerous.

You see, I didn't survive that fall. Not as far as I can tell. And the unknown, my friend, is the worst kind of bad.

"Luck snatched you just to tease the lot of us!" a woman hollered. The comment brought me back. I was used to the banter. Maybe even enjoyed it.

"Come on, Red. Just one night. It'll be unforgettable." That particular woman, Sally, with pretty green eyes, wanted to rub the muck off my body with her own, if you know what I mean.

"You won't forget it because it mucking won't happen," I said.

Mugs slammed down on tables, and Sally's mates elbowed her with snickers.

I gave the room a wink, and plucked up my respirator. All these years later this one was the real deal, with genuine filters, though I didn't think I needed it. After the day I died, I was reborn to a luckier life.

"The night is young yet, Red. We have trouble to make, you and me," a man named Tomas said. He was a decent sort.

I glanced through the grimy glass. A greenish fog swirled outside. It always did. "We can't know if it's sunup, sundown, or the air is on fire. But what I know is it's past *your* bedtime."

"*My* bedtime. You're the one with the wet nose here."

"Nah, Sally's is wetter than mine."

"I just have a cold," Sally said with a sneeze.

"Is Muck illness," an old man named Reece grunted.

"Isn't it all?" I asked.

A round of agreement rose sullenly.

"I'll walk with you," Tomas hopped up, and reached for his respirator.

"Why, so *I'll* protect you from Spring-heeled Jack?"

"Eh, don't say such things. Bad luck."

"I have loads of it."

Before another fellow with a noble heart and his mind not where it ought to be offered help, I flicked the voluminous hood of my longcoat up and left.

The metal door swung shut with a clang, and I stopped to survey the street. With the fog so thick, it was more of a listen. My ears were keen and my instincts keener—a leftover from my days as a rat. Nothing dire came to mind, so I made quick work of the street. I had better places to be.

5. HEIST

The leerie's lamps bobbed in the pea soup. It was dense tonight. I heard water trickling from pipes in a steady drip as I strode along a catwalk that skirted one of the sluggish canals.

My mark tonight was in Monger's Square.

Somewhere in the Above, I could see flashes in the fogline. Winks of light and distant explosions high overhead—thunder and lightning, we called it. We in the Below were accustomed to those sights and sounds. It was like the knock of a fan, rhythmic and familiar, and only dangerous when flaming debris plummeted to the ground. Which was unlucky for those hit by said debris, but lucky for the scavengers who made their way picking through remains. Such was life.

Monger's Square was lit bright to deter the likes of me. I swaggered over cobblestones that were scraped and kept clean of muck, and headed towards a tall structure. Everything was made of stone here, with luminous lichen clinging artfully to it. The vegetation made spots of brightness in the dim.

Merchants and taskmasters lived in Monger's Square. Their residences were spaced far apart. There were no alleyways or lanes, only wide spaces, bright lichen, and sentries behind high, stone walls. The merchants weren't a trusting lot, and the taskmasters even less so.

But all armor has a chink, and my specialty was finding it.

A hiss warned me. Silently I reached for a branch, and scurried up the closest tree to take shelter in its dark leaves. Two figures strode from the fog, encased in iron from head to toe, and spitting out steam with every step. Enforcers.

There was talk they weren't of the living. But I knew better. They were from the Above, sent to control the unruly. Like yours truly.

I forced myself to relax, to breathe calmly and evenly, and blend with the tree. These weren't Sniffers. This pair kept to the fences, away from the middle of the square. Then they disappeared back where they'd come from, into the fog. If I was the betting sort (which I was) I'd put my masques on another pair arriving in five minutes. The plumps did like their order.

I slipped from my perch on soundless feet, and walked at an even pace towards a stone wall topped with iron. The building that rose behind it was clean of lichen and muck, showing off its dark stone, with vertical grooves that made it look like a creased mourning drape.

Taking no chances, I adjusted my gloves (some liked to slick their iron with poison), and ran at the wall. At step three, I jumped, hit the wall, and exploded upwards, catching an iron spike. It was an easy, practiced maneuver. I pulled myself up, braced my left hand, and did a neat leap over the spikes. I landed and rolled in one, then kept moving towards the striated tower.

Without slowing, I tore off my gloves and tucked them away. The moment I touched the stone tower, I was safe. Here was a place no one could follow. Well, only a very few. There weren't many as skilled as my humble self.

I braced against the stone striations set at arm's length, stepped forward, and began to shimmy my way up the building.

This was my element. I didn't need a fire lit under me or a Sweeper with a whip driving me high to scrub stone. I climbed for the love of it.

I passed the first vent. And kept climbing. Then passed another, and I was out of the pea soup and into that silvery mist I craved. Where the air was fresh. In the Below, we didn't know night from day, only up and down, and cycles when the leeries lit their lamps. But I knew them now, or the idea of it. The fog was dark when I got to the Middling. This particular tower didn't stretch much beyond that.

There were layers to the fogline. Most only knew of three, but I knew of more: the Above, the Thinning, the Middling, the Below, and the Under Below.

Overhead, I could hear thunder and see lightning in the Above. The great ships that frequently crashed to the Below were battling again. When were they not?

At the top of the tower a statue of a woman stood on a ledge. She was on her tiptoes with her back to the world, her chin resting on her arms, seeming to peer down into the building's glass-domed roof.

I climbed up to share her ledge. A wrap of stone clung to her legs. It seemed sheer, showing off her body. A muscled back, not unlike my own, and a fine backside. I contemplated her beauty, and considered my options. Should I climb up to the dome and look for an access hatch or back down to an air shaft?

Over the sounds of battle above me, I could hear the steady thrumming of the building's air circulation fans. I weaved a coin between my fingers—the full masque I kept for luck. The Sage King for the dome or the Red Death for the shaft. That seemed fitting. I flicked the gold coin in the air and caught it. The Red Death it was.

Slipping it into my pocket, I shrugged out of my long-coat, detached my respirator, and took a deep breath of fresh air. It filled my lungs, made me feel alive. This is what I lived for.

I bundled my respirator up in my longcoat, and made it into a pack using straps sewn on the inside. I slung it over my back, dropped down, and turned myself around in a kind of mimicry of the statue. I hung from the ledge, dangling from a deadly height. The fog was deceiving. It was thick enough to believe I was only five feet from the ground, but there were probably a good hundred feet between me and my best mate, Death.

Hanging by one hand from the ledge, I reached for a vertical striation, grabbed it, then jammed my toes against the stone. I had special shoes designed for this very thing—a kind of slipper molded to my foot with a stiff gumshoe sole that gripped the smoothest surfaces. I climbed down, one foothold to the next. The vent I'd seen was a good ways down, and off to the right. Clinging to stone, I made my way over, with tight grips and careful steps.

A decorative mesh plate covered the air shaft. Vents were the holes that Sweepers drove children into with whips and fire. Rats, orphans, and castaways who were forced to climb (and often die) scrubbing the stones and air shafts of plump lords. My ordeal in the Bazaar from Before hadn't been a game; it was a trial to weed out weak slaves. Sometimes I wondered what'd happened to those others rats that day, the ones who made it up the chain only to be caught in the cage at the top. Most days, I tried not to think about them.

The grate swung open without a noise. No one ever locked vents this far up. If the guards, walls, and height weren't deterrent enough, the razor-sharp fans in the vents were plenty scary.

I slipped inside. It was snug, and while I was no longer short, I was still slim. The ceiling pressed on my improvised pack as I climbed down a shaft. Rough stone and four walls. It was easy enough to brace myself with my gumshoes on the sides.

Thunk, thunk, thunk, a steady sound. I let the rhythm of it wash over me, until my heart seemed to beat with the whirr of the fan. The fan soon came into view. I edged within two feet of it to rest on a lip. Though large and powerful enough to move air through the tower, the blades were thick and slow.

Thunk, thunk, thunk. A three bladed fan. *Thunk, thunk*—I dropped before the third *thunk.* The blade whooshed over my head. My hands and feet shot out to brake my fall. I braced myself in the vertical shaft and stopped to listen, but the fan's noise was all-consuming.

The air was sweet here. Rich. Moving carefully, I climbed down the shaft until I came to a maze. No matter how high the tower, no matter how fortified the building, everyone needed air and the ductwork provided it.

As I crawled through the bowels of the beast, I peeked through grates. Guards were patrolling corridors, but not many. There were gold gilt mirrors, white marble walls, statues and even blooming flowers. Tapestries and silks. The Master of the Sweepers Union lived like a king.

It didn't take long to find what I wanted: a bed big enough for four people, plush carpets, a tub that could have watered a rookery, and perfume that tickled my nose. I dug into my bundle to attach my respirator before I sneezed.

I listened; the room was empty. I checked the grate to make sure there were no bells on it. It wasn't hinged, so I stuck my fingers through its decorative openings, and pushed. It popped out of the wall. Rather than let it fall, I stuck a hook into a mortar crack and hung the cover there. Then I lowered myself down onto a wardrobe, replaced the cover, and plucked my little hook from the wall. It was a simple trick. The simplest things were usually the best.

Now this was life, I thought, surveying the master's domain. I was tempted to lie in the big bed, but I didn't want to give the Sniffers a trail. Instead, I stood in the center of the room and did a little twirl. If I was a greedy overlord of children, where would I keep my goods? *There.*

I stepped up to a large, ornate fireplace mantel, and explored the workmanship with sensitive fingers. I was soon rewarded with a satisfying click. A panel came off in my hands. Behind it was a small strongbox. I took out my lock picks and crouched to examine the lock. After a moment's thought I decided to free the box. I wedged my tension wrench between the nook and the iron, then got my spare out and did the same on the other side, using my wrenches as makeshift tongs. The entire strongbox slid out. Rather than fiddle with the lock, I bundled the box inside my coat. Mucking fool of a lord, I thought. And then paused. A bunch of papers were stuffed in the cubby. Those went into my bundle too.

Footsteps approached from outside. I calmly replaced the panel and slid under the huge bed.

The door opened, and I held my breath, watching two sets of feet enter. One with glossy boots that had never touched a muck-covered street, and the other with shiny heeled shoes. Much, much smaller.

A woman's whimper filled the room, cut off sharply by a *smack!*

"Please, m'lord. Please."

"Keep begging. I like screaming," a man's voice said. It

was heavy with threat and anticipation. Boots neared the shiny shoes, and I could hear a brief struggle. The woman was shoved against a bedpost.

I swore silently—a repeating one word mantra. Really, they decide to do this *now*? It was just my luck. I'd just lay low and let him do his business.

Clothing ripped.

You mucking idiot. Leave it be.

That was what I told myself.

I never listened well.

I unsheathed my knife, my muscles tensed in preparation for an attack, and then one blink later the woman moaned. "*Please…*" It was a throaty whisper of desire.

By the Four Elements, I was doomed. The bed groaned as the two tossed themselves on top of it. I let my forehead fall to the carpeted floor. I will not speak of the events I overheard for the next fifteen minutes. I will never utter a word of it. And to my dismay, I discovered that the bed was not as fine as it appeared. The springs were worn and the mattress sagged, hitting my head. Biting back the urge to bolt, I glared at a fancy pair of slippers that were tucked under the bed.

Here I was, a survivor of the slave market, trapped under the bed of a shagging lord and his giggling mistress. I'd show this mucking lord. I grabbed his fancy slippers and stuffed them in my bundle. These were what I came for, after all.

The life of a cat burglar wasn't always glamorous.

Eventually, the mattress stopped its knocking, and I heard a rumbling snore. I waited. The lord might be asleep, but what about… Sure enough, two dainty feet touched the carpet. With raised brows, I watched as a naked woman padded to the mantel.

I could see her, and I hoped she'd be focused enough not to look under the bed. She was a shapely thing. Porcelain skin and golden hair, with a lovely arse. A high-class sort of woman. She glanced over to the bed, then eased the panel open.

I bit my lip, tense with anticipation. Her hand slipped into darkness, questing. Her shoulders stiffened. She glanced again at the snoring lord and quickly replaced the panel. Then she padded to the lavatory.

Golden Girl was in the wrong business. There were easier ways to part a man from his wealth. She didn't seem the sleeping type so I took the opportunity to slip from under the bed and hurry to the door with my stolen goods.

6. FIRE

THE STRONGBOX BUMPED AGAINST MY BACK AS I HURRIED
down unfamiliar hallways. With an ear cocked, I listened for
approaching feet. My senses screamed to find a hole to hide
in, but I needed to find one that led out. Voices came from
around a corner. Giving a silent plea to Luck himself, I ducked
inside the nearest door.

And found myself the center of attention.

A room full of people in formal wear stopped in place,
and stared. At me. I had entered the side door to a ballroom.
Muck. Gas lamps blazed, and I blinked against the light even
as I searched for an exit. Fog swirled outside, over the great
domed ceiling of glass.

"Damn," I said flippantly. "I thought this was supposed to
be fancy dress."

And then a woman screamed. No one bought my half-
assed story. Not for a second in their silks and finery.

I bolted, as a trio of men drew their side swords. A pistol
shot rang in my ears. I smelled gunpowder and fear, and leapt
up onto a table full of food. I made mush of it as I picked my
way through a maze of delicate crockery. At the end of the

table I jumped, reaching for a tapestry hanging from a column. I latched on like a cat and climbed. My instincts always urged me to take the high ground. Another pistol shot rang out. Pain laced across my thigh. I reached the top of the tapestry and pulled myself over a balustrade onto a walkway that circled the ballroom.

The musicians there hugged their instruments for protection and backed against the wall as I loped past. Guards shouted and sabers rattled. A square bit of grate sat between two pillars. I was sure I could fit through it with some quick maneuvering. Down or up?

I glanced at the glass ceiling. Might as well be up. I wedged myself between two pillars, braced my back on one and my feet on the other, and walked up, inching towards the ceiling. Lead balls zipped through the air, but the pillars gave me some cover. That wouldn't last with a well aimed shot from right below me, though.

A group of guards were running along the walkway, their shiny metal breastplates making a racket. When I was nearly to the top, I drew my own pistol, pulled back the hammer, aimed at the dome, and fired. Glass shattered and rained on my head. I scrambled upwards, slick with my own blood, and grabbed the top of the pillar to pull myself up.

Dagger-like shards of glass jutted all around, and I could see the faces of the female statues peering down at me. They wore amused expressions. I unslung my bundle to hit at the shards.

Another explosion, and a bit of mortar punched through my trousers to stick in my calf. I bit back pain, tossed the bundle over my shoulder, and leapt up. Glass crunched under my leather gloves. I dangled for a breath, then hauled myself up with an easy motion. As glass fell on the guards, I grabbed the statue's arm. She was a saint, she was, with eyes full of mirth. Then I was up and over her, and scrambling down her back.

I stopped a moment to get my bearings, clinging to her shapely backside while sharing the ledge. Lights floated through the fog far below; thunder came from above. I looked to the rumble that was loud enough to shake my bones. The thunder was close. Too close.

A great cannon boom muted my world. Next came flames, and a great rending of wood. I cursed. No time to think. I started a hasty descent. Blood slicked my shoes, and I slipped more than once as I clumsily crimped the vertical striations of the tower.

Frantic screams joined the thunder. I wasn't sure if it was me, the guards below, or maybe Luck himself laughing. A shadow fell past me, and then another, the wind of their passage zipping down my neck. I heard a thud, and then a great fearsome crash. Stone shook under my fingertips, and I lost my grip. I fell.

Luck was with me. I didn't have far to fall, but the landing stole my breath. I had fallen to the ground only ten feet below. Nearby guards turned their rifles on me as I tried to catch my breath. I couldn't see their eyes behind their masks, but I saw a finger twitch and knew I was good as dead.

But then it began to rain. Fire. Great heaping shards of flaming wood falling from the sky. Surprised, the guards raised their rifles, but lead was useless against flaming debris. A deadly splinter the size of a tree impaled one through the chest. And the rest of the living scattered.

I rolled as a flaming sail and mast crashed near me. Heat seared my cheeks. I was blind and deaf. I didn't know what was where, or where what was. It was chaos, and my head felt like it wanted to explode.

I staggered to my feet, then stumbled as something large

fell to the ground. I glanced back, squinting through fog and fire and acrid smoke. The hull of a great ship had crashed to earth. I dove away from flying debris. Then like a fool I stopped to gape.

There were shadows moving on deck, but I couldn't hear a thing. I scrambled to my feet and ran for my life. I didn't get far. I hit stone and fell back, dazed.

For a moment I stared into oblivion. Then I remembered —the tower had a wall around it.

Mucking rat, I muttered. Crawling to my feet, I slapped a hand on brick, dug fingers into an indentation, and pulled myself up. Swords clashed behind me, along with shouting and more screams. Again the fool, I paused at the top of the fence to look back.

A masked figure fought three guards. Swords were a blur in the night. One guard fell, then another, but the third managed to land a strike in the masked figure's back. The blade must have missed their heart. The figure threw itself forward, tumbled to the ground, and came up in a roll. A dagger flashed, the blade flew, and the guard was hit in the face. He crumpled to the ground.

There was a crack in the silver mask that showed off a jawline cut from stone. Definitely male. The masked figure stumbled. He coughed, a bubbling sort of sound, and slapped a hand against the wall beneath me. He looked up at me. I couldn't see his eyes behind the mask, only dark holes that reflected the fire's light. But I swear I saw a plea in those invisible eyes.

You will not, I told myself, get involved. To each his own. Life is fleeting. Get out while you can.

I had a litany of arguments. Sensible ones, too. But I'd never forgotten that wide-eyed rat from Before whose hand had been in mine before they slipped into flaming pitch. Or their screams. Those were the sounds that kept me up most nights.

I grabbed the top of the iron fence, but instead of leaping over I reached down to offer my hand.

His bloodied hand gripped mine. His grip was weak and his hand was slick with blood, but my own grip was one a stone mason would envy. I locked his hand in a vice, and pulled. The figure used his feet as leverage. Yes, definitely a Him. I'd seen women with strong jawlines, but I couldn't imagine a woman with those shoulders and that size. And there was something in the way the body moved under the coat. When the fellow was on the top of the fence, I gave him a sort of salute, and leapt down.

My leg gave on the landing, reminding me of that bit of mortar lodged in my calf. I executed a neat roll, and came up on one knee. I clenched my jaw, pausing to swallow down pain. A heavier form landed beside me and I heard a pained cry. He tried to rise, only to fall.

The masked figure rolled over on his back, his chest rising with a sucking gasp of air. He ripped off his mask, fighting to breathe, only to choke on the poisonous fog. Blood bubbled from his lips. And I was transfixed. Not due to his dying, but because his eyes glowed amber.

A sun-touched. Here.

On the ground. Dying in front of me.

7. BACK AGAIN

Before I go forward, let me go back to what I like to call my Rebirth. That's the way I work. So don't get lost. I have a flair for the dramatic, and telling a thing straight just isn't my style.

BEFORE

I WAS FLOATING. IT WAS A SOFT DREAM THAT I'D NEVER dreamt before. Softness isn't in a rat's vocabulary. Only muck, hunger, and death. I'd spent my brief life scavenging along the River Styx, risking tides and getting stuck in the muck and having lungs full of water, but this… this softness was new.

I opened my eyes. Mist swirled lazily over me. I wondered if I was still falling from that tower with the eel wrapped around my leg.

If I was falling, it was the most pleasant thing in my life.

The mist parted. A face hovered above me. A veiled woman. I jerked and tried to scramble away, but found only air. I was falling. Again. It's a recurring theme with me. The ground came quick this time. I rolled down moss-covered steps to stop at a woman's feet. Draped in stone veils and a clinging wrap, she sat on a pedestal, her arms spread in supplication.

I had been cradled in those arms.

I pressed my palms to my eyes, took a breath, and looked again. It was a statue. There were others around me. Spread wings, gruesome visages, scythes, weeping angels. A phosphorescent steam rising from the ground. I was in a graveyard. But where? How?

Had I died? I pinched myself, and it felt real enough. Would a ghost know it was a ghost?

Stone mausoleums covered in lichen, gravestones and drooping trees surrounded me. The air smelled of rot. But also of life. Water lapped at stone steps nearby, and I realized for the first time that I was drenched and shivering. Muck streaked down my arms.

I touched my face. My respirator was gone. But I had ten toes, ten fingers, and all my limbs. Nothing was broken or crushed. What happened? Had the cage and the rats all been a nightmare? But then this was no place I had been before, so how did I wake up here? Graveyards were not for the living.

I walked to the stair's edge. A strong current of water flowed past. Luminescent creatures swirled below the surface: eels and fish and dark, lurking things. The River Styx. I'd know it anywhere.

I was cold with fear. Weak from hunger. My world spun in confusion. I looked down at my ankle. The eel was still firmly attached, but it seemed dormant. I dared not touch it.

A pebble shifted, a twig cracked, and a tall creature hobbled out of the mist. It wore a hooded coat and a shiny, beaked plague mask. I bolted. Or tried to. My legs were clumsy and I stumbled. Too late.

A second, swifter figure leapt out from behind a mausoleum and pointed a sword at my head. Oddly, I didn't pay much attention to the blade. My eyes were fixed on his feet and the red velvet carpet slippers with little gold tassels he wore. I looked up, past his trousers and a faded thief-taker's coat to the face of the man. He wore a mask. Dark leather with a built in respirator and large, round, black eye pieces. A whirring noise came from the mask as the lens adjusted to focus in on me. He seemed to stare at me in a moment of shock.

I seized fortune and sprang to my feet, but the tall creature came up behind me. My first thought was the Sweepers had found me, but this person was different. He leaned heavily on a gentleman's stick.

I scrambled in the only direction I could in the cramped graveyard. Up. I sprang up a weeping woman, and jumped off her shoulder to catch the edge of a nearby mausoleum, then pulled myself up onto its rotting roof.

But when I went to jump over to the next mausoleum, I found the man in slippers by me on the same roof. "You're a quick one," the slippered man said.

I jumped. But I was weak, cold, and confused. I miscalculated and fell five inches short of my goal to land below on an edge of stone. Pain raced through me. Air wouldn't fill my lungs, but I rolled over anyways and tried to slither down the stone steps. I thumped onto moss-covered ground and was stopped short by the pointy end of a walking stick thrust against my shoulder. It pinned my rags to the ground.

The figure in the dark hood stood over me like Death himself. "What do we have here?" His voice was crisp. Cultured. And menacing.

"A sun-touched," said the slippered man from the roof. I didn't have a mucking idea what he meant, so I kicked the tall creature in the shin, and instantly regretted it. My bare foot hit solid wood. I squirmed in pain.

The slippered man hopped down, and grabbed my injured foot.

"And a rat at that." the tall man said. "It shouldn't be possible."

"Apparently, it is. And although he's quick, he's not bright. We don't have time for this."

"Never question fortune, Gan," the tall man said.

I twisted, and opened my mouth to scream, but who would care to save a rat caught in a butcher's hand. Gan sheathed his sword and crouched down, examining the eel locked around my leg. "Fortune was the reason we came here. Not for a rat."

"I was referring to the lucky kind."

"Since when has a rat been good fortune?" Gan asked.

The tall man considered me. "Don't you think it odd? A rat here, of all places? I thought their kind avoided graveyards."

"Rats are everywhere." Gan had an iron grip on my leg, but I squirmed and fought anyway. He barely seemed to notice—until I yanked a gold tassel off his slipper. He cursed behind his mask, and his hand spasmed on my leg.

The tall man stifled a laugh. "But a sun-touched? Bring him with us; the dead will wait."

Gan ripped the tassel out of my hand. "Careful, or I'll toss you in the river."

He didn't pick me up. He wouldn't dare risk that. Instead, he dragged me through the graveyard like a half-dead corpse fighting the grave digger.

AT SOME POINT, GAN GRABBED ME BY MY RAGS AND LIFTED ME up, so I was eye level with his mask. "I don't want to make you sleep, rat. But if you try and bite me one more—" I bit at his mask and managed to snag a strap, ripping it free. He stifled an oath as he quickly righted it.

The clunking gait of the tall man neared, and a bag was put over my head. "We won't hurt you," he drawled. "Not that anyone hearing that has ever been reassured in all of time."

My arms were wrenched behind my back, and a cord wrapped tight around my wrists. "What about the other thing?" Gan asked.

"It can wait."

"I'm not sure this is worth it," Gan muttered, lifting me up to fling me over his shoulder.

"We need fresh blood," the tall man said.

I jerked at the word 'blood'. I knew it. This was the end. But at least I knew I wasn't a ghost. Not yet.

"Whatcha for?" I demanded.

"It speaks," the tall man said crisply. "Your luck has changed, rat."

"Muck off!" I screamed.

"That is precisely our plan."

Little did I know what he meant by that. That what was about to happen would be worse than anything I could have imagined back then. I shut my mouth, and concentrated on my other senses. Where were they taking me? Had I escaped one Sweeper only to fall into another's hands?

The scents of rotting life turned to familiar smells: muck, sewage, and old cabbage. The air thickened, too. I breathed in the pea soup through the sack on my head, and felt the world close in around us. They were walking down cobbled streets now. At one junction, I heard the drone of voices. A market. And the clop of wagons, powered by hissing steam.

Their footsteps echoed in a narrow alley, then the two men stopped. I heard stone grind against stone. The man named Gan turned sideways to shuffle through some tight space. Something large and heavy grated, then shut. It sealed my fate.

"He stinks like a cesspit, Mord," Gan said.

"Most rats do, don't they?"

I was set on my feet, and the hood was yanked off my head with a flourish. I blinked at the light. Gan took out a knife, and I backed up against a brick wall.

"Do you want those ropes off?" Gan asked. He had taken off his mask. His black hair was shaved so close he might as well have been bald. He had wide-set dark eyes that sloped up at the corners, pronounced cheekbones, a flat nose and a scar that slashed across his upper lip. It was rare to see an unmasked face free of muck and grime. His skin was darker than the pale flashes of flesh I'd occasionally seen.

I glared at the man.

"He has spirit. Just what we need," the other man said. The tall man unclasped his plague mask with a hiss of air. He breathed in deeply. He had longish brown hair, and his face was all starkness and angles, but his eyes were soft—a green so deep that I couldn't help but stare. "I'm Mordecai. This is Ganbaatar. And you are?"

They were high and mighty names as far as I knew. But then I hadn't heard many before. We rats didn't have names.

I pressed my lips together. But my defiance was betrayed by my body. Every muscle shook with fear. And pain. I was barely managing to remain on my two feet. It had been a long day. Dying and all.

We stood in a small room made of brick and stone, with lichen lighting the walls. A single iron door was set in a brick wall. And there was a bench.

"We're not brutes. Just two professionals in need of a small apprentice." Mordecai paused, looking me up and down, a satisfied glint lighting his eyes. "And you are most definitely small. We're not slavers, so you can remain with us or go. But you have to make a choice. And once you decide, that's it." His voice was gentle. Tired even. "Either way, I'm sure you'd like that eel removed."

I glanced down at my leg, then slowly turned to present my back to Gan. I squeezed my eyes shut as he slit the cords from my wrists. They fell away, and I rubbed circulation back into my hands.

Keeping a wary eye on me, Gan knelt and pointed at my foot with his knife. "You were caught by a Sweeper?" he asked.

I nodded.

"And escaped?"

Again a nod.

Mordecai limped towards the door, his walking stick

clicking on stones. It had a curved, talon-like silver handle that looked deadly. He wore knee-high leather boots, and walked with a stiffness that looked painful. A clanking sound accompanied every bend of his knees. He inserted a key into the iron door, and disappeared through it. A minute later he tossed a flask at Gan who caught it deftly. Gan uncorked the top and held it near the eel.

Nothing happened. Gan's brows drew together, and he unsheathed a knife to poke at the eel. He glanced at Mordecai. "It's dead."

The two men shared a look that was lost on me. Before I could reach down and rip the thing off, Gan sliced it off and collected the pieces in the flask. He stoppered it, then tucked it under his arm. "If you want to stay with us, knock three times. If you want to leave, knock four times, put the sack over your head, and wait."

"Can he count?" Mordecai said from the doorway.

I glared at him.

Gan laughed. "Let's hope so." The two men disappeared through the iron door leaving me standing in a prison room. I slumped against the wall, hugged my legs, and buried my face against my knees.

The iron door opened again, and a bowl of food was pushed into the room. My stomach rumbled. It was too tempting. I crawled over to the food and sniffed at it. I had never had a proper meal. Some crusts of bread if I was lucky. Fish, occasionally. But this. I poked at the white, grainy substance and the small white pieces of meat. And greens. I ignored those, and stuffed the meat into my mouth. Chicken. I ate so fast I felt sick and nearly puked it all up. I sat back, staring at the steaming bowl of food. There was so much left that I couldn't imagine eating it all.

I stared at the iron door. Could I trust these two? Never.

What did they want with me? Nothing good. Did it matter? I'd die for sure if I went back to the streets. I knew a dozen ways to die scavenging along the River Styx. And I knew hunger, fear, and keeping one step ahead of Catchers and Sweepers. But this? What was *this*? It was the unknown. And it terrified me.

I made a fist and stood, facing the door. I knocked once, twice, three times, and stopped, my fist poised over the iron. The unknown or the wretched known? My hand fell to my side. It felt like defeat.

Three knocks.

Slats in the ceiling and walls slid back revealing dark holes in the brick. I eyed them warily. Barrels poked out and a grinding racket echoed in the small room. I stared into the face of a muzzle. Fear clutched my throat. So they were going to shoot me after all. I ducked as the muzzle exploded.

Something hot shot at my face. I spluttered, flailing backwards from the force of it, but another jet hit me on the back, head, and legs all at once. Scalding liquid was coming from everywhere. It was worse than a driver's whip.

I screamed, but only managed to choke on water. Years of muck and grime drained off me, swirling around my bare feet, before heading to a large grate. I squeezed my eyes shut and hid under my own arms as the relentless assault battered my body. Then it cut off.

I huddled in the center of the room dripping wet. The door opened. Gan pushed a tin tub through the doorway, with a brush and some sort of floating bar sloshing inside. He stopped, and stared at me, a flicker of surprise twitched across his scarred lip.

I stared back.

"Clothes off," he ordered. "Then climb in here and scrub yourself clean."

"Not doing," I growled. "You be killing me."

"I could have done that long ago, rat."

I crossed my arms.

"Are you going to get in this tub?"

I gave a defiant shake of my head.

He lunged for me, and I bolted, but there was nowhere to go. I tried anyway. I scrambled up the uneven bricks to the ceiling and clung to the corner like a frantic cat. Gan laughed, a big booming sound of mirth. He grabbed the back of my shirt and wrenched me down. I clawed and bit, and screeched so much that Mordecai came in.

The sight of him froze me in my tracks. I gaped. He sat in a chair with wheels. His two legs were stumps in a pair of folded trousers, cut off just above the knees.

Gan used my shock to his advantage. He tossed me into the tub. There was a knife in his hand, and I felt the blade whoosh down my back. My rags fell away into the bubbling white froth. Poison! I was sure of it.

"Stay still!" Gan ordered.

I was never one to follow orders. Mordecai wheeled over, and reached out to hold my head. I tried to drag him off his chair while Gan took the white bar to my hair and back. The white bar smelled sweet, and pricked my nostrils.

"He's worse than a cat," Gan said.

"Is this really so bad?" Mordecai asked. In answer, I tried to bite his forearm. "You could have done this yourself."

It was a struggle. But they scrubbed me up. And managed to divest me of the rest of my clothing. Gan suddenly froze, then jerked to his feet and backed away.

"He's not a him," Gan hissed.

Mordecai's grip slackened in surprise. I wrenched myself free, picked up the bar and threw it at his face. The tub proved more hazardous than I imagined as I launched myself out of it. I slipped over the rim, fell on the stone, and scrambled across the floor. With my back to the wall, I turned and swore at the two. A puddle formed at my feet. My skin felt odd. I was naked. But it wasn't the lack of clothes that bothered me, it was the absence of muck coating my body.

They both stared in shock.

Mordecai shook himself. "Well, how was I supposed to know?"

"We can't train a girl," Gan growled, and stalked out of the room. He came back and threw a towel at me.

I was too young to care about modesty.

Gan pointed at the towel. "Put it on."

I snatched the towel. It was softer and cleaner than anything I had ever encountered. I gripped it in my hands and prepared to fight. If I could get it around one of their necks…

Mordecai looked up at his companion. "Girl or boy. Sun-touched or not, she's talented."

"We *can't* keep her. Not for what we have in mind."

The two seemed unaware of me. Their private conversation in semi-hushed voices carried across the room.

"Why not? She has the strength and the agility. What does her sex matter?"

"It doesn't *now*," Gan stressed. "But it will when she matures."

"How so?" Mordecai asked.

"Women have…" Gan gestured vaguely. "*Issues.*"

Mordecai rested an elbow on the armrest of his rolling chair, and rubbed his chin in contemplation. "And I don't?"

Gan frowned down at the legless man.

Why did they keep saying sun-touched? I looked down at my arm, and for the first time I saw the color of my own skin. I was dark. Not ghostly white like Mordecai, and not bronzed like Gan, but dark brown. I didn't know what sun-touched meant, but being different was never good.

"Is muck stained is all," I muttered.

Both men looked at me in surprise. I think they'd forgotten I was there.

"What do you mean?" Mordecai asked.

I waved an arm around. "My skin."

Mordecai chuckled. "It's not your skin. It's your eyes."

"What of them?" I demanded.

"They glow red in the fog. Not here, mind you. The air is pure."

"Muck poison," I stated.

"That must be it," Mordecai said. "See, Gan? Muck poison."

"That doesn't change her sex."

"No." Mordecai gave a careless shrug. "But what would you have us do? Send her back to the streets? Sell her in the market?" The last was suggestive.

Gan's jaw clenched. "Not that, never. We should hand her over to the Ministry—she's undocumented."

"You not be doing!" I shouted.

"No, he won't," Mordecai said.

"She's sun-touched. They will take her back."

"Will they?" Mordecai asked. "A sun-touched rat with no name? I can think of a number of things they will do. To us, too."

Gan gave a grunt, dropped the brush, and stalked from the room. He did not return.

Mordecai gestured at me. "The towel goes around you."

I wrapped the soft cloth around me.

"Still no name?"

I shook my head.

"Rat won't do." Mordecai studied me with an appraising

eye. And my own gaze traveled to his legs, or lack thereof. He saw me staring and a gentle smile curved his lips. "Do you know what you mean to me, Rat?"

I stared back in silence.

"You will be my legs. You will give us a new life," he said, thumping a stubby leg. "I think Evie will do. How's that for a name?"

I mouthed the name like a talisman. Who would name a rat? A crazed man in a chair with wheels. That's who.

"There is clothing, warmth, and food inside. Come if you like." He turned his chair around with his hands, and pushed on the wheels. He rolled forward to stop in the doorway, his back to me. He pointed at the ceiling. "We need to clean the muck out of here. The jets will be turning back on shortly."

The threat of water was worse than fire. I bolted through the door.

10. THE CHALLENGE

AFTER

Sun-touched. Ten years later, I knew what that word meant. And in the Below it meant trouble. I stared down at the gasping man. Blood bubbled from his lips with each sucking breath.

Fires blazed around the stronghold as the great airship burned. Metal clanked, and the bluish lights of the Enforcers seemed to float in the fog and acrid smoke. They were getting closer.

I had to get out of here, but the dying man…

Muck, I cursed, and ripped off my respirator. With a practiced hand, I attached it to his face, tucked away his own broken mask, and grabbed his arm. He was much heavier than I was, but I was a tightly wound spring. I pulled the man up until he was sitting. He got the hint, and tried to stand. When his bulk fell forward, I used his momentum to get under him. He fell onto my shoulders, and I stood. Or tried to. Pain laced up my right leg. It didn't hold, so I compensated with my left and ground my teeth until I feared they'd crack.

I staggered under the man's weight. "You're a heavy one," I grunted.

Lucky for us the Enforcers were focused on the flaming wreckage and finding surviving crew members. But Monger's Square was a checkerboard, and the great empty squares were teeming with activity. Enforcers, guards, and curious merchants were out in force. And scavengers. Shadows rushed past me in the mist as I limped under my burden. Shouts, ringing steel, and pistol fire filled the murky air.

A lead ball shattered a stone at my feet. I half turned; the man on my shoulders groaned from the sudden movement. Two Enforcers had me in their sights. Enforcer Two charged straight for me, while Number One cocked back his hammer for another go.

On a better day, I'd have been able to outrun the armored tubs. But this was not a better day. I did the only thing I could; I dropped my burden. The sun-touched fell to the stones like a sack.

My noble-hearted self kept running, but I had a plan. I reached into my trouser pocket to snatch a trick. With a deft hand, I smashed a small paper pouch to the stones. Smoke rose to mingle with fog, creating a screen. One heartbeat later an ear-piercing screech deafened the square. As expected. Next came the blinding—a blue-white fire flared from my little trick.

Enforcer Two ducked away from the blinding light. I drew my knife, and made my legs work, racing around the smoke screen. Enforcer One was aiming his rifle at the smoke. Right at his partner's back.

Moving like a breeze, I rushed the rifle-wielding Enforcer. As I slammed into his back, I reached around and squeezed his gloved finger on the trigger. All in one neat move. The rifle fired.

At this range, even armor failed his friend. Enforcer Two dropped to his knees. The first reeled back, trying to shake me off, but I knew his chink. I sliced the tubes at his knees and elbows. Now weighed down by iron, he crashed to the ground and dropped his weapon. But this would only slow him down.

I bolted for the cover of my smoke screen to grab for the dying sun-touched. Only he wasn't there.

I staggered out, confused, my eyes burning from my own trick. I righted my goggles and found the sun-touched crawling on his stomach now twenty feet away. Bloody bastard. I didn't slow. I grabbed him by the back of the collar and dragged him over cobblestones. By the light of the fires I could see the dark stain on his back. Three feet of steel would do that to you.

Soon noise fell away and the burning carcass of the airship was swallowed by fog. Finally the square ended and brick walls pressed in on us. Safe at last; the lanes and alleyways of Bedlam were a maze that changed daily. I hoisted the man down a cramped alleyway. Recessed doorways lined the brick walls, dark and foreboding portals into unknown rookeries and suffering.

I pulled him into an archway, and fell against the wall to catch my breath. The strongbox wrapped in my bundle clunked against the brick. That mucking strongbox had better be worth all this trouble.

I wrenched off my goggles and resisted the urge to wipe the sting from my eyes. Only water would help. I reached into my ever useful pockets and slid a small cylinder from a holder. With a gentle flick, the bug trapped inside glowed to life, giving me a bashful light. I glanced down at the man's back. A smallish hole cut through his coat.

Shame about the coat. That was some fine wool.

I was no surgeon, but I wagered that blade had missed his

heart and struck his lung. I rolled him on his side and tried to catch his eyes. They were a brilliant amber that glowed like fire. At present, his eyes were dazed and unfocused, though, and I'm not sure he saw me.

"Stay here, mate," I said softly.

What the muck was I doing? Angry at my heroics, I reached into a pocket on my thigh (pockets are useful things), and took out a small first aid kit. I selected one of the vials that contained a bit of whitish powder.

Tugging and jerking on his coat, I managed to expose his wounded back. His shirt had once been white. Now it was bloodstained and covered with pinkish bubbly froth. I sliced that silky material open to lay his flesh bare. He had skin so dark it reminded me of obsidian.

"Breathe out. All your air," I ordered.

The man obeyed, and the wound made a bubbling noise. I upended the vial into the wound.

His entire body went rigid with agony. Veins stuck out on his neck, and he growled out in pain. Before the waves subsided, I stuck a plaster over the hole, and sorted his coat back in place.

He fell onto his stomach. I stared down at the man panting into the muck. Right. My part was done. Finished. I dusted off my hands, symbolically washing myself clean of the stranger. He could sort his own self out.

I patted his shoulder. "Good luck there, mate. That'll hold for a bit." I started to take my respirator from his face, but stopped. He'd die without it in the Below. "The mask is on me." I felt nearly saintly. I stood, adjusted the bundle on my back, and turned to walk away. But stopped at a sweet, sweet siren rasp. I cocked an ear, and the whisper came again.

"Masques," the man wheezed again.

A long breath swept past my lips as I looked to the fog for

guidance. Of all the fog-ridden nights, I had to pick this one to burgle a lord.

I raised a brow at the fellow. "How many we talking about?"

Amber eyes found mine in the murk. They sharpened for a moment, his breath coming easier than it had a moment before. "How many do you need?"

"More than you can manage."

"Try me," he said. It wasn't a plea. It was a challenge. This noble-browed, sun-touched wretch, lying in muck with a hole in his lung, had the arrogance to *challenge me*. If ever I had a weakness (which I didn't), a challenge was a gauntlet thrown at my feet.

11. APPRENTICESHIP

BEFORE

AN INCH WIDE CRIMP BARELY LARGE ENOUGH FOR THE PADS OF my fingers stretched across the wood. It was some twenty feet to the other side and thirty feet from the floor of the empty warehouse.

"Move!" Gan barked.

I needed air. I needed a nice lie down and ice for my shaking forearms. I straightened on the platform of what my taskmaster called 'tier two'.

Down below, Gan waved a ticking pocket watch at me.

I shook out my arms. My forearms were as heavy as bricks and somehow managed to feel like noodles at the same time. I wiped sweaty palms on my trousers and took a breath. The crimp, a strip of iron slick with moisture, was bolted on wood.

I positioned my fingers and eased out into the expanse. The weight of my body was supported by the tips of my fingers, so I tucked my thumbs over for extra support and began edging my way across, one hand at a time.

"Keep your legs still. Don't swing," Gan instructed. "It will throw off your balance and sap your strength."

But I was already moving across, and my legs were swinging with every shuffle to the side. At ten feet across my fingers started screaming, and sweat from my hands slicked the metal crimp. I ground my teeth and kept going.

"You're moving your body too much, Evie! Imagine yourself as a still pond. Fluid. Calm. You can't bully the metal. You have to flow across it."

"You be talking too much!" I yelled down at him.

"And do not talk! Focus on relaxing. I can see your jaw is tense from down here."

"Why don't you come up here and do it your own bloody self?"

"I already showed you how."

"Except you be too fat for last part."

Anger spurred me. Arguing with Gan always got my blood pumping. I'd do it my way. I increased my speed and made it to the other side. Hah! There! Take that.

But I was shaking with fatigue, and that hadn't been the hard part. At the end of the twenty foot beam with the tiny crimp was a metal air shaft that went straight up. Below the shaft was the whirr of a fan—not a real one, it had padded edges.

"Brace yourself. Use every angle."

Easier said than done.

I was training in what Mordecai called a "replica of an air flow system." Whatever that meant. Gan built it. They said it was for a job that paid well. Very well. So well it was worth taking in a rat and training the muck out of her for months.

I wasn't so sure. But for the first time in my life I had a warm place to sleep, my own bed, a room even, and I hadn't known hunger since they snatched me. I didn't want to be tossed back to the street. So I kept at it.

The crimp I was dangling from ended at an access hatch to the air shaft. The outside made a corner. I braced my special shoes against the smooth surface, but there was no resting. Keeping my right hand jammed on the crimp, I reached up to the vent door and pulled it open. Like a parched man diving for water, I latched on to the solid lip with my left hand and transferred my right.

"Slower. Every movement is measured. Fluid. No action is hasty," Gan said.

I growled at him as I pulled myself up into the square opening. The fan was sucking air down. I needed to go in the opposite direction: up.

The inside of the shaft was spacious. That was an issue for little old me.

"There is no time to rest. Move!"

Here's where things got tricky. The sheet metal was slick with moisture, which meant I couldn't use friction. I had to brace myself. Only my arms didn't reach from one side to the next, so I had to use my entire body. I stretched across the air shaft, bracing my hands on one side and my feet on the other, keeping my body flat, all the while staring down at the whirring fan. I began to inch my body upwards.

It hurt. Everything hurt. My stomach quivered. My legs shook. The back of my neck strained. I wheezed with the effort, as I made my slow way up. Then I slipped. And you guessed it, I fell.

I hit the padded fan, bounced, then slid through the blades to plunge twenty feet to stuffed pillows below. The wind was knocked out of me, and I was sure I broke my neck.

Mordecai peered down at me. "Calm yourself, wait... Good. Now breathe."

I sucked in air.

"You must use pressure with your hands and feet to brace yourself. Again!" Gan barked.

"It can't get done!" I screamed.

"It can," he insisted.

"You be doing it!" I yelled back at him.

"I can't fit through the last vent."

"Maybe you are eating less."

A vein on Gan's temple throbbed.

"Let her rest," Mordecai said.

I sank back into the pillows, relieved.

"No, to the pillars. Now."

"Or what?" I growled.

Gan raised a brow. "Bath."

"You be making me anyway."

He crossed his arms, and transferred his glare to Mordecai. "How do you expect me to teach her without punishment?"

Mordecai shifted uncomfortably in his chair.

"If she were a boy you would not be so soft with her," Gan pointed out.

"Boy or girl, a beating won't help her climb."

"It will instill discipline. She has none."

"I have plenty of," I argued.

"No, he's right. A boy would have been better," Mordecai said with a sigh. "Perhaps we can find a new apprentice. Evie can cook and clean and do the laundry instead of me. We'll find her a husband when she's old enough."

"I mucking won't!" I fought with the pillows and tumbled down the mound. Then stomped over to the pillars. They were spaced a tortuous but precise distance apart. I climbed up, planted one foot on top of each, in what Gan called Horse

Stance, and punched my fist into my flat palm. I stood there, trying to ignore the quivering in my thighs.

Gan grunted. Pleased. My two captors shared a look, a small smile playing at the edge of Mordecai's long lips.

Gan hopped on a post beside mine and took up a similar stance. He was built like a whip but hard as a rock. He had muscles on his muscles, he did.

"Breathe," he said, and demonstrated. His breaths were so powerful they moved the air around him. When he exhaled his stomach turned concave and every rib in his torso showed.

We stood there for five minutes breathing until I didn't feel my legs anymore.

Mordecai had wheeled himself over to the replica. "And, Evie, it *is* possible," he said softly. Looking up, he shifted in his chair and reached for the first crevice. Long arms. Strong fingers. Before he lost his legs, I thought he must have been over six feet tall.

He wedged his fists into the vertical crevice and began climbing. With no legs.

A muscle in Gan's square jaw flexed. I knew that muscle. He was angry. Or worried. Or about to snap. I was still in horse stance with legs quivering, but all that dropped away. I watched in wonder as Mordecai pulled himself and his long torso up the wall. He moved like water. As light as air. And when he made it to the crimp bridge, he didn't hesitate. He jammed his fingers on the crimp and moved across with an ease that made me envious. Of course he didn't have legs to swing, but if he did I was sure they'd be still.

When he reached the dreaded corner, he dangled by the fingertips of his right hand and reached for the vent cover with his left. He closed it, then opened it (just to prove he could), and gripped the vent lip. He pulled himself up and I hopped down from my pillars to walk under the makeshift air shaft.

Gan didn't even yell at me. Fancy that. Instead he joined me beside the mound of pillows and we craned back our necks to watch. He was worried, though. His fists were clenched.

Mordecai reached across the inside of the air shaft to brace his left hand. How would he make the transition from vent edge to shaft without legs? With a jerk he did a little body hop off the square vent door and quickly planted his right hand on the opposite wall. I could see the strain now. With only two arms braced between the opposing shaft walls, it seemed near impossible to gain upward movement. But still he managed. A good four feet, before his hands slipped.

He fell, hitting the fan, and fell through. Gan flinched when Mordecai landed, and rushed forward to help.

Mordecai was laughing on top of the pillows. "Maybe it is impossible."

"You are a fool," Gan said.

"I'm a fool who can roll down these pillows by himself just fine."

Mordecai shrugged off Gan's attempts to help and half rolled, half pulled himself out of the pillows. Then Mordecai 'walked' himself over to his chair and climbed up it like some two-armed spider. I was still getting used to the way he moved around, and it was hard not to gawk.

Gan helped him get settled in the wheeled chair, then checked the stubby ends of his legs to make sure the stockings were in place.

"Stop fussing."

"I wouldn't if you didn't take risks."

"It wasn't a risk."

"You should have turned the fan off," Gan snapped.

Mordecai looked up at his friend. He placed his hand on Gan's. "It's a fake one," he said softly.

Gan stalked off.

Relieved to be free, I fell onto the mound of pillows.

"Why's he so worried 'bout you? It's all padded, it is."

"It is. But his memory isn't."

I looked up at the whirring fan. Then at his legs, or lack thereof. "That how you lost your legs?"

Mordecai gave me one of his crooked smiles. "I like you, Evie. Blunt and to the point. Most are too embarrassed to ask."

"Why?"

He rubbed one of his stubs. "I make people uncomfortable."

"Not me."

"Don't you pity me?" He leaned forward, eyes intent. Mordecai had a way of looking right through you, down to your bones, but his eyes were soft and kind and full of curiosity. He liked to know how things worked. Gan's gaze was also piercing, but more like a sharp knife. I'd seen killers with friendlier stares.

I shrugged. "This natty place you got and that keen chair to get around just fine." I crossed my arms. "I'm being just a rat. We got what we got."

Mordecai chuckled. "Wise words."

"Why you be climbing up there?"

"It was a lesson for you."

"How to be falling?" I asked.

"On how to try. No matter the odds."

"EAT THE GREEN PARTS," MORDECAI ORDERED.

"No," I said.

"Do it."

"No."

"I will force feed you."

"What I need for?"

"Why do I need vegetables," Mordecai corrected. He had been doing his best to teach me the King's proper. "And to answer: vegetables help you grow."

"Whole matter was you get me for being small."

Mordecai stared at me, as Gan laughed.

Mordecai shot his friend a look. "Yes, but we also need you to be healthy."

The humor died on Gan's face. He sighed, and with a small shake of his head, returned to his meal.

"What?" I asked.

"Eat."

Mordecai and Gan shared a look. They did this a lot. It took me years to finally understand what they weren't saying. At first, their silent glances annoyed the muck out of me.

I stabbed a little green tree and held it up. "What the muck this be?"

"It's called broccoli," Mordecai explained.

"Looks like shroom poison."

Gan huffed. "Broccoli is expensive. It's grown in a greenhouse under special lights, and it will keep you healthy."

"Full of the health, I am, me being a rat. You ever tried to kill us? We be living off muck."

"Which is why you are half the size you should be."

I shot Gan a look. "What you be knowing about my size?"

"Her spirit certainly hasn't suffered," Mordecai muttered.

"The sass is strong with this one," Gan agreed.

"I am what I am."

"Eat," Mordecai said again.

I stuffed the whole thing in my mouth. It tasted horrible, but it was food. I wasn't picky. It's just now I knew there were things that tasted better than the rot I'd scavenged along the Styx for years. "So what's this thing you be training me for?"

Mordecai glanced at Gan. Another silent conversation. In the end, Mordecai put down his fork and wiped his mouth with a napkin.

"We need you to retrieve something for us," Gan said. "Something that was… stolen from Mordecai."

"You said it be riches," I accused.

"It is. After a fashion. Worthless things aren't stolen," Mordecai said.

I snorted. "You be stealing me."

"You're not worthless, Evie," Mordecai said.

Gan stabbed at his meal.

I sat up a little straighter. "You sure you no misplace this thing?" Mordecai was always losing things. He worked most days in a part of the warehouse that I wasn't allowed in. The room was full of glass instruments, tubes, machines, and all sorts of steam hissing here and there. I'd ventured in there once and he'd nearly fallen off his chair in alarm.

"I did not misplace it."

"You be looking for your leg once." It had been under the bed.

Gan cleared his throat. "Some people have a great deal of wealth, more than they know what to do with, while others have nothing. We make sure things are more… evenly distributed."

"So you be thieves."

Gan crossed his arms. He never sat on a chair, but always on a stool, his spine as straight as the word itself. "We are men of opportunity."

"So who we pinching?"

"A lord," Gan said. "In a high tower. And that," he thrust a finger towards the airway replica, "is the way into his vault."

"We stealing swag?"

"More wealth than you can imagine."

"I can imagine loads. Why you need more? You got a natty place already, and food enough to make you fat."

Their home was brick with rusty pipes and a vast open space. I hadn't been outside since they snatched me from the graveyard, but as far as I could tell it was part of some underground water system. It was cold and damp, and poorly lit, but seemed to me a palace. Mordecai gestured at the room. "Gan and I aren't getting younger. We'd like to live comfortably as we get older."

Gan snorted. "He needs more padding for his chair."

"A soft bed *would* be nice."

"Mine's fine enough," I said.

"You're a rat. You slept in muck," Gan said. He did not care for muck, and waged a daily war in the warehouse against its invasion.

I lifted a shoulder. "Nicer than I know."

"Well, if all goes well, you'll know much nicer than this," Mordecai said.

"And if bad?" I asked.

Mordecai looked at me, then plucked up his empty plate, set it on his lap, and wheeled away towards a washbasin.

He was no help at all, so I looked to Gan.

"You will most likely die," he said.

Mordecai stopped and turned his head to the side, waiting.

I shrugged. "Happened already. What's one more time?"

Mordecai wheeled around to face me. "This isn't a game, Evie. Gan is serious."

"Is he ever not? What's a rat like me to lose?"

"Your life!" Mordecai snapped.

Gan stood like a coiled spring. "I told you this would not work," he growled.

Mordecai's shoulders sagged. "Fine. You're right. She won't do. We'll find someone else."

I stormed to my flaming feet. "I train harder and you beat the muck out of me. I get you what we're pinching. On the four elements, I will."

Gan looked down at me. "It's not you. Well, it is. But you don't understand."

I looked to Mordecai confused. "What it being?"

Mordecai sighed.

"He's grown fond of you, child," Gan said crisply. Then his shoulders lost some of their strength. "And so have I."

Mordecai looked to his companion, surprised.

I ran a hand over my near-to-bald head. Gan hadn't wanted to deal with my matted, lice-ridden, muck-coated hair, so he'd shaved it all off. "What's the worst that can be happening?"

Mordecai pointed to the padded fan. "You get chopped in half, or break every bone in your body in a fall."

I frowned up at the difficult spot that I hadn't ever managed to pass, not once. "Oh." Well, that might hurt a bit. I took a breath. "I'm game. For even split."

Both men looked at me in surprise.

"And even is I get half, and you two get other half."

"It can do math," Gan said.

"When it involves masques," Mordecai said.

I flashed them a grin. "Maybe I like a cushy life, too." Both men waited as I considered the little green tree on my plate. "I'm in." I thrust my hand forward. Amused, they glanced at each other, then Gan shook my hand followed by Mordecai. But he kept hold of it.

"You get a quarter."

"A quarter?" My math was limited.

Mordecai took the pot pie and made two cuts across it. He handed me a piece. "You'll get this much. We get the rest."

"Styx no," I swore.

Mordecai lifted his shoulders. "Then we're at an impasse."

"A what?"

"A roadblock," Gan clarified.

"I climb over it."

Mordecai leaned forward. "You need us to tell you where and what to steal. We hold the information, Evie."

"You be cheating me," I accused.

"We're being fair. If you took half, you'd be cheating us."

"I be doing the danger."

"There will be danger for us, too."

"Fine," I grumbled.

"And you will eat your vegetables."

I lifted a shoulder. "Food is food, mate."

"And you will not fall."

"So you be taking my share? You not being that lucky. You lot are stuck with me now."

Mordecai gave my hand a final squeeze.

I looked to the climbing puzzle, and I came to a decision right then and there. That there air shaft was standing between me and a posh life. I ate my tree, scrubbed my hands on my trousers and went over to climb that mucking thing. Masques, you see, were always the best motivation for me.

12. LOOT

AFTER

AND NOW HERE WE ARE. BACK TO THE SUN-TOUCHED promising me more coin than I can handle. As if. I lugged his wheezing hide to a punt, shoved him onto the half-sinking thing, and paid the punter his due. The punter was half asleep, likely hallucinating on shrooms. These fellas could navigate blind though. They lived in the canals.

I hauled Mr. Wheezy off at a stairway. "Drunk as piss," I told the punter, then got my shoulder under Wheezy's arm and frog-marched him into a maze of back alleys. In an empty lane, I shoved him against a wall and undid the scarf that tried to tame my hair. It was being temperamental today.

"Unless you want to spend eternity with me… put this over your eyes."

"No."

"Fine. I'll leave your arse here."

He looked around weakly. "Where is here?" His voice was reed-thin and full of wheeze.

"Like I'll tell you."

With a wheeze, he dipped his head in defeat, and I attacked him with my scarf to cinch it over his eyes. He was weak as a babe. "Mucking bad night. Don't die on me lest you want your final resting place to be in a canal."

I led him on a roundabout circuit. Not as long as I might've under ordinary circumstances, but with each staggering step, I worried he wouldn't last much longer. Which was the last thing I needed—a bloke lying dead at my feet. In short order, I steered him towards my hideout.

Now I say *mine*, but really it was only half mine. After I'd got Gan and Mordecai their riches, we went up in the world. Not high, mind you. But we lived a comfortable life.

I stopped at a brick wall, at a dead end full of rubbish, and located a catch in a corner. A small click and the brick swung inward. We went forward into darkness. When the door closed, I tapped on a solid iron door at the end of a cramped hallway.

Gan was paranoid as Styx. And a neat freak.

After the door's traps were disarmed, I dragged Mr. Wheezy into a familiar square room with a drain in the center. We've been here before, remember.

I dropped my charge and hurried to knock on the metal slat.

It banged to the side. A pair of suspicious eyes looked through.

"Don't you dare turn on those hoses. I can't spare the time, Gan."

"You smell like muck."

"I was out in it. But I got a fella wounded here."

He tried to look past me, but I wouldn't have it.

"Just open the door, Gan."

Slots in the brick slid back and familiar nozzles poked through.

"Gan! You mucking—" My string of curses were lost in the assault of water. When it was over, I was dripping wet and Mr. Wheezy was lying in a puddle of steaming water gasping for air.

"You made him a corpse, you did!" I yelled.

The heavy door swung open.

Mordecai was in his chair, disheveled, dressed in a loose, wide-sleeved shirt and trousers—clearly I had woken him. And Gan was in his usual loose shirt, trousers, and carpet slippers.

"You're limping. What happened?" Mordecai asked.

"Help me with this bloke." I started to hoist Mr. Wheezy, who wasn't wheezing much anymore.

Gan took over the hoisting with a curse. "We do not have guests here."

"Yes, yes. He's promised me a boatload of masques. Let's just get on with it. He's here already, isn't he?"

Mordecai and Gan shared one of their looks. I'd been with them long enough now to guess what they were saying. Here's about how it would've sounded out loud:

Mordecai: *What do you think?*

Gan: *I think we should have left her in the bone yard.*

Mordecai: *About the dying man.*

Gan: *Let him die. He can't stay. He'll know too much.*

Mordecai: *His corpse will attract attention. At least she blindfolded him.*

Gan: *She's more trouble than she's worth.*

Mordecai: *Always.*

Or something along those lines. Maybe throw in "the things I do for you" for the romantic sort.

Gan rubbed the fabric of Wheezy's coat between his fingers, then frowned when I took my mask back. "His mask was cracked, I had to…"

"He's not from the Below."

"Aren't you Mr. Obvious."

"Is he sun-touched?" Gan asked.

"His eyes glow as sure as mine in the fog. He's got a hole in his lung, too."

The air was good here, so the fellow could breathe without the respirator. Me and Gan hoisted Mr. Wheezy onto a table that Mordecai had cleared off, and began divesting the fellow of his sopping wet clothes. All the while I told Gan what I thought of him, and how difficult he'd made my life. Gan told me the same thing. We got along peachy, he and I.

Once Wheezy was stripped of his shirt and stretched under the lights, I got a better view of him. He was bald, and darker than me even. Like his jawline, the rest of him looked chiseled from stone, too.

I gave a low whistle. At a sharp look from Mordecai, I pretended to be examining the hole in his powerful torso. At his size it was a wonder I managed to drag him anywhere.

"I used some sealant on that hole. After I made him get rid of the air like you taught me."

Gan was the healer. He was damn good at it. But then he was good at most things. So was Mordecai, for that matter.

"You're bleeding, Evie," Gan noted.

"I got some mortar in my leg is all."

"Get me my medical kit."

I started to fetch it, but Gan growled. "I was talking to Mord. *You*, sit. Take off your trousers."

"Fix that fellow first. I can wait."

"I'll tend to her," Mordecai assured.

It was all the usual bit afterwards. I went off to a corner to strip off my soaked clothes, while Gan worked on cleaning Wheezy's wound. After, Gan started on his breathing. He held his hands mid-stomach, one palm up, one palm down, like he was holding an invisible ball.

Mr. Wheezy had gone quiet. His impressive chest was barely rising and falling. His skin had turned ash gray.

A pure light began to gather between Gan's palms. When the glow was nearly blinding, he placed his hands over Mr. Wheezy's wound. It'd be a long time before either man moved. If Mr. Wheezy survived, that was.

I blew out a breath, and took a dressing gown from a hook. When I was proper and all, Mordecai tended to my calf. The mortar had lodged in the muscle. That was why it hurt. My thigh was sliced too, but the lead hadn't stuck there.

"What did you get up to?" he asked as he plucked glass from my cheek.

I pulled a coil of my hair straight to study it, and frowned at the wet mess. It bounced back when I let go. I'd need to comb the snarls out before it dried.

"Are you my nursemaid or something?"

"I'm your—" He cut off. "We're partners. You know the rules."

"Made by you."

"How else are we going to get you out of trouble?" He gestured at the hole in my leg.

"I can take care of myself, Mord. You know that."

"Gan can too, but that doesn't stop him from telling us where he's headed. And he doesn't generally get himself shot."

"You pair barely go out anymore," I pointed out.

But he didn't rise to my bait, only waited.

"I pulled a job, is all. A small one."

Mordecai reached for my bundled longcoat, but I yanked it away. "*My* stash."

"*Evie.*"

"You both fuss like women, you know that?"

"Only where you're concerned."

"Some partners you make. I got two mothers instead."

"Being a mother is not an insult." There was a wry humor playing on the side of his lips. Mordecai had gone all gray since that day we met. I take all the credit for that. He still kept his hair longish, past his slim shoulders, but now he wore a refined sort of mustache and goatee named after some lord called Van Dyke. He looked like a lord himself.

After Mordecai slapped a plaster bandage on my leg, I stood up, tucked my bundle under my arm, and limped down a hallway to our main living area.

Plush carpets, a monstrous hearth, and walls of teak and oak hung with works of art. Even a marble statue or two. While we hadn't gotten off the ground (by choice) our hideout was top notch and the air was fresh.

I went to my room to finish dressing. I was about to leave the bundle there, but figured I'd tortured Mordecai enough already. And where was the fun in opening a stolen cache alone?

I sat in the great room waiting for Mordecai as he wheeled back into the room, a tray balanced on his thighs. He handed me a bowl of vegetable soup, poured tea, then eyed the bundle next to me.

I made him sit and wait while I used my fingers to comb cleansing oils through my wet hair. My curls had a mind of their own, and if Gan insisted on dousing me with water every damn time I got home, then they could wait until I was properly settled. When I had my hair sorted, I unrolled my makeshift pack. The bundled papers fell onto the floor, and I settled the strongbox on my lap to examine the lock.

Mordecai reached for the papers.

As I worked my lock picks, he unfurled the pages. His gray

brows drew together. "Evie… who did you burgle?" he asked slowly.

A satisfying click made me smile. I waggled my fingers over the box and lifted the lid. "Ah now… Luck is with me." I showed him the glittering box of masques and precious gems.

But Mordecai was dead serious. The blood had drained from his already pale face. He held up the papers. "Do you know what these are?"

I reached for the papers, but he snatched them back. "*Who* did you burgle?"

I lifted a shoulder. "The head of the mucking Sweeper's Union. What of it?"

Mordecai closed his eyes. "My God," he whispered.

While I had flair, Mordecai was far too dramatic. There is a drama line, you see, and Mordecai crossed it daily.

"Did anyone see you?" he demanded.

I pursued my lips. Diversion was the best tactic here. "What's lit a fire under you, ey?" I reached for the papers, again. He snatched them away. "Look here, Mord…"

"Did anyone *see* you?" He had his serious face on. Besides being dramatic, Mordecai was only slightly less serious than Gan. A rock was more amusing.

"Define 'see'."

"Do they know someone infiltrated their stronghold?"

"See there's a funny story there…" I gave him the quick version. No fuss. I tried to get him to crack a smile at Miss Hussy with the lord. He wasn't amused.

Mordecai grabbed his wheels and wrenched on them, zipping over to Gan. "We need to go. Now."

"He can't be moved." Gan said through clenched teeth. He sounded far away, his focus on Mr. Wheezy.

"Then we'll leave him."

I ran up behind Mordecai and snatched the papers from

his hand. "What's all this fuss about?" I looked at the papers. They were airway schematics: pipe ducts, airflow, fan locations. Exactly what'd you expect a Sweeper to have. Except… there was an official-looking seal stamped on the contract along with small numbers around the borders. "It's just a union contract, isn't it?" I asked.

"With longitude and latitude coordinates. That's only useful to those in the Above. To say nothing of the Sage King's own seal stamped on it," Mordecai said.

Gan's focus shattered. The healing light between his palms dispersed, little motes falling over Mr. Wheezy's chiseled chest.

"How the muck do you know?" I asked.

"I *know*."

I held up the fine slippers I'd pinched from the grunting lord. "But I got these to make up for it." I flashed a smile. It had no affect on Gan's crag-like face.

He looked down to his patient. "Who is this?"

"I call him Mr. Wheezy. He promised me more masques than I can handle if I helped him. Got into a scuffle with some guards."

Mordecai cranked on his wheelchair, and sped over to a control panel. "*After* he fell from a burning airship."

Gan cursed. "Why did you bring him here?"

I raised a brow at the half-dead man. "Can't pay me masques if he's dead, now can he?"

"It sounds like there was another thief inside," Mordecai threw over his shoulder. The two shared a look I couldn't decipher.

"I reject that term. You know I prefer professional cat burglar. And aren't you two jumping to conclusions? It's just another contract."

But then the air above us whistled. The building shook, and I had no ground to stand on.

13. FRYING PAN

Part of the roof came crashing down. I threw myself to the side as a beam pounded the floor. Dirt and mortar swirled in the air.

"Evie!" Mordecai coughed.

"Here," I called. "Gan?"

"Alive." He had thrown himself over Mr. Wheezy. As he shifted, crumbling stone slid off his back.

I squinted through the wreckage. There was an odor in the air. Black powder. Another explosion rocked the floor. This one distant.

I scrambled to my feet and grabbed the emergency respirators, tossing one to Mordecai and two to Gan. He fitted one over his patient.

"Death charges," Mordecai yelled. He flipped switches to arm our security measures, then snatched a silk cloth that was covering a giant glass bulb. Electricity crackled to life inside. A pulse showed a thousand dots: blue, green, and far too many red. "Airships are bombing West Winch."

"For a pair of slippers?"

"The Ministry could be fighting with HOOF again." Ever the optimist. That was Mordecai.

HOOF—Heroes of Organized Fury—was a rebel group opposed to the Ministry that regularly made our lives difficult when they got into skirmishes in the Above and sometimes the Below.

Gan put his ear to a listening tube. We held our breaths, waiting for death to fall from Above. Another explosion knocked loose a wave of stone. I moved away from a hole in our building.

"I hear Sniffers," Gan whispered. "Outside."

"I was careful," I defended.

"Give me that strongbox," Mordecai said.

I stuffed the contract in my waistcoat and handed him the strongbox. Gan sprinted off to make preparations.

I watched the dots in the globe, nearly hypnotized by their movements. Sniffers were… well, we didn't know much about them. Humanoid in shape, they were covered head to toe in dark shrouds, and they wore distinctive plague masks with no eyes and long curving beaks. They could track a scent through the fog, and they were called Sniffers because you could hear them sniffing the air.

Mordecai sorted through the coins and gems in the box, then abandoned care and dumped the whole thing on the floor. I winced, but took his cue and started sifting through the lot.

There. A metal arrowhead. A ferromagnetic tracer. Damn, those were rare.

"Toss it from the roof, Evie. Quick!"

I ran with a vengeance, because I was the mucking idiot. I took the stairs three at a time, bounding up three flights. Part way up I had to leap over a gap in the stairwell that had been blown out. Then I burst out onto the roof. The West Winch was on fire, the fog aglow with red. Barrel bombs continued to fall.

What the muck? That was a lot of explosives and a heap of lives to be snuffing out over a box of gems.

I threw the arrowhead as far as I could, and watched it soar through the air and disappear into the fogline. With luck the beacon would distract the Sniffers.

But the night wasn't finished with me.

I BYPASSED THE STAIRWELL AND LEAPT ONTO A SUPPORT POLE to slide down to the first floor. Gan was dumping our gear into the emergency escape hatch. I only hoped the tunnels in the Under Below hadn't collapsed.

Mordecai had his ear to a tube and his eyes on the glass globe. I didn't know how he could hear a thing between shuddering bricks and distant explosions. Just then an eerie kind of silence fell over us.

We held our breath. "The Sniffers haven't moved away," Mordecai finally whispered.

How'd they picked up my scent? Or was it something else? I glanced to Mr. Wheezy. Did they have his scent in their beaked masks? In that case, they'd come knocking on our door no matter where we took him.

Mordecai reached up to a shelf, opened a box, and carefully extracted a blinding white tube. As he did, the lights died and all the dots in the globe winked out. The lightning crackling in the tube cast Mordecai's face in a sinister light. I lit a lantern, and Mordecai slipped the glowing tube into a silk bag to tuck away. That was our real treasure. The glass tube gave lights their spark and fans their power.

Mordecai wheeled over to the escape hatch, and Gan put a tender hand over his. "We'll be right behind you."

They had one of those unspoken conversations, then Gan helped Mordecai down the chute, and dumped his legs down after.

Another explosion rocked the building. Dust swirled in the air and covered my goggles. I couldn't see a thing.

Then the big iron door shuddered.

Gan beckoned me to him. "Hurry."

I started to follow Mordecai, but paused to look over at the man on the slab.

"He's dead weight, Evie. He'll slow us down."

That was all true, but he was also helpless. I dragged the abandoned wheelchair over to Mr. Wheezy. As another earthquake shook the building, I started wrestling him into the chair.

Gan was beside me, spitting curses about fool rats with noble ideas. Together, we got Wheezy into the chair and wheeled him to the hatch.

"Incoming!" I yelled. It wasn't hard to upend the whole thing. I just hoped Mr. Wheezy wouldn't fall on Mordecai. I'd never hear the end of it.

As Mr. Wheezy disappeared down the chute, an entire section of wall exploded towards us. Stones and chunks of brick rained down. I heard nothing but ringing in my ears.

I clawed my way towards Gan. He had his mask on and his battered thief-taker's coat, but all I could see of him was a gray silhouette covered in mortar and stone dust.

"Get movin', old man!" I shouted.

Gan grunted, and got to his knees, then his head snapped up towards the busted wall. An angry mist roiled at the opening.

Something was coming.

Instinct urged me to flee, but the escape hatch was buried under a smoldering timber. Gan vibrated with intensity, and I saw what he saw: a wall of red fog coming at us like a wave.

He straddled the beam and heaved. A space opened, just big enough for me to slither through. "Go! Now!"

Not without him. I wedged the wheelchair under the beam to prop it up.

"Evie!"

I slipped inside, and braced myself at the top of the chute, waiting to make sure he followed. He moved towards the opening as the wall of fog slammed into us. The force knocked the breath from my lungs. Then came the chill, so cold it burned.

Gan met my eyes, his own desperate behind his mask. Ice crystals were forming on its glass lens. He reached for his swords, then kicked free the wheelchair and a pile of rubble knocked me down the chute.

I LANDED ON A PAD IN A SKIFF THAT WAS BOBBING IN AN underground canal. All our worldly possessions were strewn about. I rolled to the side and came up on my knees, glaring at the hatch. "That bastard!"

Mordecai's face was turned towards the hatch, unreadable behind his mask. "Where?" It was the most nonsensical thing I'd ever heard from the man.

"Something broke through. Gan sealed off the escape route on purpose," I growled.

Mordecai had his legs on now, and he stood at the stern. His knuckles were white on the quant pole. "What was it?"

"Red fog. Cold as ice. I don't bloody know!" I glared at the sewer ceiling, willing Gan to appear. "I'm going back up."

"No!" Without another word, Mordecai shoved off, the skiff gliding forward through the canal.

"We can't leave him."

"He stayed for us."

Realization hit me. Gan wasn't planning on running. He was buying us time. "New plan, Mord. Take care of my treasure hoard here. I'll meet you on the hulk."

"Evie!"

I took a running start at the side of the skiff, hit the short rail and leapt. It was a long way to the walkway at the side. I hit the edge of it at my waist, and my knees dipped into sludge. "Muck!"

Whatever these tunnels had started as, they'd ended as giant sewers. My rescue wasn't off to an elegant start.

<hr>

I HOISTED MYSELF ONTO THE LEDGE, AND RAN ALONG THE canal while Mordecai yelled curses at me. He'd be yelling more if I wasn't able to bring Gan back.

Large animals blocked my way. Rats. They were bold bastards, fat on corpses dumped in the tunnels. Without slowing, I picked my way through the biting rodents as Mordecai's shouts faded. I grabbed an access ladder slick with slime. Up I went. And shoved at a rusty grate. Locked. It took fifteen cursing seconds to pick the lock and work it free. I was up and out in another five, and standing in a street.

The fogline looked like it was on fire. Brick buildings were actually burning, turning the fog black. What had I set into motion?

I didn't stop to get my bearings. I had excellent sense, so I trusted it. I ran past fleeing residents of West Winch, then turned down a twisting lane into a maze of rubble.

The sound of marching feet had me duck down an alley. From there I took to the high road, climbing up a drain pipe to a drooping roof. I crouched and peered down at a troop of Enforcers marching down the street. The Sniffer that was leading the way was draped in a midnight shroud with a protruding bone beak, and its eyes glowed green in the fog.

I could hear it from where I was. Sniffing. Like some malformed, upright mongrel, snorting through the muck. I moved quickly over the roof, leapt across to another, then went up and over a roof peak to slide down the other side. I let the slope take me down, then leapt across an alleyway to catch a sagging balcony. It creaked, but held. I climbed through a window, ran past cowering faces, and burst out the other side, catching a drain pipe to slide to solid ground.

Catching my breath, I paused to listen. Voices, shouts, stomping feet, and hissing steam. I ran towards our hideout. Bodies lay in the streets, strewn about like rubbish. Burnt, cut, crushed.

Gan would be all right. He was way more capable than the likes of me. That's what I was telling myself, at any rate.

A wall of fog blocked my way. Not the usual fogline with visibility of about twenty feet, but a solid wall of it that blocked the narrow lane. I stopped. The fog was odd. I thrust my arm into the thick air, and snatched it back with a hiss. It was freezing in there.

I looked around to make sure I was in the right lane. Our hideout should be right on this street. I knew that was right because a familiar cart with busted spokes was off to the side. Taking a breath, I stepped inside.

I was completely blind, and shivering despite my longcoat and layers. I twitched up the hood and raised my tinted goggles. It didn't much matter who might see my glowing eyes in there. It helped a little. There was now a whole five feet of visibility. The red glow was dense. It was like walking through misted blood; I didn't much like the *feel* of it.

As I inched along, I listened for the first hissing steam of an Enforcer. Feeling the cobblestones underfoot, I came to what should have been our hideout. Instead there was a heaping mound of rubble.

I climbed broken brick and timber—all iced over. My teeth chattered from fear as much as cold. "Gan?" I called

Bad idea.

The mist shifted, drawing back. Tendrils took shape and a shadow glided towards me. There was no mistaking that humanoid form for Gan. This thing moved through the fog like a ghost. Round black eyes, no nose, no mouth, with long curving fingers of red mist.

I scrambled away, slipping on brick and wreckage as it glided forward. "What did you bloody do with him?" I demanded.

"Ssssun-touched." A long sibilant hiss filled my ears like a caress.

In one smooth move, I drew a knife and let it fly. The blade passed through the form and clattered on the cobblestones.

"Ssssun-touched, you cannot be," it hissed.

"I be!" For good measure, I drew my pistol and sent lead flying. The mist rippled at its passing, but the shot didn't slow the thing.

It raised a hand and tendrils of hellish mist whipped towards me. I dived and rolled to the side. A whip of cold fire slashed across my shoulder. It was mist. And yet it wasn't.

Self-preservation was a high priority of mine. I bolted. The hairs on my neck were screaming, but I was too cold to look over my shoulder. I raced through the red fog, and for a moment it clutched at me, holding me back. With a curse, I broke through the fog wall and nearly tripped as the air lightened. I kept running through the maze of streets, past buildings and fleeing families, back into the rain of death. Better to take my chances there than with whatever that thing was.

A rush of air warned me, and I glanced up in time to see a dark barrel falling from the fogline. It landed across the street. I threw myself towards a gutter and rammed into stone as shards of wood and brick burst outwards to bury me in ruin.

14. LOSS

The first thing I noticed was the quiet. The next was
that I couldn't breathe. At least that's what it felt like. A heavy
weight pressed on me. As I shifted, an avalanche of noise fell
around me.

Sight came next. What there was of it. It felt like sand was
in my eyes. My goggles were cracked. Slowly I moved each
limb. I was under wreckage. Or in a dark cave. Muck. I didn't
fancy being buried. But former rat that I was, that didn't cause
panic. I was breathing and hidden. Being buried in an explosion had likely saved my arse.

Scuffing and scratching sounded from above. Or was it
below? I pushed at a wood beam above my head, dislodging a
cloud of brick dust. Intense heat had scorched the timber, and
some of the bricks were melted.

I felt a tug on my boot and kicked out at the snatching
hand. "Oi! You want loot? Get me out of here and I'll pay!" I
wasn't sure if the scavengers would run or freeze. It wasn't
every day a corpse talked back. But soon enough my offer
paid off as an army of rats worked to free me.

I sat in the wreckage, catching my breath. Freedom. It felt

good. My kith surrounded me, clothed in rags and tatters, with grime covered faces and red eyes staring in wonder. They were staring at my eyes. I flashed a grin and lowered my cracked goggles, so they could get a better look.

"Free I being. To you thanks."

They scattered back an inch.

"Oi now. Payment promised." I dug into a pocket and brought out a handful of coils—a treasure hoard to the likes of them. I dropped a few in each grubby hand, but what this lot really needed was food. Pity I had none.

I climbed carefully to my feet and their eyes followed me up as one. "Alls this fall?" I asked in my old tongue.

"Alls is fall," a runt answered. This one was the smallest but the sturdiest looking. The others were bone thin. I sighed.

"Best pickins on fringe," one added. They were being generous, sharing the location of a looting spot.

"Catchers about?"

They nodded, and pointed towards my hideout.

"How you be rat?" another asked. This one's eyes were sunken and large.

"I be." I could feel their wonder. "There be dented thief-taker about?" My heart fell when no one answered. "A masque to finding him," I offered. Whispering rippled through the mischief of rats. I told them where I could be found without worry one would snitch. We rats were beneath notice except as a nuisance to crush.

I felt torn. I wanted to race back and dig through the pile of our hideout looking for Gan, but suppose he escaped and I got caught? My body was begging for rest and sense was telling me to leave. But my heart said otherwise. In the end, I limped away from the ruins of West Winch in defeat.

OUR HULK WAS AN OLD ROTTING FRIGATE THAT LOOKED ON the verge of sinking. Natty camouflage is what it was. Rats stayed clear and even Enforcers. No one wanted to go down with it and find themselves drowning in the Styx. But honestly, I didn't know if it was muck that was holding it up or the improvements Mordecai and Gan had made—those two were clever fools.

A skiff was tied alongside. The same one I'd last seen Mordecai in. I didn't call for the gangplank, but balanced my way along a thick mooring line. The Styx rippled under me. As I neared the middle of the line, clear of shore muck, I could see luminescent creatures drifting in the waters below. Denizens of the Below said the water monsters produced muck. Others said the creatures kept the deeper waters of the Styx clear of it. Whatever the case, the water below me was free of it. Most claimed that anyone who dared to stick a hand in that cool crystalline water was sure to come back without it. Of course, people said all sorts of things—lies, truth, and in between. But I didn't fancy testing that claim.

I dropped onto the deck with a faint thud. Before Mordecai could get his hackles up, I tapped out our agreed signal, then ventured below deck.

The place looked like a wreck. Rotting wood, splintered chairs, and some glowing mold growing in patches on the walls. And did I mention the creaking floorboards? Some were completely busted out, allowing the adventurous to peer down into a cavernous cargo hold. I stepped over a gap and went to a specific door. Gan and Mordecai were paranoid. Rightly so. After disarming various traps, I slipped into another world—a real posh hideout.

There were solid deck boards underfoot, not a leak in the place, and lots of oiled teak and brass. The cabin didn't have carpets and tapestries like our main hideout, but it was comfortable and spacious.

I heard Mordecai's clomping footsteps long before he arrived. When he entered the cabin he sagged with relief. Then his eyes flickered over my shoulder, searching.

I half turned, hoping Gan had somehow snuck up behind me. Only he hadn't. "I'm sorry… The entire area was bombed. It's all rubble," I said quietly.

Mordecai swallowed.

I tore off goggles and respirator and slumped on a padded bench. All I could do was stare numbly at my hands. Mordecai sat beside me. His arm came around my shoulders. I could feel the emotion in the man. I leaned into him for comfort, but winced instead. He snapped back, then carefully peeled away my ripped longcoat. "What happened?"

"There was… something." Words failed me. That shook him, for I was never quiet.

Mordecai brought out a flask from his breast pocket. I didn't argue. I drank some down and welcomed the burn. He took the flask from me and poured the expensive liquid on a clean handkerchief, then dabbed at my temple. It stung. My whole body hurt. I wanted to collapse on the bench and sleep right there. I flinched when he dabbed at a cut on my back.

"I went back to our building. It was ruined. Nothing standing that I could see. And there was a… a mist thing," I said. "In the red fog. Black eyes, no nose, no mouth, long misty fingers." I gestured as if that would help. "And it spoke."

Mordecai paused. "What did it say?"

"Hissy thing. Called me sun-touched. Said I couldn't be." I looked over at him. "My blade and bullet went right through it, Mord. What the muck was it?"

"I think you know," he said quietly.

The myths. Stories. Impossible nightmares. But he was

right. I knew what that thing was: a Ghostmaker. "What have I done?" I whispered.

"Muck happens," he said wryly.

I snorted at the rare curse from his lips. "Do you have that contract?" he asked.

Too tired to think, I fished the papers out of my coat and handed them over. "I've set rats searching for Gan——" The words sounded dull in my own ears. I had never felt so heavy, so tired.

"He'll find his way home, just like you did," he whispered. "I'm glad for that, Evie." He laid a hand on an uninjured part of my back. "Things will look brighter with some rest. There's heated water in the galley. Tend to your injuries. For what you can't reach, call me."

I climbed to my feet to go, but noticed Mordecai was staring at a wall. He looked lost. "How's Mr. Wheezy?" I asked.

He stirred. "Alive. For now."

I made it as far as the doorway before I stopped and turned. "What did the Ghostmaker mean when it said 'I cannot be?'"

"Have you ever seen a sun-touched rat, Evie?"

I lifted a shoulder. "Never seen a Ghostmaker before today."

But that wasn't entirely true, now was it? I had seen one, all those years ago in the Before, on the day I died. When it had been dragging away a man. Could it have done the same with Gan? But where did Ghostmakers take their prisoners?

He gave me a half-smile. "True enough."

15. CAUGHT

BEFORE

"So it be?" I asked.

"*Is this it?*" Gan corrected with a snap.

"Or, 'Are we there yet?'" Mordecai added.

I rolled my eyes. "I'm being likely cut in half here. Lay off."

"She has a point," Mordecai muttered.

"No one is being cut in half today," Gan growled.

The three of us were sitting easy on a skiff in a canal. I gazed up at the base of a tower and shook out my hands while Mordecai fussed over me, checking my special shoes, the satchel slung on my back, and the fit of my respirator. Not that I needed one, but he insisted I wear it. Anything to delay me leaving.

Gan used the pole to push us over to the tower. The skiff bumped against slimy stone. This was a tricky part, but not dangerous. The muck and slime along the bank of the stone canal were slick, and there was nothing to hold onto.

I settled a coil of rope around my body, and Gan assembled a pole that had been laid out in four sections. It was long and unwieldy. When he planted it in the muck, its top was lost in the fogline. Then he stood in his 'immovable root' stance on the bobbing skiff. He wasn't wearing his longcoat today, only his mask, and loose gray clothes like me. Easier to blend with the fog.

I gripped the pole and felt a hand on my shoulder. I turned to look at Mordecai, who sat on the skiff's bench, his usually calm eyes full of emotion behind the lens of his mask. "You don't have to do this," he said.

I glanced sideways at Gan. "I be wishing I was a boy too now."

"He'd still get attached," Gan grumbled.

I gave Mordecai a lopsided grin. "You make a mucking bad thief-boss, you know?" Before he answered, I started climbing, taking care to step on Gan's shoulder, then his ear, and his head. I had to stifle a laugh at his whispered curse.

I moved up the pole as easy as a stairway, up to the very top, then balanced on the end of it on one foot. When I was set, I tapped my other foot on the pole's side, and Gan, now lost in the fog below me, lifted it over his head as we'd practiced, then tilted the pole towards the tower base. Slimy moss coated the stones with a bluish glow. According to Gan and Mordecai, the water level of the canals fluctuated, controlled by levies and dams. Right then it was low tide.

I reached for the promised line of stone free of moss and slime, and found purchase. I don't know how Mordecai and Gan knew the layout of this place, but they were right. There was the high waterline right where they said it would be. I scrambled up the stones, climbing like a spider.

It was peaceful-like. The higher I climbed, the more at ease I felt. And with the fog all around, it never seemed so very high. It was like a cushion was there, waiting to catch me.

I reached the first spigot, a gargoyle with a lolling tongue, wrapped my hand around a horn and braced my feet against the stone wall. I looped one end of my rope around the spigot, hoping the gargoyle would hold, and shrugged the coil off my shoulders. The rope went taut, and within minutes Gan was climbing out of the fog, hand over hand, his feet walking up the side of the tower. Wordlessly, he nodded to me.

The eyes of his mask were as expressionless as I knew his face was beneath. I wondered how many years he had worn that battered mask. Had his real face taken on its demeanor or did the mask reflect what was already there?

Queer thoughts for a rat, I know. But my new life with these two left room for the higher contemplations. I edged out on a ledge so Gan could climb up onto the gargoyle. He gathered up the rope and attached a hook to one end. Then he moved along the edge towards a corner of the building. Small stones and mortar flaked off as he moved, tumbling far below. I heard the dull splashes, and cringed.

Gan reached the corner, and began to spin the rope. It made a whirring sound and agitated the fog. Then he let it fly.

The clatter of the hook made me grit my teeth. I held my breath listening for a call, but the guards were lax at low tide, trusting slick moss to do their job.

Gan quickly pulled the rope back up and tried again. This time the grappling hook caught. He pulled the rope taut and braced himself while I clambered over to him. The rope was at an angle. I gripped the rope and eased out over the fog. I hung for a moment to get a feel for the rope and the air, then shimmied along using my hands and feet like a rat skittering along a moor line.

The neighboring tower soon swam into view. In the fog, nothing was distinct or sharp, everything swam and swirled. Sometimes it was wise to wait, to see if your eyes were deceiving you. The fog played tricks on the mind, it did. But I was fairly immune to its deceptions.

The grappling hook had caught on a spire with a decorative cap. Why, I wondered, did they build buildings with gargoyles and decorations when it was all swallowed by fog?

At the moment, the reason didn't much matter. Only that the spire was there. The stone on this building was plated with iron for extra security. I wondered if it was reinforcement against the airships and their bombs, or to stop rats like me who liked to climb? Seemed like a lot of expense for the likes of me when a pistol would do the job well enough.

At the top of the spire, I gave the rope a tug. Gan untied his end of the rope, and retied the very end, then released the rest of it. I took in the slack, secured the hook to my satchel, then slid down to an iron bracket that was there to stabilize the spire. I was getting close. I eased myself down and crimped my fingers on the long straight rod. The edges were sharp and rusted, but months of practicing had turned my hands to calloused stone. I edged along, feet dangling, keeping my body as still as possible and my balance "as calm as a mountain lake," whatever that meant. Gan's metaphors never made much sense to me. Mordecai usually had to translate. In this case, he'd explained it as being "as still as a hunted rat." He didn't know much about rats.

My fingers ached, but I managed. Once I got to the new section, I braced myself on a corner, and reached to open a small vent door. But it didn't budge.

Muck!

It wasn't supposed to be locked. My thighs were shaking from bracing myself on the corner. The iron was smooth and there were no holds. I was using pressure to keep in place on the slick iron. Mordecai called it "stemming" for blank corners. But I didn't care what it was called in the moment.

A well of panic rose up my throat. I tried breathing the way Gan taught me, but the respirator was suffocating, so I ripped it off and let it dangle from around my neck. I gasped in air. This high up, it was clean of the toxic sludge of the Below.

The air cooled me, and I took in great heaps of it, filling my lungs until my head felt about to float. My legs stopped shaking. Calmer now, I considered the locked grate. No, it wasn't locked. It was rusted shut. I needed to place the grappling hook on the lip of the opening. If I placed it through the grate, it could fall out with Gan balancing mid-rope. That might pull it open, but Gan would plummet to a squishy death.

I braced myself on the corner with my feet and one hand, and tugged at the grate with the other, trying to open it. We didn't have time for this. The hinges looked about ready to crumble off. So I slipped out a knife and prayed to Luck himself that no one would notice the banging, as I beat at the hinges with the pommel. The whirring fan inside the passage would cover the noise, at least that's what I hoped would happen. Rust flaked off, and I tried again. No luck. There wasn't even a proper gap for my blade to pry it open. I tried anyway.

When that failed, I tucked my dagger away. Rather than risk Gan, who didn't know what was happening over here, I decided to risk yours truly.

I took my grappling hook and the loose length of rope and threaded it around the iron turret support, then stuck the hook through a grate hole.

Right. Here goes.

Climbing up a few feet along the corner, I stared down at the drooping rope and jumped. I grabbed for the rope. The combination of my weight and gravity popped the grate right off its rusty hinges. Only the grate slipped off the hook and fell into the fogline. As I dangled on the rope, I waited for it to clatter on the ground. When it finally hit, the noise was jarring.

Gan pulled on the rope from his end, and I hissed at him through the fog. He was worried. I scrambled back up and returned to my position, grabbing onto the lip of the air shaft. But my hands were bloody with rope burn now.

I wasn't going to worry about that. I had worse problems. Shouts came from Below. Mostly questions from the guards. I hung the grappling hook on the solid stone lip, and tugged three times. The rope went taut. Tired already, I folded my elbows on the lip to rest my hands and legs.

The access vent was small, but the shaft inside was wide and the fan below hypnotizing. I watched the steady rotation of its giant, deadly blades that sucked air down the shaft. We hadn't simulated such a strong air current in our replica; the drag was strong enough to pull at my respirator.

Gan soon came into view, balancing on the tight rope. He crouched near the air shaft behind me. "What was that about?" he hissed in my ear.

"This door here is sticking. You be welcome."

"Catch the grate next time," he said.

"Next time you be catching it your mucking self."

He clucked his tongue, but stayed silent.

I lingered for a minute more, to catch my breath and try to get my muscles to relax. Gan didn't press me. We listened to the guards below, but they hadn't sounded an alarm.

"It's not uncommon for grates to fall," he whispered in my ear. "Are you ready?"

I gulped. And held up a hand. A deep cut tore through my palm from grabbing the rope. Gan didn't make a sound. He reached into a pouch and took out a bandage.

"I not be climbing like that," I hissed.

"You won't be climbing with blood on your fingers either."

I let him wrap my hands. The bandages were snug and he topped them off with tight plaster. I flexed my fingers, trying to loosen them up for mobility. Then I handed over my respirator. The satchel on my back was weight enough.

I took a calming breath, and climbed through the opening.

THE SHAFT, AT LEAST, WAS THE SAME SIZE AS THE REPLICA IN Gan and Mordecai's hideout. With one foot on the vent opening, I stretched across to the other side. The stone was slick with moisture, and air tugged at my clothes. When I was settled in the air shaft, I tried not to stare down at the fan. Instead I focused on inching upwards away from it.

It was as hard as it sounds.

Shuffle, *shuffle*, move up. Months of practice had honed my body, but the down draft was strong. I panted, each inch a victory. Sweat slicked my hands and I increased pressure, but my body was stretched as far as it could go already. It seemed a lifetime before I came to a connecting air shaft. I gripped it with relief, and slithered inside the small passageway.

This one was slanted, easy enough for the likes of me. I followed the maze of shafts from memory. How did Mordecai and Gan know about these shafts? I came to the final one at last, and stopped at a golden grate. The vent cover was small, even for me.

I pressed an eye to the ornate gaps. There was a circular stone room below. A coil of metal sat in the middle like a pedestal and on top of it was a glass tube of lightning. A heavy iron vault door was the only exit. I removed my satchel, opened the grate and twisted my head, then moved my shoulders, squeezing through the vent to fall on the floor. There was no chance of going back that way; the walls of the room were too smooth to climb.

I didn't have much time. Keeping my head down, I slithered over to a pronged lever and pulled it like Mordecai had instructed. A humming sound emanating from the pedestal died. I dashed up and unhooked the strange tube. Lightning crackled and spit inside the glass. It was near to blinding, but it was also hypnotizing. Giving myself a mental shake, I wrapped it in a special padded pouch, then tucked it into my satchel and waited by the door.

Guards were alerted the moment I disconnected the glass tube. This was my exit plan. Soon enough, the wheel on the heavy iron door turned, and the door opened. I held my breath as two fancy guards stepped inside. They looked from the empty pedestal to the open grate high overhead. I took that moment to slip outside.

Sure I'd get a bullet in my back, I kept my head down and nearly ran, turned a corner, and opened a grate near the floor. Footsteps hurried down the hallway. I slipped inside this larger shaft, closed the grate, and held my breath. Feet marched right past me.

No one paid much mind to an air shaft only a rat could fit into.

Pride swelled in me as I retraced my path, and came to the final vertical shaft. Nearly home. When I disconnected the glass tube, the fans had all shut down. The air inside the shaft was still. I started down, shuffling along with my arms and legs braced.

Almost there.

But excitement made me careless. I slipped. Down I went, feeling air zip past me. The fan was still, but the shaft was deep enough to kill. Suddenly the strap of my satchel went tight, and I came to an abrupt halt, banging against the side of the shaft. I heard something crack and a strangled cry.

I craned my neck around to see Gan's arm, his hand clamped on my satchel. I dangled in shock. "Grab on," he bit out through clenched teeth.

I gripped the lip of the access vent.

He reeled backwards, and I looked out through the opening. Gan was balanced on the tightrope, his back to the corner of the building. The arm he'd used to catch me hung limply against his side, his shoulder protruding oddly in its socket. He slammed his shoulder against the tower, and there was an audible *pop*!

His knees went weak, and I stretched to press a hand to his leg, to keep him pinned against the corner. His breathing was ragged, his body slumped, but his feet stayed on the tightrope.

Bells and whistles sounded in the fog.

"Go across. I'll follow," Gan ordered.

"How you be climbing down?" We'd planned to leave the rope in place, walk across, and the both of us climb down without a rope. But his arm was hanging limply at his side. There was no way to walk across the tightrope, then detach the other end to rappel down. He'd have to make the climb one-handed.

"I'll manage. Tell Mordecai to leave."

I started to go, then turned. "You caught me."

"You had the loot."

True enough, I did. But there was nothing stopping him from taking my satchel and ordering me to stay behind to unhook the rope, so he could get back to our skiff. I was the one who mucked up, and I still had use of both of my arms.

"*Go*, Evie," he said. "Please. Get Mordecai away from here."

I balanced across the rope to the adjoining tower, climbed

down the stone wall, then slid down the pole to the waiting skiff.

Mordecai steadied me as I hit the deck. "Gan is hurt. I fell and he caught me," I panted. "His shoulder be popping. He said he can manage, and is wanting us to leave."

Mordecai cursed, and turned his face towards the fogline. Alarms were ringing and the water in the canal rippled as shadows passed in the darkness. There'd be patrol boats and Sniffers soon enough.

From the tilt of his shoulders, I could see Mordecai's struggle. The beak of his plague mask dipped, then he reached for the pole and quickly disassembled it.

"We can't be leaving," I whispered.

"Then we'll be caught and Gan will have both of us to worry about." He pushed off, and the skiff glided into the canal.

I DON'T KNOW HOW GAN MANAGED TO CLIMB DOWN THAT DAY, but he did. Later on that evening, he showed up at our hideout with his arm in a sling.

Mordecai close to fainted with relief.

As the two held on to each other like drowning men, I crossed my arms. Eventually, Gan cocked a brow my way.

"Where's my mucking masques?" I asked by way of greeting.

Mordecai untangled himself from Gan, a smile playing on his lips. "This is where the real fun begins, Evie." He beckoned me into his workshop, and even Gan walked over to study the glass tube I'd retrieved. Mordecai lifted me up, and set me on his table so I might look at the thing on a high shelf.

"What it be?" I asked.

"An invention that was stolen from me," he said. He carefully picked it up and turned it slowly. I was hypnotized by the blue crackling light inside. "A distillation process I've perfected. When you distill something, you boil it down to its essence. A distilled part is the most powerful."

"What is it?" I asked.

Mordecai's eyes danced with wonder as he watched his creation. "It's lightning. We can power Bedlam with this."

16. PAYLOAD

AFTER

I AWOKE FEELING SORE AND HUNGOVER FROM THE CYCLE before. How long had I slept? Had Gan returned?

Wincing at every bruise and scrape, I pulled on some trousers and a loose shirt and padded down the corridor. Mr. Wheezy was bundled in a bunk. He was breathing easier, but still looked gray.

More trouble than he was worth, is what he was. I wanted to shake the fellow awake and ask him what he'd dragged us into.

With a sigh, I made my way to the captain's cabin. I found Mordecai sitting on the side of a bed, the stubs of his bare legs hanging over the edge. Gan wasn't there.

I thought back to the day I'd stolen lightning. To Gan's sacrifice. His arm was never the same after he caught me. From then on it was his weak spot, but he never complained about the price he'd paid for my life. Despite all odds, I expected him to come walking into the hulk as if nothing happened. But he didn't return this time.

Mordecai looked lost. The bed didn't seem right without Gan sprawled there beside him. Dark circles ringed his eyes, his gray hair was tattered and loose, his cheeks unshaven. A bandage was wrapped around his arm and cuts crisscrossed his chest.

"What the muck happened to you?" I asked.

Mordecai pulled a blanket over his lap.

"Oh, come off it. You're decent enough." He was wearing his pants; it wasn't like he was naked.

"Have you ever heard of knocking?"

I snorted. "As if. I came to see if you needed help."

"I'm not an invalid."

I stood in the doorway, silent. To prove his point, Mordecai scooted off the side of the bed, lowering himself to the floor, and hand walked to a trunk of clothing, his torso swaying with the movement. What was left of his legs, cut off just above the knees, he held out in front of him. He had abs of steel, he did.

When Mordecai wasn't feeling prickly about his missing legs, Gan usually helped him with everyday things. Mordecai sat on the floor by the trunk and pulled out a fresh shirt.

"No word?" I asked. It was a dumb question. But it was a start.

Mordecai shook his head.

"I shouldn't have left him. I'll go out and—"

"I don't want to lose you, too."

"Gan could be buried in the wreckage. We can't just sit here on our arses," I argued.

"I agree. But you'll do him no good if you get snatched by Enforcers. At least wait until your guest regains consciousness."

I paused. "How'd you get sleeping beauty in here by yourself?"

Mordecai shrugged on the shirt. "I have my methods," he said with an air of mystery, reaching for a fresh pair of stub stockings.

"Don't you always. Just not for cooking. I'll see what the pie cart has for us, but I'm going to look for Gan after."

———

THE PIE CART HAD SLIM PICKINGS. BUT IT WAS EDIBLE. I USED the chance to poke my head into a local pub. A pint would put my body right, and the place was brim full of rumors.

"It were the Bedlam Boys, it was!" said a bloke with a hooked hand and breath to rival muck. "They were clashing with the Seven Devils."

"Nah, it was HOOF, mark my words," said another.

"Why would they bomb West Winch?"

A gnarled, broad-shouldered woman with stained fingers snorted. "Why wouldn't they? We slave away in factories to produce killing machines for the Ministry. Kill the workers, kill the production."

A round of murmured agreement rippled through the pub.

"I hear there was more than bombs there," a man whispered. He stared into the fire's light.

"Come off it, Pete. I'm sick to death of your talk of phantoms."

"A cousin of mine saw Spring-heeled Jack," yelled a young bloke.

It wasn't a night at the pub unless Spring-heeled Jack came up in the conversation. His crimes ranged from setting homes on fire and slashing whores to stealing apple carts. I'd even heard a woman claim he got her up with child. Her mate hadn't been convinced, though.

"No!" yelled a woman. "That bombing was revenge for the Night Witches raiding the Union Lords. I heard something was stolen," she boasted.

"From who?" shouted one-arm.

"My sister's husband's cousin's friend. She's a lady's maid for one of those proper sorts in the towers. "There's a fugitive on the run, too."

"They'll have to round up the whole Below, then."

Laughter filled the pub, but when it died the silence left a queer sort of emptiness. That's when the whispers started. Voices turned low, and patrons clutched their mugs, as talk of the Red Death rippled through the pub. But the only agreement they came to was that West Winch had been leveled.

Itching to return to the place, I took my pies back to the hulk, and walked straight into a standoff.

WELL, NOT SO MUCH AS A *STANDOFF* AS ONE MAN LEANING heavily in a doorway, panting, while a second sat legless on the floor with his arms in the air trying to calm the first man down. Wheezy had found a pistol.

As soon as I walked into the main cabin, Wheezy turned the muzzle on me. His eyes, now a pleasant golden hue without the glow, were glassy and confused. I couldn't help it. Humor took me at the oddest times.

"Now there's a sight," I said, laughing. "Holding a legless man at gunpoint. Scared he'll rush you? That's it, point that thing at me. I assure you I'm not harmless."

"Evie," Mordecai warned. He'd never much cared for my carefree ways.

"We'll just wait a tick, and he'll keel over soon enough."

Wheezy blinked through his daze and straightened his

arm, trying to hold the pistol steady. If I knew Mordecai, he'd dosed our guest with laudanum or some such concoction. Wheezy was only wearing pants, and I distracted myself from the pistol by admiring his physique. The man was pure muscle. Shapely calves, powerful thighs, and a stomach I could use as a washboard. His bald head gleamed dark in the lantern light, and I thought I could sharpen my knives on his jaw.

"You drugged me."

"I didn't," I said, crossing my arms. "But it's a good thing someone did, considering that hole in your lung."

He wheezed in confusion.

"You owe me masques."

I noticed Mordecai was inching over towards a work table. There was a holster bolted to its underside with a loaded pistol in it. We kept things like that, being in the business we were in.

"Do you remember a thing from the last cycle?" I asked.

"How many days?" Wheezy asked.

I looked to Mordecai. "Nearly two," he supplied.

I whistled low. I must've been tired as muck to sleep that long.

"You. Get over there with him," the man ordered.

I raised my brows. "Aren't you a proper scoundrel. Here I saved your life and all. To think I gave you my respirator. You don't even know what that means down here, do you?"

The pistol faltered, as he wheezed and tried to stay upright while his mind was as muddled as the fog. I wasn't the waiting sort. And I had no illusions that noble-minded folk existed. I rushed forward, grabbed the pistol barrel from underneath and pushed it up towards the ceiling. To his credit, he didn't pull the trigger, but I had miscalculated. He let go of the grip, and grabbed my wrist, then bore down on me with all his weight.

I slammed into the bulkhead, the pistol barrel still in my hand. His other hand clamped around my other wrist to stop the knife I had poised at his groin.

We locked eyes, his heart thundering against mine. Me straining against his might. "I'm more than you can manage," I said.

My words struck a chord, because his eyes flashed with memory.

The click of a pistol came between us. "I'd let her go, if I were you," Mordecai drawled. He had the business end pointed at the back of Wheezy's head.

The man stiffened. I hooked a leg behind his knee and dropped him on his arse. Before he could roll, I went down on a knee, pinning it against his solar plexus and wrenching the pistol from his hand. My knife was at his throat.

What little energy he'd stored up was spent. He grunted in pain, and his head dropped to the floor like a rock. "You saved me," he rasped.

"How convenient that you remember it now."

"A knife at the throat will do that," he said. "Ease up on the pressure?"

I did, but only because I didn't want that hole in his back to start bleeding all over the deck boards. Gan's healing had its limits. "Where's my promised masques?"

"Do I look rescued?"

I snorted. "You look half-dead."

"You'll get paid when I've contacted my people."

"So you can tell them where we are? Do I look like a fool?"

His eyes sharpened. "Is that your name?"

"Sure, why not. What's yours?"

He considered me a moment. "Wil."

I waited for more. But his jaw was set. "Do they call you Wee Willy?"

He showed me his teeth. "Can't you tell?"

I made a disgusted sound and got off the man. For good measure, I pointed the pistol at his head. "What faction are you with?"

"That pistol isn't primed."

"I can still hit you over the head with it."

"Answers weren't part of our deal."

"Neither were Enforcers and Sniffers, and my home being blown to bits along with a missing father." I faltered at that last, then got angry over it. "Give me a reason not to hand you over to the Ministry."

He sobered. "I promised you masques. You'll get them. But not if I'm dead and not if you turn me over to the Ministry."

"Just let me know where to drop your hide."

Wil hesitated. "There's the catch…"

17. THE CATCH

THE "CATCH" AS WIL PUT IT WAS ON THE DIFFICULT SIDE. As a sun-touched, he belonged in the Above, and that was a whole other world away.

How to go about smuggling someone back to the Above? There were ways, of course, or so rumor went. Ideally, a sun-touched could just saunter up to an M.U.W. (the Ministry of Ungentlemanly Warfare) building, identify themselves and be whisked home. But Wil wasn't exactly on the upside of the law.

"I'm with the Seven Devils," Wil had said. Pirates, raiders, and hoodlums with a penchant for chaos.

"Were you a cabin boy?" I asked.

"A raider."

"What happened?" Mordecai asked.

"We were raiding a tower and the Ministry caught us. Our airship crashed, I survived, and you know the rest."

"Right, you got your arse kicked."

A muscle in his jaw flexed. I expected him to defend himself but he didn't. Mordecai and me waited for more, but

Wil was a tight-lipped sort. A pity, since his voice was deep and rumbly, and gave me a thrill.

"How come the Sniffers got you in their beaks?" I asked.

Wil raised his massive shoulders. "I smell good?"

I stuffed his quiet arse and ballooning ego into the brig. It felt good to turn the key. I flashed him a grin as I tucked it down my shirt. Then I was off to Mordecai's workshop. He had a workshop in every hideout, even our cramped bolt-holes. A tinkerer, he was, and a damn good one.

I picked up a hinged-contraption and leaned against the workbench. "He's lying," I said.

Mordecai snatched the device from my hands. "Or withholding truth."

"Same thing."

Mordecai raised his brows. "You make a habit of withholding just about everything."

I crossed my arms. "And you don't?"

Mordecai gave me a rueful smile. "I worry what you would do with all my knowledge." He was bent over a table, tinkering with a leg. The socket was made of leather and vulcanized rubber, with steel knee and ankle joints, and wood bits for the bone parts.

"You going to connect the lightning thingy to the hulk?"

"I call it an electric coil," he huffed. I knew the term, but I liked to get under his skin. "And no. I don't want to risk attention."

Always the safe one.

"So what do we do with Wee Willy over there?"

"He's your guest." Mordecai glanced over his shoulder. "Prisoner now, I suppose."

I shrugged. "Maybe I'll turn thief-taker."

"Gan will have something to say about that." Mordecai drifted off into silence.

"Do you have contacts in the Above?"

"Just middlemen."

"You mean Poe."

Mordecai chuckled. "He's an acquired taste."

"He's pure slime and you know it."

"I never told you to trust him."

"No one else?" I asked, hopefully.

"I'm afraid that's Gan's department. I'm a denizen down to my bones."

"You and me both."

"Aren't you ever curious about the Above?" he asked.

I considered the question. It was a common enough one in the Below. Some denizens dreamed of escaping to the Above. It was like heaven, they said. Fine living, fine bodies, not a worry in the vast sky. Considering the number of airships that plummeted to the ground, I doubted it was as heavenly as they dreamed.

The Below was home, and Mordecai and Gan the only family I had. But was I curious about the Above?

"Sounds fanciful to me. I don't know what's true and what's bollocks," I said. "No muck? No fog? And a blazing hot sun?" That last was true, I knew. I'd seen it with my own two eyes right before I died.

"I imagine sun-touched, yourself excluded, feel the same about the Below," Mordecai mused, glancing back towards the brig.

I snorted. "'Cept sun-touched can come and go as they please."

"Can they?" Mordecai asked. That was a good question. Could sun-touched visit the Below without restrictions?

"Gan's been to the Above, hasn't he?" I asked.

Mordecai gave a slight nod.

"More reason to find him."

"Do we need another reason?"

I started to say something flippant, but I didn't have it in me. "No," I said quietly. "And that's why I'm going to look for him and you can't stop me."

"West Winch is crawling with Enforcers."

"How do you know?"

"I have eyes and ears in Bedlam, Evie." He gestured at the strongbox of burgled jewels. "Between you and Gan burgling every lord in the district, and my inventions, we have plenty of coin to pay snitches."

"Which attracts attention," I pointed out. "I'm going anyways. Besides, I got to figure out how to get Wee Willy back to the Above." How often did a strapping sun-touched fall from the fogline? These last cycles had been one pile of muck after another.

"Do you buy his story?" I asked.

"It fits."

"Should we ask him about that pale beauty burgling the lord's suite?"

Mordecai set down his tool, and considered the matter. "Not yet, I think. We keep our cards close, as usual."

"Can we afford to with Gan missing?"

"We're not there yet. And I'm coming with you."

"Are not," I countered.

"If you insist on putting yourself in danger at least have a partner to back you up."

"You got no legs."

"True, but I have these," Mordecai tapped his artificial ones, "and I have a mouth. If I go along, I'll deal with Poe later."

"You'll slow me down. Beside, who's going to empty the piss pot in the brig?"

His calm facade cracked. "I can't just sit here and wait!

Gan's out there. He could be injured or—" Mordecai gripped the side of the table. The two of them had been together for longer than I'd been alive. He sighed and dropped his hands to his stubs, absently rubbing the ends like he could still feel his legs. I knew he could. He'd told me once that he could still feel his toes curl.

I put a hand on his shoulder. "I'll be back in four hours," I said. "If not, come rescue me."

Before he could argue, I swept my longcoat over my shoulders, only wincing slightly at the ache in my thigh and the bruises on my body. Rats like me are used to pain though. It's the only constant in our lives.

On my way down the hallway, I passed the brig. Wil was gripping the bars. "I can help you," he said.

"Sure thing!" I said, cheerfully. "I'll just let the bloodthirsty pirate out, so he can put a pistol to my head again."

"I was disoriented."

"You can barely stand, mate."

"Are you always this stubborn?" he yelled as I walked past.

"Ask Stumpy back there."

18. SLIPPERS

Mordecai was right. West Winch was swarming with Enforcers. I wasn't surprised, but I was frustrated as muck.

I ventured in, dodging patrols, and finally taking cover in a stone skeleton of a rookery tottering in the fogline. Red eyes stared from a nearby sewer grate.

I nudged up my goggles and winked. The eyes widened, and I sat in the rubble to listen and wait. Rats were cautious by nature. We had to be to survive any length of time on the streets.

The hiss of steam from an Enforcer's casement passed. Then my patience paid off when I heard a faint scuff to my right. I didn't turn.

"Got a snitch for me?" I asked.

A muck-covered form crawled over the rubble on all fours to sit back on their hunches, ready to flee. Their red eyes darted from me to the fog, body alert for any approaching danger.

"Metal heads be taking flesh in eels." Meaning Enforcers were rounding up the survivors. But for what? Slaves?

"How many?"

They glanced back at the grate, where more red eyes blinked from the darkness. Numbers were hard for rats. We tended to count with fingers. A few of us could even manage all our toes, too.

"Many."

That meant more than twenty—or it could mean more than five.

"Cartloads," a voice hissed from the grate.

"Did you eye a battered thief-taker?"

No answer.

I jerked my head towards the sewer grate. "I need to be getting to the West Winch middle. Tunnels caved?" I asked.

"Most. Metal heads, too."

I grunted softly. "Lead me where you can." I flipped a coil in the air, and the rat caught it deftly. They skittered back to their hole and I followed, wrinkling my nose as I lay down in an all too familiar muck. It wasn't as unpleasant as it should've been. As I slithered through the grate into the Under Below, I pondered what Wee Willy would make of this.

THE SEWERS WERE A MESS. A MAZE OF CAVED-IN PASSAGES FULL of debris and sludge. And bodies. My kith had already picked them clean of their belongings, and now the animal variety feasted on flesh.

They took me as far as they dared, then waited as I climbed back up through a grate that led to a cave of stones. A smoldering timber on the verge of collapse made for a dubious doorway. I poked my head out, and strained my ears. Nothing about.

I don't know what I expected to find in the ruin. Some indication that Gan had escaped. Even his body would do, though not preferred, if only to put his ghost to rest. It was a slim chance, but coming back here was a start.

Fog swirled around me as I picked through the debris of our home. Anything of value that had survived the destruction had long been whisked away by Enforcers, dead-lurkers, and rats.

The fog made my skin crawl. There was something different about it here. But was it my imagination or memory? I couldn't get that Ghostmaker out of my head.

How do you fight a wraith?

What had it done with Gan?

A bit of color caught my eye. I shifted away stone and timber, and dusted away ash to find a tasseled carpet slipper. My heart lurched. But no, this wasn't the slipper Gan was wearing. It wasn't attached to his foot. This was one I'd pinched from the Union Lord. I dug around until I found its twin. Charred and rough around the edges, but still posh.

Taking this as a sign from Luck himself, I tucked the slippers in my satchel, and continued my search.

Gan could be buried under all this, and I'd never know. I sighed. It seemed futile. My eyes were keen and used to the fog, but I'd have fared better with a lantern. Light would attract attention, though. I resisted the urge to holler his name like I'd done before.

Maybe my name *was* Fool.

A rat came skittering towards me, their eyes darting this way and that. Ah, it was the runt from the cycle before.

I crouched down to their level.

"Word?" I asked with hope.

"Word," they said. "Battered thief-taker be with Ferryman now."

"Show me."

The runt led me through a maze of wreckage. Corpses lay

in the streets, some half-buried, others cut down as they ran. A number were nothing more than charred husks. I followed the runt numbly. They could be leading me straight to a trap and I wouldn't have noticed. Gan. *Dead.* But I had to see it with my own eyes to believe it.

The runt led me to a mess of bodies strewn about in an intersection. A charred crater in the middle of the road hinted at the cause of death. The whole lot of them had been blown back from the crater. Runt checked the fog for noise, then skittered to a twisted corpse.

Bile rose in my throat. Though charred, I'd recognize that leather thief-taker's coat anywhere. The back of the coat was slashed and blackened from the blast. Steeling myself, I turned the corpse over. There wasn't much left of the face. Or the head.

"This be kith?" a voice asked.

I must have fallen, because I was sitting in the rubble. "This be kith." As I dug into my pocket for a masque, I paused at a bit of leather clinging to a burnt calf. Boots. The corpse was wearing boots.

19. RUMOR

I SAT IN A CORNER OF A PUB AND SIPPED MY PINT, WATCHING firelight cast shadows around the room. A whirr of fans undercut the drone of conversation. And since the air was fresh, respirators and masks dangled from belts or were slung from hooks on table edges, as was proper. The patrons here were posh and free of muck; their laughter belonged to idle youth with a hand in their parents' coffers.

I'd stopped by a bolt-hole we kept in the Rook to clean up. My eyes were safe from glowing here in the fresh air, but their red hue still attracted notice. There weren't many rats who made it to adulthood (lucky me) let alone ones who could afford this kind of establishment.

The *Laughing Donkey* was where the Above came to mingle with the Below, dipping their toes in filth for a thrill. I only hoped no one recognized me from the Union Lord's ball.

A tall, sleek figure slipped into the booth across from me. Slick black hair, large black eyes, and petulant red lips. He wore a black velvet suit and was as pale as death himself. A mechanical raven named Rumor sat on his shoulder, the firelight playing on its blued body.

"Really, Red? Mead?"

He snapped his long fingers, and a server swept in with a glass of blood-red wine. Rumor hopped down on the table with a whirr of gears.

"I'm a practical sort."

"So I've heard," he drawled. "Did you enjoy the Union banquet?"

"That obvious?" I asked.

He lifted a slim shoulder. "Who else would have the bollocks to burgle the Union Lord? It's the talk of the Above."

"I neither admit nor deny your accusation." With a man like Poe, it was a matter of life and death to keep your cards close. He was a first-class genie with no loyalties. Aside from himself. That suited me just fine, because I knew where we stood.

"You've got style, Red. And I'm not just talking about that delicious coat of yours." He eyed my cowled longcoat with envy. It wasn't 'working' garb, but a coat to wear when I mingled with high-class criminals and the 'Middlers' as we called them. As deep a red as his wine, it was serviceable but still stylish in a pinch, and had pockets hidden in the liner.

Never go anywhere without pockets. That's my motto for life.

"What do you know about the West Winch bombing?" I asked.

Poe sighed. "You know I like a bit of foreplay," he purred.

I slid a ruby so red it was nearly black across the table. He pursed his lips, waiting for Rumor to react. The bird poked at the gem and squawked. "We like that too, but where's the *wordplay*? The tit-for-tat followed by a proper tongue lashing?"

"You're just sore I didn't bring Mordecai along with me."

His eyes flashed. "How is the old devil?"

"He's just peachy," I said.

"Really? Considering…" Poe let the word linger, as he took a sip of his wine, humming with appreciation.

I took his bait. "Considering what?"

"Rumor says his partner is dead."

I glanced at the bird, who gave me the evil eye in return. To say I was pissed and itching for a fight would be an understatement. I was livid, but I kept my emotion in check. "What else does she say?"

"A great many things. It's Rumor, after all."

One could bottle the essence of a thing, but that didn't mean one could control it. Even if one happened to make it a pet.

I slid another gem across the table.

"Those better not be marked," he said. Rumor dropped her head to eye the gem.

I lifted a shoulder. "The Sniffers aren't here yet, are they?" They weren't, because I had tossed the marker off a rooftop.

Poe leaned forward. "Have I ever told you what beautiful eyes you have?" To any other, it might have seemed an intended compliment, but I knew better—Poe had a fascination with eyes. In jars.

"You've mentioned it. And my lips. And my legs. And my arse. It gets redundant after a bit, don't it?"

"The things I could teach you. Proper grammar, for instance."

"Words are there to muck about with. Where's the music in a flat note?"

He laughed softly, a tinkle of music, and raised his glass to me. "There is a charm to you," he admitted.

I flashed my teeth. "My middle name. That, and I'm all ears."

"I'd rather whisper in those ears of yours." I doubted they would still be attached to my head.

"Isn't that what you tell Mordecai?" I asked.

"I'm a man of many tastes."

"West Winch?" I prodded.

He draped an arm on the back of the booth and dipped his pointy chin towards the gems on the table. "Retaliation. Typical, I know."

"But it was the Union Lord who was burgled. Not the Ministry."

"The Ministry is Law," Poe quoted.

"They slaughtered an entire quarter for a few gems."

No use playing like I didn't know what happened. A banquet full of lords and ladies spotted me in their ballroom. At least I hadn't been wearing anything overly distinctive. Like this coat. But I had something of an underground reputation —I was the best cat burglar there was.

"MUW has a long history of overcompensating. An unfortunate side effect of inflated egos and small cocks."

"I heard an airship crashed next to the Union Lord's tower. Any ideas?"

Poe toyed with a gem. "Pirates. One of the Seven Devils."

"What were they after?"

"The obvious—an entire ballroom of bejeweled peacocks makes for a tempting target." He tapped a gem. "You can't mine these in the Above."

I leaned forward. "Do the Above factions have operatives in the Below?"

He gave me a devilish grin. "I imagine so."

I knew that look for what it was. Poe was fishing for information, even as I was. I should've brought Mordecai along. He had more patience and finesse for these sorts of meetings, but me and Gan were protective of him.

"How would I go about getting to the Above?" I asked.

"Tired of me already?"

I nodded towards the gems. "I can get a better price if I cut the middlemen out."

"Careful, Red, I *am* the middleman."

I flashed a grin. "I won't cut you too badly. I swear it on the fifth element."

Poe brushed a speck of nonexistent dirt from his lacy sleeve. The mere mention of muck stained him. I took a moment to imagine him sprawled in that very same muck. He must have seen the look in my eyes, because his mood shifted. "You're wasting my time."

"Then stop dancing around, mate, and tell me what I need to know."

"I'm not the one who's dancing."

The gems on the table were only for the pleasure of his company. Poe's real price was information. Thus far, I had offered him crumbs from a meal he'd already eaten. What he really wanted was dessert.

"How do I smuggle someone to the Above?" My question lit a fire in his dark eyes. The unspoken spoke volumes. I'd just told him that there was a sun-touched fugitive in the Below, and considering my proximity to the Union Lord's affair and the downed airship… Well, Poe wasn't a stupid man.

"The Librarian."

"The librarian?"

He waved a hand. "I've spoken." He reached for the gems.

"How does Rumor know Gan is dead?" I asked.

The hand wavered. "She's Rumor. That's her curse."

I glanced at the bird. "But it only just happened. We were caught in the bombing. There's heaps of dead rotting there now. How did you hear about Gan so soon after?"

He raised his eyes to mine. "I'm going to need something more substantial than the rubbish you've been dishing out."

"There was a Ghostmaker in West Winch."

Rumor squawked in alarm, and Poe's pallor turned a shade closer to the grave. I'd just dropped a flaming cannonball on the table.

Poe swallowed. "How do you know?" he whispered.

"I saw it with my own two gorgeous eyes."

Poe stared at me with a look between wonder and dread. "We're done here." He shoved the gems back at me and made to rise, leaving his wine. The game was over.

I caught his wrist. "Gan?"

"Why do you think they call them *Ghostmakers*?" He wrenched his arm free and hurried away, with Rumor flapping in his wake.

20. OUT FOR BLOOD

Boots. The corpse had been wearing boots. I kept reminding myself of that as I hurried back to our hulk.

As far as I knew, Gan had never worn a pair of boots a day in his life. He preferred cloth slippers with rubber soles. As a joke, Mordecai had once stolen a pair of tasseled, red velvet ones for him, instead of the functional ones he wore every day. It had turned into a thing. And for the past ten years I had been pinching slippers from the lords. Gan had quite the collection. The Union Lord's slippers were to be the cherry on top of the cake.

If the charred corpse in West Winch wasn't Gan, then how did his thief-taker's coat end up there? Unless the booted man took it from Gan's dead body. Maybe the booted man was a dead-lurker, someone who robbed the dead. It fit. But then that meant… I sighed as I balanced along the moor line. Should I take what Poe said about Ghostmakers literally or was he being flippant? *Why* did they call them Ghostmakers?

If I hadn't been preoccupied with thoughts of Gan, I might have noticed a few things. As it was, I didn't spot anything amiss until I walked into the main cabin. Drawers had been dumped on the floor, the galley was overturned, and my strongbox had been emptied on the table, leaving a scattering of gems and coins.

Muck!

"Mordecai!" I raced into his cabin. Empty. The mattress was on the floor, the bedding dumped in a pile, and his clothes strewn about. It was the same in all the rooms. With rising dread, I checked the brig.

My fist tightened. Mordecai was an old softy. A plate of food lay overturned just outside the open door. That pirate bastard had attacked a legless man bringing him food.

After I got my breathing under control, I did a more careful search. Some of the gems were missing, along with a pouch of my hard-earned coins. The gold and silver were intact, but Mordecai's workshop was a mess. His artificial legs were gone, along with his coat, which likely meant Wee Willy hadn't dragged him off without legs and proper clothing. At least Mordecai wasn't out there in the fog freezing his arse off.

I took stock of the armory. A saber was missing along with a pair of pistols, a dagger, and a jerkin. And a full respirator.

The question was… where was Wee Willy taking Mordecai? And why the muck was my life being turned upside down?

A STEVEDORE GAVE A SHRILL WHISTLE FROM A NEARBY DOCK. It was a warning to the smugglers and lowlifes who posted lookouts at every alleyway and wharf.

I raced to a porthole, and cursed. How could this cycle get any worse? I'll tell you how—when an armored steam wagon rattles to a stop and a patrol of Enforcers clunk to the ground. Their weighted selves sank right into the muck.

That bought me time. I started towards the nearest hatch, but backpedaled to check on one item. Mordecai had left behind his lightning coil. There's no way he'd ever part with that willingly. While I was carefully stuffing it in my satchel I heard a gangplank being hoisted onto our hulk.

There was a Sniffer at the lead. Bent close to double, its queer beaked head shifted like Poe's mechanical raven. Sniffing. I could hear it in the air—a great searching breath that permeated the fog.

I started to slip over the rail, but noticed the skiff was gone. Yes, this was precisely how my day could get worse. I scrambled back up on deck and did what came naturally. I climbed the masts. Up and up, until the fogline swallowed me.

As Enforcers swarmed the hulk, I perched on the tops and cocked an ear. It sounded like a herd of bulls rampaging in a pottery shop.

I held my breath and considered my options. But that sniffing sound put me on edge. It was like a clawed predator thirsting for blood.

Were the Sniffers following my scent or Wee Willy's? I knew their beaks weren't precise. Scent trails only led them to a general area, but at the moment I didn't care one jot. I needed to get off this bloody hulk.

Minutes passed. Long ones. The crashing continued and I began to fully appreciate my precarious situation. How long before someone would get the bright idea to climb to the tops?

Not long apparently. The rigging began to shift, and I edged around the mast to wait. Soon a nimble thief-taker appeared on the platform. Sleek mask, and a wool coat with a Ministry badge pinned on the breast. I knew by the vibrant blue of the new coat that this was likely a fresh face straight from the ranks. He was looking towards the other masts.

Wood creaked and I felt the bending of a plank underfoot. Maybe Luck would intervene and the fellow would fall through a rotted plank. As the thief-taker edged around the platform, I moved around the mast, keeping the heavy timber between us. The thief-taker suddenly tensed. I didn't hesitate. I zipped around the mast and drove my knife into the small of his back. Right into a kidney.

The man didn't scream. He couldn't, because the pain was too much, but his entire body arched and tensed hard as a log. Before I could finish him off, he stumbled forward, and fell.

Muck.

I was already moving before he crashed to the deck. I leapt for a dangling line, caught it and swung, and latched onto the shrouds. Every Enforcer aboard pointed their pistols at the masts and fired. The fog exploded with gunpowder bursts. But they'd aimed at the main mast, not the foremast.

As I stretched for a rope, someone got the bright idea to take an axe to the shrouds. I slipped down the rope, over the rail, and found myself near the anchor. Now I've mentioned before that Gan and Mordecai liked to rig traps, so I reached into the hawsehole and found a latch. Then pulled. The chain rattled as it slipped through the hole, triggering a ripple effect of carefully designed mechanisms.

The balance of the hulk shifted, and it began to sink.

With a cocky grin, I braced my feet against the sinking hull, with my back to the wharf. Then like a spring, I launched backwards, turning in midair to grab a pylon. I scrambled up the pylon, then leapt ten feet to the wharf. As soon as my feet hit the wood I was running, leaving a squad of armored Enforcers on a sinking hulk.

I WAS OUT FOR BLOOD. A SWORD BUMPED AGAINST MY HIP AND I had a pistol primed and ready. If that pirate bastard had hurt Mordecai, I'd make him in a eunuch.

As I walked the streets, fog swirling in agitation, I pondered my next move. Or rather, Wee Willy's. If he was to be trusted (I was quite sure he wasn't) then he didn't know the Below, or its ways. But suppose he did know his way around, or had some idea of it—where would he go?

To find his people. But who were his people? The Seven Devils. Did I even trust that? As I had nothing more to go on, I mulled over my conversation with our friendly genie.

I'd never heard of the Librarian before. But Bedlam was vast and the Under Below a maze of shadows and lurkers. There was a heap of people I didn't know. If it didn't involve coin and a challenge, I never paid it much mind.

I knew where to fence my goods. I knew where to go for information on a good mark, where to peddle Mordecai's inventions to the highest bidders, but I'd never thought much on the Above, or about the politics of the Below.

I was a mere mortal. And a once dead one at that.

It would have been peachy if Wee Willy had left a note along the lines of: "I have Stumpy. Meet me at **X** location if you want him back alive." Wasn't that the way of pirates?

I didn't know. This was my first "pirate falling from the sky" experience. I was in virgin territory. And I hadn't been in that sort of territory for a good long while.

So I did what any diehard denizen would do, I went to my local pub.

"Red!" Mick called, waving me over to his table. I tore off my mask and sat without hanging it up.

"Can I buy you a pint or two?" Ah Tomas, ever hopeful.

He was like a loyal dog. Only he would pinch your billfold in a blink.

"Not today."

"You look on the warpath," said Sally.

"Got caught in the bombing."

The table fell silent. Tomas hopped up and got me a pint anyway, setting it down. I drank half of it, ignoring the froth gathering on my lips. Sally was rubbing my back. "I hear it was awful. They say everybody's dead."

"About." I looked at the table. "Look, I'm in a spot of trouble."

"You? Trouble?" Mick snickered. "Never."

Any other day, I'd have put my feet up, joined in with the ribbing, and talked nonsense till the wee hours, but not today. "Have any of you heard of the Librarian?" I asked in a confidential tone.

Mick sat back, and took a sip of his pint in contemplation. Sally drummed her fingers on the table. And Reece searched for the answer in his remaining teeth with a toothpick.

Sally looked up, a blush spreading across her pink cheeks. She was all curves and prettiness when she was deep in thought, and I hate to say this, but I wondered how much there was between her ears in the ways of brains.

"Have you, um…" she blushed, looking embarrassed.

"Yes?" I asked, encouragingly, though I didn't expect much.

"Have you tried the library in the Rook?"

Silence. The others looked at me expectantly. I shifted and stopped the quick reply on the tip of my tongue. The library?

"You know, Sally," I said. "That had not occurred to me."

She beamed. And I leaned over to kiss her cheek. "You're brilliant, love."

I bought the table a round and took my leave, feeling like a proper dolt.

Could it really be that obvious? That this famed Librarian, as was whispered to me by the foremost Genie in Bedlam, was in fact… a librarian?

Stranger things have happened.

21. THE LIBRARIAN

The Rook was impressive. Great stone buildings rising out of the fog, complete with gargoyles and angels perching on them like birds on a limb. The streets were wide and paved with cobblestones, and one of their decorative grates would fetch enough coin to feed a swarm of rats for a lifetime. Ornate bridges spanned stone canals and fancy rigs piloted by handsome men in striped shirts drifted down the Rook's wide waterways. Their cabin tops were all glass so the fancy lords and ladies inside could appreciate the fog drifts and trees.

Walking these streets always made me feel like I was being watched. It was too open. The fog too light—more wispy than thick in this part of the city. But considering where I'd come from, being watched might not be far from the truth. The Ministry's Cloudhall building was only one street over.

As wide as the streets were, they were clogged with traffic. Leeries walked on their stilts keeping the fog at bay with their bright lamps. Markets bustled, carriages rumbled past, thief-takers patrolled the corners, and smartly dressed women strolled with their children under the watch of paid bodyguards.

This was not a place for trouble, and I was glad for my posh red coat as I strolled up the stone steps of a columned building that made me itch to climb it.

There were no guards in front of the library, so I trotted right up and pushed open the double doors. The inside was vast. Floors were smooth underfoot and the shelves climbed to the rafters. Books. Tens of thousands? I didn't know.

Mordecai was a keen reader, but I was a more practical sort. Unless a book was going to give me an edge in life, I tended to shake my head at works of poetry and those so-called 'exciting romances.' That's right ladies, stick out your breasts, flutter your lashes, and pop that first hook on your bodice. Then play helpless. Sure, there were heaving bosoms and broad chests aplenty, but I wasn't one for damsels in distress. Life was complicated enough without being saddled with someone who couldn't pull their weight. I preferred my lovers to be competent.

A black cat sat on a rail that divided the entryway to the stacks. We regarded each other with mutual suspicion.

"You the librarian?" I asked.

The cat meowed, sarcastically.

"I don't judge," I said as I pushed a waist-high gate open. My shoes didn't make a sound on the marble. Gumshoes were good for that. I walked to the center of a domed ceiling, and stood in the middle of a giant compass rose mosaic set in the floor. The cat followed, two more joined it, then a fourth popped into view. Each was a different color, and all four soon sat on the points of the compass. White, black, orange, and gray.

My hand strayed to my sword hilt. And I shook myself. What were they going to do? Claw me to death?

I picked a direction, northeast, and walked between the

white cat and black cat, losing myself in the stacks. Books and more books. All dusty tomes that hadn't been handled in decades.

A clicking drew me deeper into the stacks, until I came upon a desk. And a woman. Her silver hair was piled high on her head and her eyes had a decidedly feline shape, while her collar was stiff and starched and snowy white. She wore a waistcoat that hugged her ample breasts, and sported a tie. The tapping soon became apparent: her fingernails. They were long and curving, and of a silver so bright I felt sure they were metal. Her feline eyes were glued to a book.

Master of the Tides was stamped on its spine in gold gilt.

I stepped in front of the desk, and cleared my throat. A nameplate read Ms. Silvernails.

"Yes?" she asked without looking up.

"Are you the Librarian?"

"I'm reading."

I crossed my arms. "Can you point me in her direction?"

Her eyes flickered up at this. Yes, her pupils were slits rather than round and those claws weren't glued on her fingernails. Either all these books had seeped into her blood, or she had a touch of the Feen in her.

I glanced around and noted the four cats were there, positioned on various high places. I had no idea how they'd got there. They were a silent group. "Now why do you assume the 'Librarian' is a woman?" she asked.

"You're the only person I've come across in here."

"Have you been everywhere?"

"I haven't," I admitted.

She started tapping a claw on the desk. Something about the gesture raised my hackles. "Are you looking for a book?"

"I'm looking for the Librarian."

"What book?" she asked. Her voice was high-pitched and shrill, like a cat mewing for fish.

I considered. "A book on the Above."

"Ah." She considered me. "For theory or practical application?"

"Practical application."

The black cat hopped off its high perch, and the others followed suit. They all sat in unison around me. I wondered what would happen if I failed whatever test this was.

She pushed forward a form. "Fill this out."

I frowned at the form. She tapped a fountain pen with a long claw. Definitely metal.

The form had all the usual business: name, place of birth, residence, sex, age, and a box for sun-touched or not.

"Look, Ms. Silvernails, have you seen my father by chance? Longish gray hair, pale, no legs? Might've been walking with a limp."

"How could he be walking if he hasn't any legs?" she asked.

I paused.

Then she started laughing, a shrill note that pierced my sensitive ears. The tails of the cats waved lazily with pleasure. Then her humor died in a snap, and she was all business. "Fill out the form."

I leaned forward and placed my hands squarely on the desk. "A man abducted my father. He's headed to the Above. I need to find him. Have you seen them?"

The librarian closed her book. "Do you need help filling out the form?"

With a growl, I snatched up pen and inkwell and hastily made up a load of drivel.

Name: Red

Place of birth: Muck

Quarter: Piss off

Sex: None of your business

Age: That's just rude.

And I just circled both boxes for sun-touched.

I pushed the paper back at her. Her brows rose as she read the form. "Red?" She glanced at my eyes. "How distinctively unimaginative."

I nodded at her metallic claws and nameplate. "Distinctively unimaginative seems to be in style."

Ms. Silvernails huffed, and tucked away the form. Movement caught the corner of my eye. The cats were agitated. Their tails were twitching and their faces were turned towards… Where was I?

The stacks were a maze. I had walked northeast, but the domed ceiling was still directly overhead. I glanced over my shoulder, then slowly turned. Red mist was crawling through the stacks.

Muck.

Silvernails picked up a stamp and pressed it to my form. "I highly suggest you run." The words were said so calmly that it took me a moment to register the urgency. I drew my sword, then glanced back to her. She nodded to her cats.

The cats darted off, all four in the same direction. I ran with the herd, weaving in and out of stacks until my guides stopped at a far wall. It seemed solid, with books climbing clear to the ceiling and a rolling ladder.

The white cat meowed at me. Then all four sat on their haunches, waiting.

I sheathed my sword and prepared to climb, which was always my first thought. As I placed my foot on the second rung, a claw slashed my calf. It was razor sharp and sure to have torn my trousers. Not to mention my flesh.

I looked down.

The gray wove back and forth along the lowest shelf, purring. I dropped to my haunches and scanned the books. On that shelf in battered leather with faded gold lettering on its spine was a book entitled "The Above."

Could my life get any stranger?

I pulled the book out. Something clicked. But instead of a wall opening, the floor dropped from under my feet.

I LANDED ON A PAD, TANGLED WITH MY SWORD SHEATH AND pained by the sword's hilt jabbing me in the ribs. A pistol cocked by my ear, followed by its barrel pressed to my head.

"I'd nearly given up hope," said a deep voice.

Muck. I clearly was a fool.

"What'd you do with Mordecai?" I demanded.

"Careful, now," Wil purred. "Don't make any sudden moves. I'd hate to brain you."

My eyes, keener than most, had adjusted to the near darkness, but he was behind me so I couldn't get a proper view anyway. The room was empty, aside from the landing pad on the floor and a heavy iron door.

"The Ministry's in the library," I said. "Best get on with it quick."

"I'll not fall for that one," he said. "Get rid of your weapons. Slowly."

I wasn't intimidated. It takes more than a pistol to my head to get under my skin. Now a lead ball would do the trick, but I wasn't keen on thinking about that at the moment. "Where's Mordecai?"

"He's safe. Unharmed, for now. For as long as you do as I say. And if I return in one piece."

"You're that frightened of little old me?"

The man laughed, a short burst that he quickly stifled. "You're about as tame as a sky drake."

I started to turn, but the pistol dug into my skull. "*Weapons.*"

"Look here, if we don't get moving my weapons will be the least of your worries. One of us is being hunted, or maybe both, and I don't have a clue why."

"Don't you?"

"Do I?"

He reached around me to grab the pistol from my belt. It clunked onto the stone floor, and he kicked it over to the far wall. He did the same with my sword.

"At this rate it's going to take all day to disarm me. You don't know your way around a woman, do you?"

"I know how to disarm a woman."

I had to laugh. "Practiced much? Is this the only way they'll let you near them? With a pistol to their head?"

"Normally I'd parley, but I don't trust a word out of your mouth."

"The feeling is mutual."

His hand came around, searching. He brushed the underside of my breast. "Oi!" Pistol barrel to my head or not, I jerked to the side and twisted, striking out with a well-aimed kick.

Wil leapt out of the way, and I dove for my sword, coming up like a spring to face him.

"That was an accident," he said.

"You have a bloody pistol aimed at my head!"

"You have a sword."

"I saved your hide," I countered.

"And then you put me in a brig."

"You attacked me."

"I…" The man ground to a halt. I could hear those white teeth of his grinding on each other. His shoulders stiffened. "*Who* are you working for?"

"What?"

"What faction are you with?" he demanded.

"Myself."

His eyes blazed with anger, but my sword didn't waver. He might be able to get a shot off, but I was quick. Far quicker than most. He might hit me, too. He might not. But I'd be sure to finish the job the guards had started with another hole in his hide.

Then Wil did something unexpected; he lowered his pistol. "When my airship crashed, you were there burgling the Union Lord, weren't you?"

I did not lower my blade. I only raised a brow.

"I saw the strongbox…"

"When you turned over everything in my hulk."

"I searched it."

"What were you looking for?" I asked.

"The union contract that was in the strongbox."

"There wasn't a contract in the strongbox." Notice I said, *in* the strongbox. There wasn't, technically speaking.

"I was afraid you'd say that." He strolled over to the iron door and I turned with him, keeping my sword pointed his way. I could dive for my pistol, but he'd be sure to fire off a shot first.

He slid a slat to the side. "Kill the cripple!" he called.

"You're bluffing," I growled.

Wil arched a brow. A scar ran through his left eyebrow, giving him a rakish air. "Hold," he called, then looked at me. "You don't know who I am, do you?"

"Of course, I do. You're Wee Willy." The corner of his lip twitched. "You sure as muck don't know who I am."

"I asked, but you never introduced yourself," he said.

"You told me my name was Fool. Why should I?"

"I gave you my name."

"A lie," I stated. "You're a scoundrel."

"And you're not?"

"I'm not holding a legless man hostage."

"He's my insurance."

"For what?" I demanded.

"For you telling me where that contract is."

"I don't trust you."

"I assure you the feeling is mutual. But I have the upper hand here. Give me the contract, and I'll return Mordecai unharmed."

I shrugged. "Maybe I don't care a whit about him."

"That's unfortunate for him."

Our stares clashed in the tiny room. I wasn't backing down, and neither was he. And yet… he had all the cards. I relented.

"The contract is at the bottom of the Styx now. Enforcers sank our hulk."

His eyes narrowed. "I searched it."

"You did a bloody poor job of it."

His gaze darted upwards to the hatch, and his face turned ashen. I hesitated for a moment, then followed his gaze. Red mist was seeping through the cracks around the hatch.

"Told you so," I said.

Wil tapped his pistol to his temple in a salute. "I wouldn't linger if I were you." With that he yanked open the iron door and darted through.

HERE'S THE THING. WEE WILLY HAD ALL THE CARDS. HE HAD Mordecai. He had the weapons. And apparently he had all the answers. As much as I hated to admit it, I needed him. But then it seemed he needed something from me, too. I took one look at that chilly red mist, and ran after him.

There were no guards beyond the door waiting to kill Mordecai. And, of course, no Mordecai. Just an empty spiral staircase. I cursed the scoundrel's back, and myself for falling for his bluff. He was a sly one, he was.

The staircase came to a dead end. Keeping an eye on me, Wil grabbed an accordion style lattice work screen and wrenched it open. A seam split the wall behind it. He mashed a button on the wall.

I kept one eye on him and the other on the stairwell. "What is that mist?" I knew, but I wondered if he knew.

"A Ghostmaker," he growled.

"Why's it after you?" I asked.

"We're both unregistered sun-touched in the Below."

"I've been here all my bloody life."

His gaze flickered to my eyes. So he remembered them glowing in the fog when I rescued him. Yet another card he held.

"It's after me then, I suppose."

"How do we stop it?"

"We don't," he said. "Not down here, at any rate."

"Then why are we standing here!"

"We're not." A bell dinged, twin doors slid into slots in the wall, and a small room reminding me of a vault appeared. He stepped inside. It was so small we'd be standing shoulder to shoulder.

"I'd hurry if I were you."

"You really do think I'm a fool."

He crossed his arms, pistol held casually.

"Piss off."

"Suit yourself."

The doors started to slide closed. I lunged for the opening, and slipped through just as they slammed shut. But my long-coat was caught in the seam.

"Get it out. Quick!" he said.

The room started moving up. But my long coat was going down. With a curse, I swiped my blade across that fine fabric. The patch caught in the door disappeared. And I gaped. Only for a moment. When I turned back to my companion, I hoped none of my surprise showed on my face.

"You really haven't been to the Above before, have you?"

"I've seen some of it," I lied. It was only partly a lie. I had seen the sun. Wasn't that close enough?

We retreated to opposite corners of the... "What is this thing?"

"A lift," he said. "It's a room that moves up, like a crane, only it works on a pulley system."

I nodded, impressed. I'd seen open platforms on pulleys, but never a solid room like this. "How do you kill a Ghostmaker?"

"You can't kill the dead."

"Are you sure they're ghosts? They look like mist to me."

"We don't really know."

"So you just... run away from them all the time?"

He frowned. "No. Most times we die."

The lift stopped and the doors opened. Wil swept through without a word. He trotted up another spiral stairwell, and I was forced to follow. At least we'd left the mist behind.

Wil paused at the topmost door. "What is your name?" He was standing a step above me. I had the disadvantage here. I was eye level with his chest, and had to crane my neck back to look up at him. It was irritating.

"Fool, isn't it?"

"As you wish."

He shoved open the door and walked through.

A gust of clean, cool air blasted me, licking at my coat and sweeping my hair backwards. It stung my face and stole the breath from me. And yet, I moved into it. I stepped out onto a platform, air battering me from all sides.

The door slammed shut behind me, but I barely noticed. My eyes were on the sky. Midnight black, with a million twinkling lights. I stumbled forward. Struck. There was no fogline. Just a vast open space with no end and a giant glowing white orb lighting the endlessness.

My world was spinning, tilting.

A hand snatched at my coat, holding me fast. "Careful," Wil warned.

I fell to my knees, fighting the urge to retch. That's when I looked down. I was on the edge of a small platform. Air thrashed me, tugged me, invited me to fall to the sea of fog so far below.

I gripped the side, and retched my guts out. When I finished, a handkerchief was thrust before my eyes.

I couldn't reach for it. I couldn't move. I was frozen in place like a cat clinging to a log in the Styx.

"Happens every time. I apologize in advance." An eel latched around my ankle, and it did what they'd been doing since my rebirth. Absolutely nothing. I couldn't handle the vastness, but I could bloody close my eyes. I did just that, and found that if I imagined fog surrounding me, my body worked just fine.

I kicked at him, connecting with his knee. He went down with a thud, and I punched the center of his chest. Solar plexus for the win. Gan had taught me every pressure point, weak spot, and vulnerability in the human body. And he'd taught me how to kill.

I was on Wil in a flash, leaping up… Ugh. The world spun. I dropped to the platform. As I tried to get my bearings, a heavy weight came down on the back of my head. I was almost thankful when all the lights in that vastness winked out and the world went black.

22. TABLES TURNED

FROM THE THROBBING BETWEEN MY EARS AND THE QUEASY feeling in my gut, I determined that I'd been drinking for half a cycle. The world was swaying. Rocking. And I was floating.

I cracked open an eye, and my stomach lurched again. I managed to rip off a respirator attached to my mouth, and grab a thoughtful bucket nearby. When I was done, still bent over the bucket, I moved the hair from my face and wiped a sleeve across my lips.

This was not my room.

Not an alleyway, either.

The first thing that registered were the bars on the door, and then the sturdy hatch for passing food and slop buckets. There were no windows.

Memory came next. The sky. So vast. My stomach lurched again, and I buried my face in the bucket. It stunk like muck, but at least it was familiar. The air here was… sharp.

Taking my bucket with me, I collapsed back and was happy to have a solid wall at my back. Only it wasn't quite solid. Cold air whispered against my back. The walls were woven like the side of a thick basket, and air seeped through the weaving. Some brig.

The air had a funny smell that I couldn't place. Maybe it was what real air was supposed to smell like. Using my toe (they'd taken my boots), I pulled the respirator over. It had a tube attached to a canister. I sniffed at the inside. Sharp air blew from a nozzle inside. It wasn't a respirator, then, but meant to deliver fresh air?

Whatever it was, I didn't have the energy. I dragged a heavy blanket over me and braced against wall and floor, stretching out my arms to steady the world. But it wasn't steady. Nothing about it was. Everything rolled and swayed.

A boat. I was on water. Only it felt empty.

I'd been stripped down to shirt and trousers. All my pockets were empty, even the secret ones. Muck. I clonked my head against the wall. Muck. Again. And one more time for emphasis. Muck.

Disarmed, and in a brig. Both fathers missing, or dead. I growled in anger.

A tan, freckled face appeared at the barred window. Tattoos adorned her forehead and cheeks, curling down her chin. Earrings decorated her nose, ears, and bottom lip and her red hair was in a multitude of braids, decorated with beads. "You should put on the mask," she said.

"So you can poison me?"

"The air is too thin for you here."

"If you can breathe, I can breathe."

The girl considered me a moment. "Hungry?"

"Just muck off, will you," I growled.

"Captain Steel warned me about you," she said. "I'm Bran, by the way." She spoke proper with a heavy, lyrical accent I couldn't place.

"Unless you plan on unlocking this door, I don't bloody care."

"The captain didn't give me your name. Do Belowers have names?"

"'Course we do. What do you think we are?"

Her fingers curled around the bars and she stood on her tiptoes to peek down at all of me. Maybe she was more my age (whatever that was), it was hard to tell from here. She had knowing eyes with a twinkle of humor in them, and freckles along her nose and cheeks that made me want to count them, which made it hard to be rude to her.

"You're not what I expected," Bran admitted.

I hugged the bucket to me. "What the muck did you expect?"

She wrinkled her nose. "Shorter, for one. Pale, kind of sickly, hunched. You know, from the toxic fog and all."

"We have respirators."

"Do all of you have red eyes?"

"Do all of you have red hair?" I shot back.

She laughed. "You're stuck in there so guess you'll never know."

I glared.

A corner of her lip twitched. "Lighten up, whatever your name is. Life can't be that bad. We gypsies don't usually eat our prisoners."

Gypsies? I wanted to ask, but I bit my tongue instead. Best to act like I was in control. "Look, that bastard Wil abducted my legless father. Is he in a brig, too?"

"No."

Before I could ask more, Bran sank back down on her heels, and disappeared. The hatch at the bottom of the door opened, and I dove for it. I didn't get very far. The ground lurched under me, and I thudded to the planking. Bile rose up, but I forced it down, pressing my forehead against the reassuring wood.

"Don't worry. I've heard it's normal for denizens to get sick up here." Bran nudged a wooden cup through, along with a wooden plate with some type of root. "Drink the tea, and suck on the root slivers. It will help with the air sickness."

I eyed the offerings.

Her face appeared in the food hatch. Her eyes were a striking blue. "Look, if we wanted to kill you, you'd be dead. Captain Steel said to look after you."

"So he can keep me as a bloody slave to do his bidding."

Bran snorted. "I don't even know your name, but I can tell you'd make a piss poor slave. You'd likely brain me the second I turned my back."

I ignored her. "Is that drugged?"

"No."

I carefully picked up the wooden cup and managed to sit crosslegged. It smelled sharp and bitter. "Would you tell me if it was?"

Bran grinned through the hatch. "No."

Maybe I was already drugged. What did it bloody matter at this point? I drank, then sucked on the strange root. My stomach instantly settled. Still weak with sickness, I reached across the cramped room and pulled a mat off the bunk, then curled up on it with my blanket to sleep off whatever this sickness was.

Keys rattled. An oiled door opened, then shut. I sat bolt upright, and tried to leap to my feet. Only the floor lurched and I ended up on my arse.

Wil frowned down at me. He was as clean and fresh as I

was disheveled. I spat, aiming for his shiny black boots. Dead on. But his chiseled face didn't show a reaction. It might as well have been cut from stone.

I glared up at him. A light in the hallway cast shadows over his freshly polished head. He wore a dark longcoat and a red-brocaded waistcoat with an open-collared shirt beneath. A cutlass hung from a wide belt, and his trousers were too fitted for pockets.

I leaned back into a corner. I hoped it looked casual, but really I needed the reassurance of two walls and a floor. "You're a bastard," I said.

"I'm also a scoundrel."

"Where's Mordecai?" I asked.

"He's safe."

"I want to see him," I demanded.

"Most prisoners grovel and beg for mercy."

I summoned every fiber of my body that wasn't sick to the bone and met his amber eyes. "I wasn't the one gasping for air in the muck with a hole in his lung begging for help."

A muscle in his jaw flexed. "I haven't forgotten. For all my ways, I am a man of my word and I believe I promised you masques."

"So I can buy my freedom from you. Is that it?"

"I need that contract," he stated.

"Should've asked for it instead of assaulting us."

"Don't push me, woman."

"Or you'll what? Toss me off the nearest tower?"

Wil cocked his head. "Despite what you told me in the lift, I don't think you've ever been to the Above."

"Why does that surprise you?" I shot back.

"You're sun-touched. But you have red eyes."

"So?"

"I've never seen a red-eyed sun-touched before."

I lifted a shoulder. "What of it?"

"You're a rarity."

"Look here, Wee Willy, I'm not inclined to be part of your harem." Fine, all right, maybe I'd read *a few* of Mordecai's romance novels.

He snorted. "I'm not inclined to keep one. And if I were, I wouldn't trust a woman like you in my harem. You'd have the other women staging a takeover in under a day."

I clicked my mouth shut. That was quite possibly one of the nicest compliments I'd ever received.

"Can you stand?" he asked.

"Of course I can."

He waited.

"Why should I?"

"Do you want to see Mordecai?"

Keeping the wall firmly at my back, I pushed up with my legs, sliding up the wall. He held out a hand.

"What do you take me for?" I asked.

"A woman in need of support." He made a beckoning gesture. He had large, calloused hands with a gold signet ring on his index finger. That hand was a good two steps away though. The bastard wasn't going to make this easy for me. The ground felt like it was heaving. I took one step, then another, and grasped his hand like a lifeline. His grip was like steel, and yet he gently drew me forward. I felt weak as a newborn calf.

"You'll grow accustomed to it. You just need your air legs."

"My what?"

"Air legs."

My sluggish brain finally kicked into working order. "I'm on an airship, aren't I?"

He dipped his chin. "In the Above."

"And I'm your prisoner."

"You are," he said with a wry grin.

I sighed. "You're Captain Steel, aren't you?"

"I'm afraid so."

"You claimed your airship went down," I accused. "Are you even with the Seven Devils?"

"Oh, yes." He tucked my hand through the crook of his arm. I could feel his muscles beneath the fabric. He was as hard as stone, and the only thing that felt solid here. "I'm the Seventh Devil, himself."

"Muck."

23. THE SEVEN DEVILS

and the various factions. It was a mess. That's what I'd been told. The Above was fractured territory where pirates, the Ministry, gypsy clans, and enterprising organizations battled for supremacy. Of what, I didn't know. It was the sky. How did you divide that up?

Before the Seven Devils came along, pirates battled pirates as often as they raided other ships. That was until a pirate captain united the disorganized mess into the Seven Devils. Each devil brought his own pirate fleet. And it just so happened that this fractured group was brought together by the Seventh Devil. Wee Willy, apparently.

"Is your name really Wil?"

"Willem Steel," he said.

"I prefer Wee Willy."

He smirked and opened a door. He had insisted I bring my respirator, or breathing mask as he called it.

"We're on the *Swale*. My ship, the *Crow*, did go down." His voice was grave as gravel. "Captain Jacapo is the second captain here. The crew know me as Captain Steel."

"And your friends?"

He glanced sideways at me. "I don't have any. I'd put on the breathing mask if I were you."

"Bran told me the same. Why do I need it?"

"The air here is thinner than the Middling."

"I can breathe just fine."

"Suit yourself. I'm not going to wrestle it onto you."

"A pity."

He arched a brow; the scar slashing through it made the gesture menacing.

A crew member trotted up, a man with hair so blond it was close to white. He was heavily tattooed and wearing fur-lined clothes. The man put fist to chest, then handed Wil a pair of tinted goggles.

Wil handed the goggles to me. He didn't say a word as he walked me to the end of a corridor. "Since you won't listen to me anyway…" He threw open the door.

Light blasted me. Bright. Stunning. Powerful. And cold. All at once, a gust of frigid air hit me and I staggered backwards as sure as if I'd been hit by a wagon.

Wil kept me upright as I fumbled to put on the tinted goggles. I blinked past tears. It was like staring into a fire. Only brighter.

Blindly, I let him lead me forward. Air whipped around me, tugging at my hair and clothes, and urging me onward. It filled my lungs and made me heady with delight.

I bumped into a waist-high rail. Good solid wood.

"Open your eyes and see the sky," he murmured.

I squinted past the brightness. Into a vast vibrant blue world. My knees went weak. Swirls of air climbed and dipped, and white billowing masses drifted in the endlessness of it all.

I felt like retching again, but I was struck with awe. Then I saw a familiar sight. It burned so brightly I couldn't gaze at it. Not even through the tinted lens of my goggles. The sun.

I stood on an airship, its ballooning sails drifting above. Rigging shifted with each gust, but I barely noticed. I couldn't take my eyes off the air currents.

"I can't even imagine," Wil said at my side, "what it must be like to see this for the first time. Living your entire life in that fog with no light."

There were no words. I drank in the sky and it filled my heart to bursting.

"This way."

I planted my feet.

"Please?" he asked, his voice low. "There's a better view."

I let him draw me away from the rail. I felt better on my feet now, though the vastness was unsettling. Visibility for twenty paces was considered a clear day in the Below. The only time I had seen farther was when Gan and Mordecai took me to a greenhouse called the Crystal Palace. I'd gawked at the waterfalls and all the different plants while they'd plotted our next burglary.

As we walked along deck, I looked upwards at the ballooning sails. Some were round, while others were stretched to catch the air. I could hear a whirr of fans, too.

"Why's the air pushing at the cloth?"

Wil cocked his head at the question.

I gestured to the sails.

"It's *wind*."

I tasted the word. It felt good. I could see translucent currents, moving like eels under water. I was so caught up by the sight that I barely noticed walking up stairs to the poop deck.

The helm was shaded by a balloon sail. The pilot at the wheel nodded to Wil, but my gaze was on a familiar figure who sat at the taffrail, perched on a barrel. His arms were folded on the rail, and he was gazing down.

I must've made a noise, because he turned, surprised. Then relief washed over him, followed by disappointment. Nearly stumbling, I let go of Wil's arm and rushed forward to pull Mordecai into a crushing embrace. He hugged me back just as fiercely.

"I'm in one piece. Well, as much as I usually am," he whispered in my ear.

I pulled back and grinned. Although his paleness was near to translucent in the sun, he looked rested and in good health.

"I haven't been mistreated. Only manhandled."

I tossed a glare over my shoulder. "Wee Willy is good at that, isn't he?"

The pilot, a bullish man with a perpetual scowl and skin like leather, turned that gaze on me. Then glanced at Wil.

"This is *Captain* Jacapo," Wil said.

I tossed back a glare. "Like I care."

"You should, woman," Jacapo said. "You're on my ship."

"Play nice, Evie," Mordecai murmured under his breath.

"As a prisoner," I said.

Jacapo showed me his missing teeth. "I'd nearly forgotten. It appears Captain Steel did, too."

Wil's eyes flickered towards his second captain. He wasn't as in control as he'd like to be on this airship. "I haven't forgotten. This woman saved my life in the Below," he said.

"We are all very grateful to her."

Wil looked hard at the man, then barked an order to a nearby sailor. "Escort these two to quarters. Post a guard."

"Aye, aye, Captain."

"Damn it, Evie," Mordecai hissed. "What are you doing here?"

"I came to rescue *you*." I looked at him like he was mental, which he was. "Things just went sideways."

"Don't they always," he sighed.

"Best of life, that is."

We'd been stuffed into a small cabin with a double bunk. I eyed the second tier wondering if my stomach would recover. Instead of finding out, I opened a shutter and had my breath stolen. The window looked out into the open sky. I stuck my body halfway out, craning my neck to get a better view of the airship. Then just stared down. I couldn't even see the ground.

"Your rescue could use a touch of diplomacy."

"That's your expertise."

"Yes," he said with a clipped tone. "Jacopo and I were discussing poetry until you blundered your way up there."

"I didn't like the way that fellow was looking at me," I said over my shoulder. The wind snatched my words away, but from Mordecai's sigh, I gathered he'd heard me.

Mordecai squeezed in next to me. "Clouds," he informed me.

"Can we walk on them?"

"I don't know." He glanced at me. "You can breathe up here?"

"I am, aren't I?"

He adjusted his mask. His hair was being blown all over the place, and so was mine. I'd pinched a leather cord from a sack, and now used it to tame my hair. A bald head or braids made perfect sense up here.

The wind was blowing, so I leaned close to hear him. "I'm relieved you're all right, but I can't say I'm glad to see you, Evie."

"That warms my beating heart, it does. Here I thought that bastard killed you."

"After he waited for me to put my legs on, dress, and put on a proper coat?"

"I was worried, all right. Why'd you open the brig?"

"I thought our guest might be hungry."

I frowned at him.

"Fine, I was a fool."

"You're no fool," I muttered, and looked away, my heart twisting. I'd left Gan. I should've known he wasn't planning on following me down that hatch. All of this was my fault.

"It's not your fault, Evie," he said, somehow reading my mind. Usually that knack of his annoyed me, but not today. "I just… I need to know why Gan died.

"He's *not* dead," I said.

"There's a reason they call them Ghostmakers."

"Funny, Poe asked me why they called them that."

"It's obvious," he snapped.

"Is it? Because I'm still here."

"You have the luck of Luck himself."

I smirked. "So does Gan. Look, I found his longcoat."

"Where?"

Hearing the hope in his voice, I hesitated over the next. "On a charred carcass, but that body was wearing *boots*."

"And?" The glimmer of hope was gone. "Can you think of no reason for him to abandon his flimsy slippers for a pair of boots in a bombed out quarter?"

"It wasn't Gan," I insisted.

"Evie…"

"*No!*"

In the ensuing silence, we turned to the sky below. "I just don't believe it," I whispered after a time.

Mordecai swallowed. "Then let's work on the assumption that Gan is alive."

I nodded.

"When Wil escaped…"

"*Wee* Willy," I corrected.

"Oh, I think everything is quite proportionate."

"Have you been ogling my prisoner?"

"Hard not to, isn't it?"

"I'm telling Gan."

"I wish he were here, Evie. Jealously and all."

"Gah, don't start. We'll find him."

"Actually… that's the reason I'm here."

I frowned. "You're here because you were daft enough to trust the man and open the door to give him food."

"But I learned what Wil was after—the union contract. He ransacked our hulk, ignored the gems and masques, and demanded to know where the contract was."

"What did you tell him?"

"I told him I didn't know what he was talking about. He was convinced you had the contract, so he took me hostage."

"And you just let him go on thinking that?"

"As long as he was busy with me, it meant you were safe. I didn't want to put you in any more danger."

"I'm touched," I said dryly. "But I don't have the contract. Far as I know it's at the bottom of the Styx."

"*What?*"

"Good thing you lot left. 'Forcers showed up, so I triggered our 'last resort' defense."

Mordecai's face fell.

"Look, snatching that contract wasn't high on my list of things to do. I did snag the coil though."

Relief washed over his face. "That's my girl."

"You know I wouldn't leave *that* behind. But they took all

my gear, so now they have it, and Wil knows we don't have the contract."

"Don't we?"

I gawked at him. "What'd you do? Stick it up your arse?"

Mordecai looked to the sky, and sighed. "No," he said in a clipped tone, then tapped his head. "The contract is safe, as long as I'm alive."

I stared. I knew Mordecai was brilliant, but I hadn't thought he'd memorize the entire air shaft schematics. Then realization dawned. "You let him escape, didn't you?"

"It seemed the quickest way to get answers."

"You're a sly old devil, you know that?"

"I'm not all that old."

I snorted. "Pushing fifty, you are."

"Pushing from afar," he drawled.

"You could have left me a note."

"I did," he insisted.

I gawked.

"The coil, Evie. Do you think I'd leave that behind if I didn't intend on returning?"

"I thought you'd been brained and dragged away."

"All things considered, Wil was an extremely courteous captor."

"That's because he's hoping to use you as leverage to get to me, Mord. Why else would they let us blather on and reconnect. They're trying to pull our heart strings before they torture me to death."

"Perhaps."

"You could sound a dash more concerned over that last bit," I muttered.

"I'll toss myself off the airship before it comes to that."

I frowned at him. "Not funny." Joking aside, I'd ruined

that plan of his. If you call risking life and limb a plan. "So what do we do?"

"We use this to our advantage."

I gave a pointed look over my shoulder. "We don't have much advantage."

"We have something they want. And they have something we want."

"And what's that?"

"We're assuming Gan is still alive."

I gave a firm nod. "He is."

Mordecai looked down at his intertwined fingers. "If Gan isn't buried under a pile of rubble, I'm hoping he escaped. But barring that… the Ministry likely took him."

Blunt and logical. I didn't like the taste that left in my mouth. Denizens taken by the Ministry were never seen again.

"These pirates knew there was a contract with the Sage King's seal in the Union Lord's suite. That means they have contacts in places we don't. Contacts in the Ministry itself, perhaps. Or inside the unions."

"Like the pretty blonde shagging the lord."

"She may be an operative of HOOF."

"Are they that organized?" I asked.

"'Organized' is part of their acronym," he said dryly.

"I'm beginning to see where I get my sassy tongue from."

"You were near to bursting with sass when we found you, my dear. I simply nourished it."

I stuck my tongue out at him, and he tried to snatch it as he always did. The childhood routine cheered me greatly.

"If I tell them I have the contract memorized, we may be able to negotiate for information."

"Well, that's an issue, isn't it? I'm here. What's to say they won't threaten to harm me if you don't cough up the goods?"

"Then I'll cough up the goods and hope they don't toss us overboard."

There was nothing for it. I was here. Mordecai was here. We were so neck deep in muck our captors didn't even have to worry about us escaping. Short of jumping overboard with an express ticket to the Styx, there was no going anywhere.

I bent over the windowsill to reach for an air current. "They're like eels drifting in the Styx, aren't they?"

"What is?" he asked.

I glanced back at him. "The swirls. The… wind here." I dipped my fingers in the twining air currents and splashed one his way. It snatched at his hair.

"Evie, my dear, I think you need to put your mask on. The thin air is getting to you."

24. PIRATE TROUBLES

I EXPECTED OPULENCE. THE KIND OF GILDED GOLD ROOM THAT lords preferred, with silks and a bed big enough to house an entire family. My imagination always got the best of me. It was an airship after all. Weight was crucial.

Still, surprise was plain on my face as Mordecai and I were marched into the captain's cabin by four toughs who acted like Enforcers without their casings. There was hardly a cushion in sight, only a large table bolted to the floor that was strewn with maps.

I comforted myself by imagining that Wee Willy's cabin on the *Crow* had been a study in ego. This was Jacopo's cabin, after all.

I started to help Mordecai to one of the few chairs in the room. He was unsteady on his fake legs in the air, even with his walking stick. And I knew his pride didn't like to scoot around in front of strangers. But the guards held me fast.

A curtained alcove I assumed held a bed was off to one side, along with two massive chests. The other side of the cabin was a wall of pigeonholes, filled with charts and instruments. The aft was taken up by a large window. Thin metal slats that could be closed for battle were currently open to let in light and air.

Wil didn't look up from the table of charts. Jacopo leaned against a wall, arms crossed, appraising us. And Bran was perched on a trunk, flipping a fat water droplet in the air like a coin.

My brows drew together at that. It was definitely water—a clear, quivering blob, but it wasn't behaving like ordinary water. Noting my surprise, she blew on the droplet and flipped it my way. I caught it despite the ropes around my wrists. It had turned to ice.

She gave me a wink.

Mordecai inclined his head. "Captains."

Neither captain returned the greeting. We stood for some minutes as Wil continued to study his chart. He had planted his palms wide on the table. I rocked forward on my tippy-toes to see what I could spy. Freehold. Isle of Skye. Wails. Roaming. The Wasteland. Gloom. A heap of other meaningless names dotted the vast space, but there was only one I recognized: Bedlam.

At long last, Wil looked up from his charts. "Did they cut out your tongue?"

"I'm supposed to behave," I said.

"What would you be doing if you weren't behaving?"

Since he'd asked… I grabbed the hand on my arm, found a pressure point, and twisted. The guard screeched, and the next closest to me got an elbow to the throat. He staggered back and clumsily drew his sword. I tensed to grab it, but a third guard put a knife to Mordecai's throat. I froze.

"You cut him and I'll kill—" Guard One drove a fist into my lower back. I grunted.

"Enough!" Wil barked. "Leave them be."

Jacopo sobered, and came off his wall. "I'm not known for my hospitality, woman. Take care here."

I started to open my mouth, but Mordecai placed a hand on my arm. "We thank you for the comforts you've provided, Captain. And the chance to finally see the Above."

"Have you remembered where the union contract is?" Wil asked, glancing to me.

"Did you enjoy searching my things?" I countered.

"No, because I didn't find what I wanted. Where did you hide it?"

"It's safe," Mordecai said.

"At the bottom of the Styx?" Wil asked.

"That's right," I said.

Wil stood with his arms crossed, striking a commanding pose that let him look down his nose at us. He managed it, despite me being nearly his height. I was only two inches behind him, but it was enough.

"Then I'll dump you in the river and have you fetch it."

"Go ahead. Dump me in. Mord's been trying to get rid of me for a while now."

Mordecai cleared his throat. Loudly. "I'd like to negotiate," he said.

The Captains looked over to him. "Go on," Wil said.

"My partner was lost during the bombing of West Winch. The Ministry seems to be after the same contract as you."

"The one your…" Wil hesitated, puzzling over our relationship.

"*Apprentice*," I said. I hadn't been an apprentice for years now. I was a full-fledged partner. But partner was the word Mordecai used for Gan and I didn't want any confusion. Though I supposed they assumed Gan was a *business* partner.

"Stole?" Wil finished.

Mordecai ignored the exchange. "A Ghostmaker showed

up at our hideout. I don't know if it was hunting you or the contract, but Gan bought enough time for us to get you in a skiff and escape. I think the Ministry has him. I'd like you to use your contacts to track my partner down."

At the word Ghostmaker, the room went still. Bran was off the trunk and standing now, and I noticed the top of her head barely came up to my shoulders.

"Prove to me that you've seen the papers," Wil said.

"They bear the Sage King's seal, along with pipe schematics to an unnamed structure, complete with longitude and latitude."

"Which is only useful to someone in the *Above*," Wil said. "Tell us where you hid them and I swear I'll do what I can to find your friend."

Mordecai considered this.

"We need more than your word," I said. "You're not exactly trustworthy, now are you?"

Jacopo growled. "Enough of this. Talk or *she* dies."

The guards seized me.

"No!" Wil barked. I was so shocked by his concern that I forgot to fight. I'd expected Mordecai to say that.

The two captains faced off.

"Have her look into the abyss," Wil said.

Jacopo's face cracked into a smile. He slapped Wil's arm. "There's the man I know. Lower the plank!"

Before the guards could drag me off, Wil moved around the table to grab my arm and haul me out of the cabin. I glanced over my shoulder and saw the guards manhandling Mordecai. I tensed, and an urgent voice whispered in my ear.

"You've insulted captain and crew. Don't look down, and you'll be fine," Wil said. "It's this or a lashing, and I don't have the stomach for that."

I was hauled out into a red sky. A section of railing swung

open like a door, and a plank was fitted to the edge of the airship. Crew on the rigging above us stopped to cheer, while those on deck gathered to watch the show, which apparently was featuring me.

When I saw what they were after, I started backpedaling, or tried to. The crew laughed, while Bran stood on the sidelines, tight-lipped and ashen. Wil marched me straight to the start of the plank and let go. I stumbled, but caught myself on the ends of the railing. The sky swirled below with all its vastness.

Men with hooked spears stepped forward, points tipped at me.

"Please, Captain Jacopo," Mordecai said. "This is unnecessary."

"You're right, it is. Where's the contract?"

Mordecai glanced at me. I gave a firm shake of my head. "I've memorized it," he said.

Gah, he really was the worst thief-boss ever.

Jacopo grinned, showing off his gold teeth. "Good. Let's give you a taste of what happens if you don't deliver. What do you think, boys?"

A cheer went up around the airship.

I shot Wil a glare. I saw what was happening. He needed to maintain his reputation in front of Jacopo and the crew. They wanted me to grovel. But I didn't like this game, so I decided to play one of my own. I took a step out onto the plank.

Wind snatched at me and played in my hair. The plank was flexible and I bounced a bit, getting a feel for it. I looked down at the clouds, at the swirls of air, and all the wonder in the sky. It drew me. I stepped farther out.

"You lot can muck off!" I shouted.

Mordecai sighed and closed his eyes. He knew full well what I was about to do; he had that queasy look about him.

Wil turned ashen. His game had backfired. And even Jacopo hesitated. That's what usually happens when you played with me. I moved to the end of the plank, and bounced comfortably.

"Enough of this," Bran said. "She's earned her wings."

From the looks her mates shot her, I gathered she had just fallen a rung in their estimation. "Shove her overboard. See if she flies!" someone yelled.

So here I was with few choices. Go groveling back, and beg for mercy as Wil supposed I would, or… I leapt off the plank. My hands clamped onto a dangling line—the ship was full of them. Before the line even stopped swinging, I was climbing. When I reached the rail, I leapt onto the shrouds, and shot up to the tops. Pure joy filled me. This was bliss. Wind swirled around me, goading me upward. Here was freedom: no fog, no ground, only air as far as my heart could stretch. I wanted to climb to the sun.

A sailor tried to intercept me on the rigging, but I dodged him, quick as could be, and leapt to another dangling line. This was no different than one of Gan's obstacle courses. I was in my element here. Well, nearly.

The airship was different than what I was used to on our landlocked hulk. Giant balloons, sails jutting out every which way, and propellers whirring in the wind. The whole thing resembled some multi-finned fish I'd seen swimming in the Styx.

I flew up the shrouds, avoided what would've been a lubber's hole, went past the tops with their converging crew, then walked across a boom at the highest point on the ship. The boom stretched well past the deck, like a wing bone. There was nothing below me but sail and clouds.

I sat on the end. "I don't like your hospitality," I called down.

Jacopo scowled from deck. Wil was stone-faced, but I thought he might've cracked a smile on one lip's edge.

"Why don't you come and get me, Captain Jacopo? I promise I'll play nice."

The crew started ribbing him on. I'd put him in an awkward position, I knew. He either had to accept my challenge or walk away. Either way, I had him where I wanted. He was set to lose face.

Wil took that moment to seize control. His mask cracked, and he started laughing. "Bran's right. She's earned her wings. But let's see how she fares in a storm! Pilot, due east!"

Down below, I watched as Mordecai shook his head, and hobbled back to his cabin.

———

WATER PELTED ME, LIGHTNING RIPPED THE SKY FROM BELOW and above, and I clung to the boom like a wet rat. This really did top the cake of bad ideas. Never try to one-up a scoundrel on his own turf.

Growing up, Mordecai's tube of lightning had fascinated me for endless hours, but out here, unrestricted, it was terrifying. Every crack shook my bones. Then the sky rumbled a laugh at me. I was drowning, I was. And frozen in terror.

The airship rattled, creaked, and shook violently. The whole thing was sure to be pulled apart. The crew had reefed the sails and the armored shutters were closed tight. The giant balloons rippled with wind, but held fast.

A slash of lightning hit a pole that extended high above the top of the mast. Naked metal poles bristled all around the ship. I thought they were for intimidation purposes, not for practical use.

The sun vanished. The moon wasn't out. I didn't know if it was day or night, or even if we were level. I just buried my face in a rolled-up sail, and tried not to heave.

Then I heard a voice, but the wind snatched the words from my ears. A familiar hand touched my back.

I looked up to find Mordecai. His eyes smiled at me.

"What the muck are you doing up here!" The wind snatched my words away, but I was sure he got the gist.

"Rescuing you."

"You got no legs."

"But I'm not petrified of water," he shouted back. The entire conversation was shouting.

I bristled. I was *not petrified* of anything. Well, maybe I did have a grudge against water.

Suddenly, I no longer felt the rain pelting my back. I ventured a peek behind Mordecai. "You both need to get down!" I saw more than heard her words. Bran stood on a ratline just under the boom, gripping the straps that secured the reefed sails. The rain formed a sphere around us, as if we were in a glass globe.

She beckoned us forward. Without the water slamming into me, I felt a little better. With her encouragement, and Mordecai's, I edged along as the ship shuddered and rocked below me. It dipped down and up, and heaved to the left battered by winds and rain. I was nearly sick to death worrying about Mordecai, but Bran kept a hand on him as she navigated the line.

The more I moved, the more confident I became, until the three of us were climbing down the shrouds.

Through the sleet, I spotted Captain Willem Steel at the helm, all sure-footed and confident. He spared me a glance, then turned his eyes back to the bowsprit. He was in his element. And I wanted to put a chunk of lead between his eyes.

I hopped onto the deck, and reached up to help Mordecai down. He didn't have his artificial legs, so I settled the man on my back. He hated to be carried this way, and I felt bad knowing it was my actions that led to it. But he endured the humiliation with his usual stoicism. Bran waved us down a hatch. I climbed down the ladder and stood dripping in the corridor. Bran was completely dry.

Without a word, she took my hand and led me deeper into the ship. We passed by crew quarters with sailors lounging in swaying hammocks. They didn't seem to mind the movement of the ship or the noise of the storm. As we stumbled through, they eyed me and Mordecai. I expected insults, or sneering over the man clinging to my back, but they kept it to themselves. Wil might have won that round, but I had gone up a peg or two.

Bran led us to Mordecai's cabin. I put my back to the bunk, and he dropped off, landing on the mattress. Then I turned on him. "You're mad," I hissed.

"You get it from somewhere."

I scowled down at him. "'Bout gave me a heart attack."

Mordecai flashed a roguish grin. "I used to be you, Evie. I still have a bit of daring in me."

Bran laughed. "Runs in the family, I think. Either way, I doubt the crew will give you any more trouble." With a tip of her head, she left us.

"I'm surprised your guards let you do that."

"They didn't," Mordecai said, peeling off his waistcoat. "But no one expects a legless man to climb on deck in a storm."

"What do you think they'll do to us after you make a copy of that contract?"

He shrugged. "Does it matter?"

I knelt on deck, so I could look up at him, and took his hand. "Hey, now, don't go into one of your black moods. Gan's not here to drag you out of that hole, and I'm no good at it."

Mordecai brought my hand to his lips. "Some days you're the only light in my life, Evie. Even when Gan is here. You're beyond good, my dear."

"Now you're getting sentimental on me."

"It happens."

I gave his cheek a kiss. "You're still a mucking bad thief-boss."

"Sassy tongue."

"Wanker," I called over my shoulder, as I shut the door. His answering chuckle cheered me, and I stopped to lean against the door for a moment. I was soaking wet and still dripping puddles on the flooring.

"I'm to escort you back to the brig," Bran said.

I started. She was leaning against the bulkhead, in the shifting shadows of a swinging lantern. I hesitated to leave Mordecai unguarded.

"He'll be fine, I swear it. The captains don't want anything to happen to him."

"Ah, right," I said, following her. "Because he has what they want in his head. What's so special about that contract?"

She glanced over her shoulder. "That's not for me to say."

I stepped willingly into the brig, but she didn't lock the door. Instead she left it open and came back with hot tea and more root slivers. I was busy combing my fingers through my wet hair, trying to work out the snarls.

"I want to shoot that captain of yours," I said.

"Most do. Hold up, there." She set the tray down, and reached out with fingers splayed to pull water from my clothes. I stopped shivering.

"How did you do that?" I whispered.

She tilted her head up at me. "You're sun-touched. You should know."

I sat down on the bunk, and held the tea in my hands. Bran sat beside me, folding her legs, and putting her back to the wall. "But I don't know. I don't even know what it is," I admitted.

"It's my Knack," she said. Color spread across her freckles. "I'm a Waterdancer."

"A what?"

"An Elemental Knack. I control water. Every ship needs at least one to keep the buoys dry, else they get waterlogged and a ship can go down in a storm."

"How do you use your Knack?" I asked.

Bran lifted her shoulders. She was slim and sleek, with long graceful muscles. I doubted she topped five feet. "It's—" she dipped her fingers in her own tea and drew them out. Droplets formed in the air, swirling around her fingers. "—instinct. I just *do*."

"If you control water—"

"I don't control it. I coax it. I speak to it. It's like a... wild animal. One you have to make friends with."

"Sure. Right." It sounded crazy, but who was I to judge?

"Sun-touched can't use their Knack in the Below. Because the fog is toxic. That's why our eyes glow down there."

So that much was true. The air in the Below was certainly toxic from all the factories and mines. I'd been breathing it in since my... birth, I supposed. All rats did. None of us remembered how we ended up in the muck along the Styx, and most never lived long enough to see what happened when we matured. Everyone just assumed we were born of muck and died in it. There were heaps of ways to die as a rat. I could go listing them for days.

"Any idea why?" I asked.

"We don't know. The Gloom is expanding though. Even I can remember when the fogline wasn't anywhere near the foothills of Wails."

"It's fog. That's what it does," I said.

Bran shook her head. "No, I know fog. That fog over Bedlam isn't natural. It's polluted. Altered. And it's heading towards the mountains, towards the Wails."

"Won't it stop there?"

"No one wants to take that chance."

She told me more. Of villages, of cities in caves, and of tribes that roamed the mountains. Of white snow—frozen water that was soft on the ground.

I sat and listened, and worked on my hair, marveling at a world I didn't know. "It sounds… vast," I whispered.

She smiled. "It is. You can sail the skies forever."

I shivered slightly. All that open space scared me.

"Don't you want a comb or something? You could braid it like mine."

"My coils just frizz with a comb. And I'm partial to them. I could use a scarf and some…" When Mordecai realized my hair wasn't like his own, he had come up with a special concoction. It worked like a charm, and kept Gan from shaving it all off again. "What do you use up here to keep your hair from drying out?"

She hopped up, and returned shortly with a glass vial with some sort of light oil in it, and a bright scarf. I gazed at the fabric in appreciation. Were all colors so vibrant in the Above?

"I still don't know your name."

"Everyone calls me Red."

Bran laughed. "Same here. I hate it."

"The name's Evie."

"Just Evie?"

Years ago, Mordecai and Gan presented me with official papers of birth in case I was ever stopped by the Ministry. Mordecai had claimed me as his own, and even given me his surname. It was a touching gesture, even more so because he'd forged those papers with his own skilled hands. "Evie Scarrow. Is it just Bran?"

She snorted. "By the Mother herself, you don't want to know."

I raised my brows at her.

She relented. "My clan name is Wren. So my parents were tickled to death to name me Bran Wren."

I didn't get it.

"Bran*wen* is a common enough first name up here." She shook her head.

"I like it."

"You have to. You're being held prisoner."

"Do I strike you as caring about that?"

"No, and nice to meet you, Evie. But a word to the wise, I don't know why you're goading the captains, but I'd stop."

"Because I'm bored?"

She laughed. "You put them in a tricky situation here."

"It's my nature."

Her eyes danced. "I can tell. But look here. Captain Steel's ship went down. He's the Seventh Devil to be sure, but he holds a tenuous thread on the other Devils."

I sobered. "Did he send you here to coach me?"

"He sent me to rescue the man with the plans in his head. You were a bonus."

"Sounds like you got the muck job. How'd you end up here?"

"I'm a skyrider, from one of the gypsy clans."

"Is that what your tattoos are?"

There were swirls of blue in the ink that matched her eyes. They reminded me of air currents. "Most anyone with a tattoo belongs to one of the gypsy clans. Though I suppose they're growing in style."

"So why are you with the pirate Devils?"

"Gypsy is a race, like the city you're from. It's where you were born, your kin, but that doesn't mean you can't be a tailor or an airship captain." She toyed with a braid. "The sky isle where I grew up was attacked by the Ministry. My parents fell with a section where the balloons gave out. I just happened to be on my eagle."

"Wait, what? Your eagle?" As an afterthought, I added, "Sorry about your parents."

"It happens, I'm afraid. But I still have my bird, Otter. We ride the currents together, usually at the head of the airship to calm storms."

"She must be big."

"She is."

"Where does she live?"

"She has a perch on the underside of the airship, or some-times the bow, which throws off the navigation. She does what she pleases, and flies off to hunt when she feels like it. She never stays away too long. After the attack, we were adrift with nowhere to perch, until a pirate airship came along. Willem wasn't even a captain then, but he stuck his neck out for me."

"What's his Knack?"

Bran snorted a laugh and turned all sorts of bright colors.

"What?" I asked.

"It's not polite to ask."

"Why not?"

"It's like asking… how you like to shag."

"Whichever way gets results," I said.

Her laugh was as musical as her voice, and I found myself smiling for the first time in days. "Right," I said. "So what other Knacks are there?"

"*Firestarters*," she put emphasis on this one. "Airtalkers, Stonetongues, and Waterdancers. One Knack for each element."

"What about the fifth element?"

She frowned. "There is no fifth."

"Muck."

Bran tilted her head, puzzled. I missed my mates in the Below. And I wondered suddenly if we'd ever get back.

The thought made me sober. "Bran," I said. "What's the captain going to do with us after we cough up that contract?"

"It's not for him to decide."

"Who then?" I asked.

"Aoife. The Gypsy Queen." It was pronounced EE-fah.

"Why does she have say over the Devils?"

"Because she hired them to get the contract."

I smirked. So the Seventh Devil himself, Captain Willem Steel, was a man out for masques after all. It figured.

"What will she do with us?"

"I'm not sure, Evie."

"Would you tell me if you knew?"

She gave me a lopsided grin. "No."

25. WILES

WE MOVED THROUGH CLOUDS FOR WHAT SEEMED LIKE DAYS. The cloud formations reminded me of fog. Sometimes they turned dark and angry, while other times they seemed wistful and carefree. Shapes moved inside of them, a whisper here or there.

"Do you see those?" I asked Mordecai.

"The birds?" he asked without looking up.

I'd met Bran's eagle. Otter was nearly as large as one of the skiffs that attached themselves to the great airship. Otter also tried to bite off my head. There went that escape plan.

"Yes, but…" I shook my head. "I think there's more than just birds out there." We were in Mordecai's cabin. A table had been brought in along with parchment and rulers. He'd been busy working on recreating the contract when the airship wasn't heaving.

"The world is vast." The whimsy was gone from his voice. There was no wonder in it anymore.

"I'm sorry, Mord. I am."

He looked up. "For what?"

"I got us into this mess. If I hadn't stolen those slippers…"

Mordecai set down his instruments and gripped the bunk to steady himself as he stood, so he could join me at the windowsill. "Something else would have happened eventually. If anyone is to blame, it's me, isn't it? I talked Gan into taking you on all those years ago."

"Come on now. Trying to make this about yourself?"

He bumped my shoulder with his own. "Muck happens. We live a dangerous life."

"And now we can't go back, can we? Not with the Ministry hunting us."

"We've been hunted before, Evie."

"Not like this, have we?"

"No."

I never thought of the word home. Never thought I had one. But Bedlam was, wasn't it? And I'd never be welcomed back. Not as long as the Ministry was hunting us.

"What do you suppose Poe meant when he asked me why they call them Ghostmakers?"

Mordecai was silent for a time. "I think he was answering your question about where Gan was taken. And I think he was terrified of the answer."

I shivered. Not much could terrify a genie. All this idleness was leaving room for my flourishing imagination to come up with all the ways a man I loved and considered a father could be tortured.

Mordecai went back to his drawing. He had a good start. I only hoped his forgery was exact.

"Any idea what Ministry building this is?

He gave a shake of his head. "When all is said and done, we in the Below know so very little of the Ministry."

"The fog sees to that."

Mordecai was toying with his fancy goatee, as he studied

his progress. "I imagine even the most fortified building needs its pipes cleaned."

"Ah, muck," I muttered. "Fine. I'll go use my wiles on Wee Willy."

Mordecai looked up, startled. "I wasn't suggesting…"

"You were thinking."

"I was not," he said firmly. "That was the farthest thing from my mind. You've already brained him. I don't think attacking him again will help."

"Har, har. I'll have you know I do have wiles of a delicate nature."

He grimaced. "Do be careful."

"Who knows, maybe he swings your way and he'll keep you on as his cabin boy after all this."

Mordecai was not amused.

***

THEY WERE KEEPING ME IN THE BRIG TO SEND A MESSAGE: don't forget you're a prisoner. But I could leave with guards on my tail whenever I asked permission. I think that was the point. To make me ask.

When I ventured out, the crew gave me nods, and as long as I stayed away from the armory, the engines, and the cannons, my guards didn't seem to care where I walked. They looked about as bright as baked rocks. Everyone on the ship, dark-skinned or pale, had a cooked look about them. Bran claimed it was the sun. Whatever it was, it had turned Mordecai's usually pale face a painful shade of red.

After some enquiries, I found Wil in his cabin. Charts and instruments were spread over the table every which way. Wind ruffled their edges, but they were clamped down.

Captain Willem Steel stood in front of the large stern

window. He was wearing a simple shirt, open-collared with wide sleeves, and trousers that were too tailored for pockets. The slats were open and light streamed in. Air currents snatched at his collar, and he had his face turned to the sun. Or maybe the wind. I wasn't sure.

"So let me get this straight," I said by way of introduction. "You have no issue attacking me when you're a guest, but when I'm a prisoner, you keep a guard on me. Worried I'll bite?"

"You're a denizen of the Below, aren't you," Wil said, without turning around.

"Sure as muck. I'm surprised you're letting me move about freely on your ship. Who's to say I won't get into the gunpowder?"

My guards scowled. Well, look at that. They were bright enough to spot a backhanded insult.

Wil looked to my guards. "Leave us."

One of the guards, Mason, smirked at me as he left, no doubt thinking his captain was going to teach the mouthy woman a lesson or two.

When the door shut, Wil turned to consider me. "Refinement isn't your strong point, is it?" he asked.

"Not everyone has a stick up their arse."

"Noted."

"Are you this uptight in bed too?" I liked to get under people's skin. It made them react and it showed their true colors. Though maybe I was a fool for goading a dread pirate on his own ship.

"Are you always so..." he searched for a word.

"Impertinent. Brash. Brazen. Ill-mannered. Insolent. Infuriating... I could go on. Mordecai has a large vocabulary. He likes to practice on me to show he cares."

The edge of his lip twitched. "If you prefer I can lock

you up."

"I do not prefer."

"Then I'll ask you, politely, not to disrespect me in front of my crew."

I crossed my arms. "Oh?"

"Mutiny is always a concern."

"Did the little game you played with me boost you up a peg?" I asked.

He placed his hands on the table. "This isn't a game. You don't know our ways up here, and if you value Mordecai's safety, then show some respect. At least in public."

"Respect is earned," I said.

Amber eyes met my own. They smoldered. And I mean smoldered like fire. Smoke hissed from his open collar. "I earned respect with an iron fist."

"Should I act terrified and beg for mercy?"

"That's the typical reaction."

"To you?" I asked in surprise.

He lifted his mighty shoulders. "I'm the Seventh Devil."

"Pfft," I waved a hand, "Means nothing to me."

"I know." He sounded amused.

"Maybe I'll play nice with Jacopo. This isn't your airship, now is it? Or maybe I'll just start a mutiny myself and take over."

Wil didn't rise to my bait. "I wouldn't put it past you," he muttered, looking back to his charts.

I edged closer, studying the charts. "Not much of a talker, are you?" I asked.

"Words are bluster and wind."

"You'd be dead in the sky without wind," I said.

He inclined his head. "And I would be dead without you."

That gave me pause. I cast around for a distraction, and tapped the charts. "Where are we headed?"

The smoke vanished, but the smolder in his amber eyes didn't. He held my eyes with his own. It was hypnotic. "I still don't know your name," he said, his voice deep.

"You said it. Fool."

"You actually said that," he pointed out.

I relented. "People call me Red."

"People call me Dread Pirate. And Captain. They don't use my name."

I locked eyes with the man. "Why do you care? Going to carve my name on your flesh after you use me to threaten Mordecai with?"

"You saved my life. I'd like to know your name so I can properly thank you."

Ah, muck. I was too vain to pass that up. "It's Evie Scarrow."

He gave me a little bow. "Thank you for saving my life, Evie Scarrow."

Well, now. This bastard was buttering me up. "You promised me more masques than I could handle."

His face turned hard. "Right."

"What's so important about that contract?"

He didn't answer. Why would he. Instead he asked, "Are you always motivated by greed?"

"Greed? I want food in my belly and a warm place to sleep. For me and my crew. That's not greed."

"You don't need more masques than you can handle for a full belly."

"Says the Dread Pirate with a stick up his arse. What would you know about hunger? By the look of you, you eat a larder for every meal."

"I'm surprised you don't accuse me of cannibalizing my captives."

"Nah, that's what hunger drives someone to do."

He searched my eyes. And I think he saw some of the things that haunted me. Life for a rat wasn't pretty. We witnessed all sorts of bad in the fog.

"Any road, I'll try to show you proper respect," I said, and turned to go, but stopped at a tap of a finger.

"Our location," he said, pointing to a spot on the chart with an intersection of lines. He traced a finger along one line. "Our course: where we started, here, and this is our destination."

There was no name. Just gridlines. "Which is?"

"How did I ever think you were Ministry agents," he said under his breath.

"How the muck should I know?"

"We're rendezvousing with a sky isle—a band of gypsy ships."

Wary over his sudden change, I edged forward to look at the spot on the chart. It was nonsense to me. All intersecting lines and numbers on the sides. But my gaze was drawn to one chart in particular, with the name Bedlam on the edge.

With a glance to him, and a nod of permission, I pulled the chart out from under the others. It was a map of my world. A sprawling city. There were just dots and labels for the towers that poked above the fog. No streets, or buildings, or pubs. I noted the Union Lord's tower, and vague border lines for the districts: West Winch, the Rook, Snettish, Cruel Barrow, Huntsmorrow, Monger's Square.

"You don't have the Below mapped," I realized.

"We don't. No one does, as far as we know. The fog, the Gloom, as we call it, sees to that. What's on here is what we can see from the sky."

"Makes it look sparse, don't it?" I muttered.

"Aside from the Rook, I'd never been below the fogline

before. I never realized how… close it was. It's a maze down there."

"If you'd behaved I would've given you a proper tour." And I meant that.

"I didn't have time to behave, Evie. I need that contract."

"So you can get paid?"

"My crew, captains, and operatives need pay. Yes."

"But not you?"

Wil ignored my question. He pulled out another sky chart, the one dotted with landmarks. "Do you see this? The Gloom. Every year it takes over more land and sky. It's inching towards the Wails. And as it expands the Ministry's reach goes with it. Along with the Sage King and his general—the Red Death."

"So just sail to the other side of the mountains. There's plenty of sky left."

"Do you think the Red Death will stop there? He wants it all. The skies. The land. The sea. And… the people."

"Greedy bastard after my own heart, eh? Is that why you united the pirates?"

"It is. I'm working on the other factions, including HOOF and the Gypsies."

"Who was that pretty blonde in the Union Lord's tower?"

He glanced at me, surprised.

"I was under the bed."

Wil raised that scarred brow of his.

"Not something I like to recall."

He cleared his throat. "That was Charlotte. An agent of HOOF."

"And your airship was there because…?"

"We were her exit plan."

"That went sideways."

He looked like he might be sick. "Things go wrong."

"So who mucked up?" I asked.

"I did," he bit out.

There was a flash of vulnerability in him. I realized he likely wasn't much older than me. Maybe by six years or so. Here I was, stealing carpet slippers, while he was busy uniting pirates, rebels, gypsies, and terrorists to fight the Ministry. I felt a bit like an underachiever.

"We were hiding in the Middling, waiting. When the alarms sounded we swooped in to provide a distraction, only the Gloom was higher than we thought. The *Crow* got caught in erratic air currents, and my Airtalker couldn't keep the ship afloat. We were already dodging Ministry ships when the Gloom pulled us down."

"Well, I suppose I mucked that plan up."

"No, I should've accounted for surprises."

"Not much of a surprise if you can account for them."

Despite my efforts, the weight on his shoulders didn't leave. Why did I care whether he felt guilty? This wasn't my concern.

"So what's that contract got to do with all this?"

He pulled out the chart of Bedlam. "Do you see this large empty space in the city?"

I nodded.

"Do you know what's there?"

I studied the map with its districts and picked out buildings I knew. A compass was no good in the Below. The arrows just spun in a circle. But the way the Quarters were arranged... "The Quarters here butt up against the Styx. It's the shore-line, isn't it?"

"My contacts believe so. And beyond the Gloom, there's the sea. But no one knows what's in the rest of this area. The air currents are... chaotic. It's the thickest part of the Gloom, and heavily guarded by Ministry ships. Our scouts never return.

"Some weeks ago, we got word that the Union Lords were fiercely bidding for a sweeper contract for the Sage King. It was all very secretive. We think the coordinates on the contract will point to an important Ministry location inside this blind area."

"And you plan on doing what?"

His mask slipped back on. "I can't tell you that, now can I?"

"Still think I'm a Ministry operative?"

"No, I think you work for the highest bidder. You'd sell us out to whoever offered the most."

"Pot. Kettle," I said. "I don't care what you bloody claim. You're in it for the same. And if that's not it, then it's power you're after."

"Think what you like."

"Set me right, then. What's in it for you?" I demanded.

"It's personal," he said, then turned his back on me to stare out the window. "You may go."

26. GATHERING

THE SKY ISLE WASN'T WHAT I EXPECTED. NOT AT ALL. Mordecai and I stood at the *Swale's* rail gawking like a pair of starving rats at a pie cart.

"Why the muck is there a chunk of earth floating in the sky?" I asked.

I couldn't see Mordecai's expression beneath his tinted goggles and mask, but from the way he stood, I was sure he was shocked.

"It defies everything," he muttered.

"And your distilled lighting doesn't?"

"That's science," he defended.

I glanced sideways at him. Wil had returned our gear. Well, most it. No one was trusting me with weapons. Lucky for everyone on the airship they'd had sense enough not to fiddle with Mordecai's electric coil. Once he explained it was a power source for lights, Wil handed it back.

The floating chunk of earth had roots and greenery hanging from its underside. Waterfalls streamed off its sides, and trees grew on top like fake flowers bedecking a lady's hat.

Colorful tents and awnings had been erected, and large sails jutted out in odd directions to catch wind currents.

Close to a hundred different types of airships were docked at platforms along the isle, while birds soared in the sky.

I spotted Bran on Otter, as she darted by, heading for the isle.

Captain Jacopo joined us at the rail.

"Captain," Mordecai said.

I muttered the same.

"How does it float?" Mordecai asked.

Jacopo was cleaning his nails with a dagger. "Pick any gypsy clan or pirate crew, and each will give you a different story."

"What's your favorite story?" Mordecai asked.

Jacopo grunted. "I don't care as long as the thing stays afloat." He flashed his gold teeth. "Eh, I tend to think the Airtalkers know what the sky isles are about. They say when an air elemental crashes, it imbues a bit of earth with its essence. And that bit of ground tears itself free to get back to the sky."

A farfetched story if I wasn't looking at a sky isle with my own two eyes. Now it seemed perfectly plausible.

"Stonetongues believe that the sky isles are stars that have fallen from the heavens, and they're trying to get back to their brethren." He tilted his hand and made a face. "Who am I to say?"

"And the Wrens?" I asked.

He glanced at me, but his gaze lacked its usual glower. Captain Jacopo was in a good mood today. All the Devils were. As Bran had told me, Gatherings on sky isles were week-long drunken orgies that likely accounted for most births. Enjoyment aside, Bran claimed a child conceived on a sky isle was more likely to have a Knack. But in case I didn't fancy being saddled with a child, she gave me a root to chew on. I wasn't planning on putting the preventative to the test.

"The Wrens claim the ground is sacred. That the earth was imbued with the lifeblood of their kin and all those bones seeped into the ground until it broke and drifted away." He chuckled. "Everyone wants to stake a claim to a sky isle."

"Do the Devil's have one?" I asked.

Jacopo slapped Mordecai on the back. He rocked forward on his legs and caught himself on the railing. "We will soon! Thanks to you, my good friend."

The captain walked away chuckling to himself. I wasn't amused. "So that's the payment," I said. "And that's why the Gypsy Queen gets to decide our fate. We're part of the transaction."

"At least I'm useful," Mordecai quipped, then turned serious as orders were shouted for the *Swale* to dock. "Somehow I don't think they'll simply release us."

When we docked, Captain Jacopo had my wrists clamped in iron, and we were escorted across the gangplank.

Wil helped Mordecai across. I was thankful for that. The gangplank bowed and flexed underfoot, and the clouds were far below.

"I should warn you," Wil whispered at my side. "The gypsies live by a code. Break their code and all things are final."

"Is there a handy guidebook or something?"

The corner of his lip raised. "I wish there were."

"Right. Then I'll just have to rely on my charm."

Mordecai grunted. "How about you let me do the talking."

"Sure thing, thief-boss."

We were led past tents and awnings that made up a kind of marketplace. The gypsies were as varied as their tents and clothing. Some wore bright, festive clothes; others wore dark robes, thick eyeliner, and were reserved; some were scantily clad, while others were covered head to toe in flowing scarves and robes. All of them bore tattoos, even small children. I even saw a circular design on the upper arm of a baby.

Some were as dark as Wil, and others fair-haired and light-skinned with that sun-kissed look to them.

As curious as we were, they watched us pass with equal curiosity. Children jangling with bells ran up to Mordecai and giggled as his legs clicked and clanked. They admired his gentleman's walking stick, and marveled at the silver drake wrapped around its length with its head perched on the handle.

Their parents pulled them away with stern words. I couldn't understand the lilting tongue. It was quick and musical, but I understood the tones—*Keep away from the foreigners.*

"Makes our life in the Below seem rather dull, doesn't it?" Mordecai said to me.

"We haven't tasted their ale yet," I said, flashing him a grin. He chuckled. But I knew how he felt. Small wonder the Above called us 'denizens of the underworld.' Living in toxic fog as we did, we were as good as dead, though we managed to eke out an existence, and maybe even thrive.

We were led to a bright blue awning stretched under a sprawling tree. The tree was tall as a tower, and its branches spread like wings. The leaves were green, nothing like the ghostly pale things with red leaves that we called trees in the Below. This one was vibrant and alive. Green carpet climbed up its sides and the gypsies had placed chimes in its limbs. Air currents played in the tree, knocking the chimes and rustling leaves, dancing to their own music.

I was so entranced that I stumbled over a thick carpet on the ground, but Wil steadied me, his strong hand bringing me back to the present and our tenuous circumstance.

We stopped in the center of a banquet of sorts. Men and women lounged on plush cushions, with trays of food laid out in front of them.

The gathering fell silent, and my eyes were drawn to a woman sitting on a cushion. She was stout and strong, her skin dark like the tree's trunk, her hair white but full of luster.

She looked us over, as she plucked at a grape bunch in her hand. Her gray eyes were as sharp as those of the men lounging around her. My gaze was drawn to another. A redhead in the mix. Bran sat off to the side, and gave me a small smile of apology.

I compared Bran to the older woman, and sure enough I could see a hint of resemblance. They were clearly related. And I was certain the older woman was Aoife, the Queen of the Gypsies.

Willem Steel stepped forward, and gave a slight bow. He spoke in their tongue, though there was nothing musical about him. Aoife gestured to one of the men by her side. He hopped up like a spring, and held out his hand.

Captain Jacopo and a few of his toughs stood behind us. They all had cutlasses and pistols. The gypsies didn't seem to mind, but then they were all armed, too. I'd even spotted curved knives in the sashes of small children.

Wil brought out the copy of the contract Mordecai had produced, but he didn't hand it over to the man. He stepped directly up to Aoife and presented it himself.

Interesting, I thought. I didn't speak the language, but I knew a power play when I saw one. This was all about respect.

Aoife unfolded the contract, and studied it for long minutes, then addressed Wil. He replied, and her eyes darted to Mordecai. I could imagine the conversation by their expressions and gestures. Rats were good at that. We learned early on to read the body rather than listen to the words.

Aoife: *This is a copy.*

Wil: *The original was lost. This man has it memorized. He made the copy.*

Or did he tell her we hid it? Or that Enforcers destroyed it? That part I didn't know. Was he tossing us under a carriage?

Despite her seeming age, Aoife rose like water, and stepped towards us on bare feet. Bracelets on her wrists and ankles jingled softly with movement. She was the same height as Bran, but with more curves, and there was a grace to her that commanded the eye.

She circled us, appraising me, and I half followed her inspection. She didn't seem to mind.

Aoife stopped in front of me and looked up. "I've never seen red eyes before," she said. "You are what they call a 'rat' in the Below?" She spoke the King's proper with barely an accent, but it was precise and careful.

"That's what they call us," I said. "I'm more cat than rat though." I flashed her a grin.

She frowned. "Do you bear a mark on your flesh?"

"A what?"

She tapped one of the tattoos on her cheeks.

"Not that I've noticed, unless scars count."

She made a disappointed noise and moved on to Mordecai. "So pale," she said clucking her tongue, then tapped one of his fake legs with her sword.

I glared, but Mordecai only inclined his head. "They slow me down, but they also speed me up."

Aoife didn't react to that bit of humor. She spared his facial hair a look, then returned to her seat to speak to Wil. He glanced our way, hesitant.

There was a lengthy exchange, until the two fell silent. I didn't like the little crease forming between Bran's brows.

Ah, muck it. Behaving was getting us nowhere. I raised my chin. "Where I come from we at least have the decency to speak directly to our prisoners," I said loudly.

"Evie," Mordecai said out of the corner of his mouth. "*Shut. It.*"

I raised a brow at him. Too late now. A very deep hush had fallen over those assembled and Bran's pretty blue eyes had flown wide. Wil rubbed his forehead.

But I'd drawn the attention of the only person I cared about. The Queen. That's right. Look at me.

Aoife stared at me in the ensuing silence. She turned her head slightly, and asked a question to Bran, who replied quickly.

"Where *I* come from," Aoife stressed, "We cut off the legs of cowards." She inclined her head towards Mordecai.

I bristled. "He's not a coward!"

"*Only fools are free of cowardice,*" Mordecai quoted… someone. Probably himself. He liked to do that sort of thing.

Aoife smiled, showing her teeth. "It was a joke."

I felt my bristles droop.

"And a test, perhaps?" Mordecai gave her one of his charming smiles. I'd seen women near to swoon after one of his looks.

While I don't think it was lost on Aoife, she only nodded. "That, too." She gestured, and one of the men passed back the contract. "*This* is a copy. Where is the original?"

"I don't know," I said truthfully. "Far as I know it went down with our hulk. Enforcers attacked us."

"What is a hulk?" she asked.

"A piece of junk," I said.

Mordecai gave a proper answer. "It's a retired sailing ship with no sails that floats on the Styx."

Aoife looked to Wil. "You promised the contract. Instead, you bring me a rat and a rogue from the underworld, and expect me to trust them."

A muscle in Wil's jaw flexed. "I will vouch for them."

"I will, too," Bran added.

I'm afraid my mouth fell open. Now why the muck would he do that? And Bran, too, for that matter.

"Why?" Aoife asked.

Hah, that's what I wanted to know.

"This woman saved my life. And their friend, Gan, saved it again by sacrificing himself when a Ghostmaker came looking for me."

Murmurs traveled around those assembled. Some shook their wrists causing bangles to speak.

Mordecai cleared his throat. "If I may…"

Aoife made a slight gesture, and the gathering fell silent. She settled her pale gaze on Mordecai. "Speak."

"I have what is called an eidetic memory. Call it my knack. That copy you have there is exact."

"One thing I have learned over a long life is to never underestimate the Ministry," Aoife said. "That includes their spies. How do we know we can trust what you've given us? So what, your thieving partner is missing. I know some men who would *pay* the Ministry to take away their business partner. And that includes many here."

A ripple of laughter traveled around those assembled.

"He's closer than a brother to me," Mordecai said.

Laughter turned to whispers and sidelong glances.

"What does that mean?" Aoife asked.

Mordecai glanced at the crowd. "He's my husband."

The whispering stopped. What I'd taken for distaste turned out to be confusion over the meaning of "closer than a brother."

"Why did you hesitate?" Aofie asked.

Although Mordecai appeared at ease in front of the gathering, I could see his hands shaking on his gentleman's stick. His relationship with Gan was not something he openly talked about. With good reason.

"Our relationship is illegal in Bedlam."

"Do you know why?" Aofie asked.

"I do not. The Ministry has a great number of laws that boggle the mind and yet grant permissions that go against human decency."

"Hmm." Aoife nodded in agreement. "Do you know what cattle are?"

Mordecai blinked at the change of subject. "I do. Though there are very few in the Below."

"A cow wonders why it can't be free. Why it can't graze on this grass or that grass, and then it screams at the slaughter of its young. The people of *An Aisling* are the Ministry's cattle. They want us to breed."

I'd read about cows in a book. I'd even seen one kept in a little pen. It was such a sad, miserable thing that it'd reduced me to tears. Gan went back with me later that night, and we popped the lock and set it free. I don't know what became of the cow, but at least we gave it a fighting chance.

"Our people have few laws. But many strong opinions." A chorus of bangles shook with laughter. "This mate of yours… what is his element?"

"We don't have Knacks in the Below," he answered.

She gave a dismissive gesture. "It does not matter."

"He's earth," I said. "Stubborn as a stone."

Aoife nodded in approval along with the rest of the people.

Mordecai cleared his throat. "I would be suspicious of us if I were in your place, too."

"You are not in my place."

"True, I do not sit so easily as you," Mordecai acknowledged with a smile.

Aoife gestured. "Bring him a chair."

"Thank you." Mordecai settled himself and his legs, then rested both hands on his walking stick. "Gan disappeared fighting a Ghostmaker. I think the Ministry may have taken him prisoner. For leverage, in exchange for the contract. Or… to interrogate him." Mordecai's hand tightened on his walking stick. He swallowed down a wave of emotion. "I've copied it down just as it was in hopes you will use your contacts to help us find him."

"Ghostmakers are not natural," she said. "They are a blight on *An Aisling*."

"We don't know much about them in the Below, I'm afraid. They're more myth than reality."

She shook her head. "Your world view is small in the Below, with good reason. I'm told denizens can live an entire life within a single district."

Mordecai nodded. "Between the Ministry and criminals, our streets and canals are dangerous. It's safest to stick with what you know, especially considering how easy it is to get lost in the fog."

Wasn't that the truth. I knew a bloke who got so pissed one night, he went for a walk and didn't find his way back home for a full year.

"Do you know what we call Ghostmakers?" Aiofe asked.

Mordecai shook his head.

"This land, *An Aisling*, is the Dreaming. We call Ghostmakers, *Itheoir aisling*. Dreameaters."

"Why's that?" I asked.

She spread her hands, bangles jingling. "Because my mother told me so."

Mordecai sighed. And I felt that same sting. It meant the gypsies didn't know much more about the Ghostmakers than we did.

"I've heard rumors that Denizens have the ability to distill elements and trap the essence of a thing."

I made it a point not to glance at Mordecai. Far as I knew he'd perfected the process when he somehow managed to distill lightning. "It's rare," Mordecai said. "But it does happen. With great cost."

"Myth and legend are truths seen through a veil," Aoife said. "We call them Dreameaters because they feed on our future. They kill but cannot be killed. They are the essence of death. I'm sorry, but if your husband was taken then he is dead."

That was a final sort of word. Like a punch to the gut. But I was never one to go down after that sort of punch. "I survived," I said. "And if I did, so could Gan."

All eyes went to me, including the Queen's. "Impossible."

"I went back to help Gan, and found the bloody thing roaming the wreckage. It spoke to me."

"That cannot be," she said.

"Heh, that's what it told me. That I shouldn't be."

No one in the tent moved. There was fear in their eyes. Aoife stood and walked up to me, searched my eyes as she had before, but there was an intensity to her now. She grabbed my wrists, and I started to resist, only a ring of steel at my back told me that would be unwise.

She studied the palms of my hands for a time. Then

looked at me with a widening of eyes, and whispered for my ears alone. "Only the dead can talk with the dead, child."

Her words shook me to my core. I was back up on that tower with an eel around my ankle, desperate to escape the Catchers. And I was falling, all over again.

I must have rocked back on my feet, because her hands clamped around mine, tethering me in place.

"Cage them," she said. "But see to their comforts."

I was so shaken that I didn't even put up a fight.

27. VISITORS

"Evie?"

As far as prisons went, ours was posh. Narrow beds with blankets, and in each cell a table, chair, and plenty of cushions. Our cages were half-buried, tucked in the roots of a towering tree. I could look out the bars at the markets, and at night look up at the moon and stars. I was staring at them now.

"*Evie?*" a voice came again. "Are you all right?"

I stirred on my cot. Mordecai had his face pressed to the bars between our cages. "Sure, we're in prison. Why shouldn't I be?" I asked.

"You haven't said a word in hours."

I blinked and sat up to lean against a wall. Usually a comment like that would've sparked some good-natured ribbing. But I didn't have it in me.

"I haven't given up on Gan." Mordecai worked his arm through the bars, and reached down for my hand. "You're freezing, my dear. Put that blanket around you. And don't worry, we'll get out of here. I have my picks."

I didn't answer. I just held onto his hand and stared at the twinkling lights of distant festivities. Music and laughter drifted on the air. It felt so very far away.

His hand anchored me.

"What did the Queen say to you?" he asked. "I thought you'd faint."

I didn't give him a straight answer. "I was just thinking about that day you found me in the graveyard."

"Our lives were never the same." I could hear the smile on his lips, and he gave my hand a gentle squeeze. Because I imagined him standing at an uncomfortable angle, I got up so he wouldn't have to reach so far. But he didn't have his legs on like I thought. He was holding himself up with one hand on the bars.

Mordecai lowered himself back to his cot, and it was my turn to stare down at him. He leaned against the wall, absently rubbing the ends of his stubs.

"Are they all right?" I asked. "No sores? Anything rubbing? Do you need clean stockings for them?"

"They're fine," he said. "I'm worried about you."

"Did you ever wonder why I was in that graveyard?"

"Does it matter?"

"I don't remember."

"You know I don't remember getting my legs cut off. I recall what led up to it… to an extent, but…" He trailed off, rubbing at his residual limbs. "I always assumed you couldn't remember because something terrible happened to you."

I frowned down at him.

"The mind protects itself, Evie. There are horrors our minds aren't equipped to deal with."

"But I want to know… That time I told you I touched the sun and fell, I wasn't making up one of my wild stories," I whispered.

Mordecai sat in silence for a time, his pale skin nearly

glowing in the light of the moon. "What did Aoife say to you?"

"That only the dead can talk with the dead."

He didn't laugh. Instead he pulled himself up to place a kiss on my forehead through the bars. "Whatever happened," he said against my forehead, "you're very much alive to me, Evie. And I'd like to keep you that way."

"Tough time you'll be having."

He huffed a laugh, and let go of the bars, falling back onto his cot.

"What were you doing when you lost your legs?" I'd never really gotten a straight answer before. And I didn't expect one. But he reached for his coat and dragged it onto his lap. We'd naturally been denied our weapons, but they'd returned the rest.

Mordecai pulled out the electric coil I'd stolen all those years before. Blue white light filled the room. It was nearly blinding. He gazed into its luminance, hypnotized by the tiny storm in the glass. "A miscalculation on my part." He glanced up at me. "I was struck by a bolt that burned my legs." He gave me a sad sort of smile. "Gan had to saw them off."

I gawked at him. "Are you having a laugh?" I blurted out.

"Do I appear to be laughing?"

I stared at him. Hard. He was a sly one with an odd sense of humor. It wasn't the first tragic story he told me about his legs. A fan cut them clean off. He was hit by a wagon while saving a dog. His knees shattered in a fall. And my favorite, he got pissed in a graveyard and a ghoul on the lookout for good legs mistook him for a corpse.

"Wanker," I grumbled, and dropped back down to my cot.

We said nothing for a time, but he'd gotten me out of the dark.

"Psst," I said

"Hmm?"

"You sleeping?"

"Not anymore."

"Do you think it's true, about the Ghostmakers being the essence of death?"

"Until proven or disproven, anything is possible."

"Like getting out of here."

"That too."

"What's your plan?"

"I was planning on sleeping," he said with a yawn.

"Well, I'm not planning on rotting in this cage."

"Where do you plan on going, Evie?"

"We can use those picks of yours and steal an airship. There's plenty moored to the isle."

"Do you know how to pilot one?"

"You can figure it out," I boasted. "I'll do all the legwork."

"Or we could win their trust."

"Has that ever worked for us?"

"I won yours."

I scoffed. "Blasted me with water and bribed me with food and coin."

"And yet you're still here."

"I never claimed to be the brightest," I said.

"I'm beginning to regret getting you talking again."

I laughed. "Too late now. What do you suppose they're doing down there? Aside from waving their nethers at each other." As the night progressed so had the music and merrymaking. I tried but had trouble picturing Aoife joining in the fun, or even Wee Willy. But Bran... now I wagered she was having some fun. 'Course that thought made me sour.

"I think they're making plans to attack whatever is at those coordinates."

"Won't they scout it out first?" I asked.

"I would hope so," he said. "But there was vengeance in their eyes."

I blew out a breath. "Suicide, that is. We really are muck deep in it."

———

WAITING WAS THE ABSOLUTE WORST. I DIDN'T DO IT WELL AT the best of times. But waiting with grief gnawing at my heart was unbearable. It was thoughtful that they'd put us close together. So there was no worrying about Mordecai. But maybe it was for more sinister reasons—like one of us having to watch the other being beaten senseless.

See where my thoughts were straying?

Mordecai slept mostly. He wasn't eating either. I nagged at him, but then I wasn't taking my own advice.

I spent the next day watching children climb trees while giant eagles circled overhead and airships drifted past. It was all so… vast. A life that was unfamiliar yet seemed right.

Captain Willem Steel came by to check on us.

"Aye, we need something," I said to his question. "We need letting out."

"I'm sorry, I can't do that."

"Then you can piss off," I said.

"If you hadn't stolen that contract, then you wouldn't be here, and my crew would have their payment."

"Where's *my* promised payment? What was it you said? All the masques I can handle?"

Wil flexed his fists on the other side of the cell door. "You're a greedy bastard," he bit out.

"And you're a liar," I shot back.

"There's more at stake than you know."

"And what's that?" I demanded.

"*Lives.*"

"What do you care?" I muttered.

"I care."

"If you cared, then you'd knock those ideas of an air assault out of their minds."

"Who told you about that?" he demanded.

"Hah!" I knocked on the wall between our cells. "You were right, Mord. The bloody lot of them *are* planning an air assault."

Wil's jaw worked when he realized I'd goaded him into revealing more than he intended.

"I usually am," Mordecai drawled. "And not to worry, Captain. Evie is talented like that."

"Apparently," Wil said, his shoulders deflating. "The less you know, the better chance you have of being freed."

"Do they plan on keeping us here forever?" I asked.

"No, just long enough to ensure you can't sell any information to the Ministry."

"Oh, right, 'cause we might be *spies*. I think that's the highest compliment anyone's ever paid me."

Mordecai snorted from the adjoining cell. "What about the time that fellow mistook you for a winged feen?"

I laughed. "All right, so it's a close one."

"This isn't something to joke about."

"That's all we have left, Wee Willy."

"I've done everything I can for you. I apologize. I do." He turned to go, but hesitated. "For what it's worth, I argued against an air assault."

"You're joining the attack?" Mordecai asked.

Wil gazed into Mordecai's cell. "I have a bone to pick with the Ministry," Wil growled.

"An air attack is suicide, Captain."

"We have to try."

"*Why?*" Mordecai hissed. "Why not draw them out? Why fight on their terms?"

Fire erupted from Wil's hands, it burned up his forearms, licking away his sleeves. "Because they take our children!"

I watched Wil walk away. Then sat down hard on the cot. From afar, I watched children running through the tents, laughing, carefree, their near to naked bodies touched by the sun and gleaming with life. And tattoos.

"They mark their children," I realized aloud. "In hopes of identifying them."

Mordecai was silent. I could imagine him perched on his cot, toying with his goatee as the gears of his mind worked.

I realized now why Willem Steel was so desperate for that contract. I wondered who had been taken from him. "Well, I feel like a proper scoundrel," I said.

"He could've just told us."

"Why would he?" I asked. "I wouldn't trust us."

"True," Mordecai conceded. "He's an intriguing man, don't you think?"

"You're just admiring his arse," I grumbled.

"I was wondering if you'd noticed."

"What's that supposed to mean?"

"Nothing at all, Evie," he said innocently.

"Cough it up."

"The tension between you two is… striking."

"Shut it. And start working on a plan."

Bran Wren visited at noon. I wanted to be properly mad at her, but when I saw her freckled face drop from the branches above, I could only smile till my cheeks hurt.

"I'm not supposed to be here," she whispered. She was crouched on the top of my cage. "I hope you're comfortable, at least?"

"I've slept in gutters before," I said.

She leaned over. "What about you, Mordecai?"

"As usual, Evie is talking my ear off."

"What now? Did Gan *talk* your legs off?"

"I admire him for his *silent* nature."

"You admire him for his physique," I shot back.

Bran stifled a laugh. It was like the beginning of a song cut off too soon. "Do you two ever stop?" she asked.

"Don't get Evie started," Mordecai warned.

"I'm talking with *my* visitor," I warned. "And I'm fine. Just bored." When Bran arrived I'd been climbing around the bars of my cage, and she'd caught me hanging from the ceiling bars. It wasn't much of a challenge, but it felt good to stretch. From the sound of it, Mordecai had been doing the same.

She gave me a sympathetic look. "Look, I'm sorry about my aunt…"

"So you *are* related?"

"My mother's sister."

"Why did Gan's element matter?" I asked.

Bran looked surprised. "Your element means everything here."

"What do you mean?"

"Water is always attracted to earth," she explained.

I was still lost.

"It's plain to see that Mordecai is water."

"But he doesn't have a Knack."

"No, but if he *had* a Knack, I'm sure that would be it."

I thought about this, and couldn't argue. Watching him climb was like watching water flow over a rock. He was that fluid, he was.

"The four elements affect everything in our lives. An earth and water pairing is steadfast. It's unbreakable. Water always seeps into the rock and carves a path straight to the heart."

I heard a sniffle in the adjoining cell, but pretended not to notice.

"Now fire always goes after air, and let me tell you... there's usually knives thrown, but those couples are the most passionate. Sometimes it burns out quick, but other times it smolders on for a lifetime. Then you have the more common pairings, like earth and fire, and air and water."

"What about fire and water?"

Bran grimaced. "Opposites are forbidden."

"Why?"

"It's *unnatural*. Any hint of such a relationship is instant grounds for exile. Or... death. Depending on your clan leader."

"But *why*?"

She lifted a shoulder. "That's the way of things. The Balance. Fire and water don't mix, and the same goes for earth and air. Children born from those unions are abominations."

I didn't know about all that. It sounded like the superstitious talk I heard in pubs, but then I'd seen some strange things in my lifetime. So who was I to judge?

"What about a pairing of like kind? Air with air? Or fire with fire?"

She wrinkled her nose. "It happens... but not all clans allow it. Some are more lenient than others, as long as the relationship is kept secret."

"What am I?"

Bran's forehead creased. "Considering the stunt you pulled on the *Swale*, air would be obvious…"

"But?"

She reached through the bars and touched my cheek. "I don't know, Evie. You're a hard one to place."

"Are there any without an element?"

Her eyes dimmed. "There are."

"Is that bad?"

"It's just sad. Like a child being born without sight, or…" She glanced at the other cell. "Hands."

She'd been about to say legs. Sure, Mordecai had no legs, but I didn't consider it sad. He just got around a bit differently than me. All in all, he did all right for himself.

"Is it true? That the Ministry takes your children?"

"Every time they attack."

"What do they do with them?"

"We don't know."

"Haven't you ever recovered any?"

Bran shook her head. "We thought they were conscripting them into MUW, so we started tattooing every baby born to our clans. We check all the bodies of Ministry soldiers when we can, but we've never found a soldier with one of our marks."

I considered what that meant for a nomadic race who valued tradition and family.

"The Ministry takes us in the Below, too."

She perked up. "Do you know where they're taken?"

I shook my head. "We never see them again, either."

"I'm sorry."

"It's just life in the Below."

"That's no kind of life, Evie."

Now that she said it out loud, I had to agree. But it was an uncomfortable subject. What were we in the Below to do? It was hard enough scraping by down there. "What's your aunt have planned for us?"

"Nothing bad," she said.

"Would you tell me if she did?"

Bran's eyes sparkled. "No, but I promise I'll come back later tonight."

THAT NIGHT I LAY ON MY BED LOOKING UP AT THE MOON AND watching the wind play in the stars. The night was dim enough that I didn't need to wear the tinted goggles. I tried counting the stars, but they reminded me of Bran's freckles, and I soon lost my way. Then my thoughts turned to the pain in Wil's voice and what his words meant. *They take our children.*

I rubbed at a scar on my upper arm, the skin smooth in the center and jagged on the edges, an uneven circle of flesh that gave me shivers to touch. I didn't remember how I got that scar, but then I remembered so very little of the Before. I remembered hunger, fear, and cold. And darkness. *Pain.* It made me queasy to dwell on it.

I listened for any noise from the adjoining cell. Mordecai had silently wept for the better part of the afternoon, and I wanted so badly to wrap my arms around him that I considered using his picks to escape my cell so I could break into his. But that would only alert our guards.

Eventually he passed out, and I could hear his gentle breathing. A mad old woman once told me that 'Sleep is a sip of death.' And that we dream dark dreams to remind us to stop drinking death's sweetness. I was terrified to sleep for a straight month. But now I understood what she was getting at: Sleep was a mercy, and sometimes death was too.

The festivities were in full swing again, and I lay awake waiting for Bran, hoping she'd keep her promise. Anything to distract me from my thoughts.

But it wasn't Bran who came, it was Wil. He spoke some words to our bored guards. I wondered what they'd done to get stuck with guard duty while the rest of the isle was having a snog fest.

After a moment's hesitation, the pair of guards trotted away. Wil walked up to my cage door, but didn't speak, only sat a safe distance away and gazed out at the lights.

I sat up. "Come to let us out?" I whispered.

"I'm afraid not," he said softly, so as not to disturb Mordecai.

"What did the clans decide?"

"You'll be released after we're gone. You can hitch a ride with a trader to a port, then make your way back to the Below, or anywhere you wish."

That sounded like it'd take time—time lost searching for Gan. I swallowed down a well of grief.

"Revelry isn't your cup of tea?" I asked.

"No."

I sighed. The man was as talkative as a rock. I started to lie back down, but a movement of shadow stopped me. Wil had turned slightly. "It used to be, but not anymore."

I moved off my cot and sat on the floor in front of the cell door. He shifted to the side, one eye on me and one on the sky.

"Why not anymore?"

"I got a woman with child," he said gravely.

"Oh, what a surprise. Never heard that one before," I said dryly.

"I happened to be back in port when my baby was born. She stole my heart." I saw a flash of white teeth in the dark. "So I stayed around."

"And the woman?"

"A girl, really. I wouldn't call myself a man at the time either. But we got on well enough. We were both young and… dumb."

I chuckled. "I've been there."

His eyes, near to glowing in the moonlight, smiled.

I didn't press him. In some ways he reminded me of Gan. Strong and severe, and with a heart of gold.

"We still needed to make our way, though. I tried my hand at a few things, but sailing is in my blood. My captain at the time needed me, so I went, but I came back as often as I could. After one of our raids, I returned to find the sky isle in ruins. My baby girl had been taken."

"What of her mother?"

He swallowed. "She held on for a year, but grief got the better of her. It's the not knowing that gnaws at you."

I knew that feeling. It was gnawing at me now, and it was eating away at Mordecai. It's one thing to lay your hand on the body of a loved one, but it's a whole other beast to never know their fate.

"After she was taken, Niamh (it was pronounced *nee-iv*) always heard our daughter crying. Couldn't get it out of her head. It drove her mad and she threw herself off a sky isle." His voice was hoarse. And I felt that same gravel in my own throat.

"What's your daughter's name?" I asked.

"*Was*," he corrected.

"You don't know that," I said.

"Hope is poison."

I shook my head. "No, it's what we don't know about that

does the killing. The unknown is the worst kind of bad there is."

He looked at me for a long silent while. I was speaking from a hard lifetime of experience, and that kind of place left no room for argument.

"Her name... *is* Saoirse," which he pronounced *Sersha*. "She's a Firestarter. I knew it the moment I saw her."

"I'll help you look for her," I said. "Along with Gan."

His visage turned grim. Anger blazed in his eyes. "Is this another one of your angles? Trying to get me to free you so you can run off?"

"What the muck?" I hissed. "Are you always so distrustful?"

"Of you," he bit out.

"What did I ever do?"

Wil sprang to his feet and I followed suit. "You turn up at the tower. You steal the contract from under our noses." He ticked off his fingers. I could feel heat rising from him. "Then you demand masques to save me."

"Why else would I save your hide?"

He ignored this. "You douse me with water. Then it turns out a man in your hideout can use some mystical healing force from Yonder Veil to mend me. And do I even have to mention the brig?" He drifted closer until only bars separated us.

"I didn't put you there till you attacked my father."

"You drugged me."

"That was Gan."

Wil made a growling noise, his hands working.

"Say it," I said.

He smoldered at me.

"Go on, now. Say it. Everyone does."

"That you're the most capable person I've ever met?" His words were rough, pained. "Aside from myself."

I stared at him. Speechless. My mouth worked, until I decided to click it shut. His hands gripped the bars. I could feel the heat of his breath near my lips.

Instinct told me to take a step back. The bars where he gripped the metal were glowing red. "Well, that's a new one," I whispered.

"It shouldn't be."

I took a breath, and then a small step backwards. It was getting so hot I was sweating. He glanced at the bars and quickly let go.

I felt some of the fight leave me. "Is dousing a Firestarter bad manners?"

"It's beyond insulting," he said. "But I could use some cold water right now."

Despite myself, I glanced down. And quickly returned to his eyes. "Are you sure you don't want to let me out of this cage?" I said, cheekily.

He made a sound in the back of his throat. "I'm not falling for that one."

I flashed a grin. "Your loss."

A sudden movement across the moon caught my eye. A large eagle darted across the sky, a rider hunched on its back. The white eagle spread its wings wide, and barely stopped itself before landing.

Wil turned as the music stopped and laughter died. A commotion stirred in the main camp, and a moment later a frantic alarm bell began to holler in the night.

"What is it?" I asked.

Wil moved off to search the night sky. "The Ministry."

"Get your legs on, Mord," I called.

"Already working on it."

For a long frantic moment, I thought Wil would keep walking towards the camp, but he turned back without hesitation and placed his hands on the hinges of my door.

The gypsies were in a frenzy. They streamed towards their airships, as sails began to unfurl. In the starlight, off in the distance, I spotted a formation of heavily armored airships heading for us.

A few gypsy ships and air pirates rose in the sky to meet them. Cannons boomed in the night amid clouds of smoke.

Wil tore the door off its melted hinges and I stepped out. He started to work on Mordecai's door, but the man had already picked the lock.

"We need to get to the *Swale*," Wil said.

"Will they leave you?"

Wil's lips tightened.

"Run, then!" I said. "They need you. We can look after ourselves."

"I'm not leaving."

I moved over to help Mordecai, and between Wil and me, we were practically dragging him along. I was worried his legs would fall off.

As the fleet drew near, I could make out smaller vessels flying at the gypsy ships. They were the size of the great birds, but wooden with stiff wings. A skyrider leapt from her eagle onto a Ministry airship's balloon. I cringed. Was that what they did? Was that Bran?

"What are those smaller craft?"

"Ministry aeroplanes," Wil yelled over cannon blasts and pistol fire.

A shadow swept over us, then thudded to the ground. Otter flapped her wings in agitation. "Told you I'd visit!" Bran said. "I'll take Mordecai to the *Swale*. Get him up here."

"How many?" Wil asked, as we loaded Mordecai behind Bran.

Bran grimaced. "Too many. Ten warships. I don't know how they found us."

He cursed under his breath. There were hundreds of gypsy ships, but they were lighter and smaller. And from the look of things, the Ministry ships were armored.

A rapid fire of popping joined the fight. I watched tiny bursts of light follow a skyrider like baleful wasps. The trail came from the top of a Ministry ship. I wagered those were lead tracers from a gatling gun.

As soon as Bran and Mordecai were off, Wil started running and I followed. Aeroplanes were swooping down on the fleeing gypsies, the pilots dropping canister bombs on women and children.

I nearly ran into Wil as he skidded to a stop. He stood with legs apart, his hands wreathed in flames, then thrust his arms in the air. A giant, roiling ball of fire roared towards the aeroplane. The entire craft was engulfed in flames and it spiraled over the edge of the isle. Wil turned and obliterated another, then turned his focus on an approaching Ministry ship.

I staggered back from his heat.

A great cannon burst from the sky isle. The closest Ministry ship screamed with a rending of metal. Coupled with Wil's fireball, the balloon burst into flames. The airship started losing air, falling towards the ground. But there were plenty of enemies left, and they were drawing near.

We started running again, gypsy ships falling from the sky like so many moths to a flame. Their sails punched full of holes, their hulls aflame, and their balloons deflated. Distant screams whispered between bursts of cannon and gun, and the air turned acrid with black smoke.

War was bad in the Below; it was worse when you could see the destruction.

Bran thumped to the ground with Otter. "Take her!" Wil shouted, and leapt for a line dangling from the *Swale*. It was ten feet from the edge of the dock. My heart skipped a beat, then his hands clamped on the line, and up he went as the ship rose.

I slipped onto the saddle behind Bran and wrapped my arms around her waist. She was all taut, coiled muscle. It felt like I was holding a whipcord.

"Hold onto the straps, not me!" she yelled.

I adjusted my hands as Otter hopped into the air, but she didn't flap her wings, she just leapt off the side of the isle. The breath was torn from my lungs for a stomach-dropping moment. Then the eagle's wings snapped open and we soared in a great arc. I gave a shout of excitement, and Bran laughed in answer. It was glorious. And I thought if I was about to die, this would be a grand way to meet the Ferryman. I had my coin and all.

We were soon flying high over the airships. The sky isle was being pounded by barrel bombs, while the gypsy ships swooped and dived at the slower Ministry ships. I realized they were giving the larger gypsy airships time to flee.

An aeroplane shot towards us, aiming its propeller straight at us. Bran swooped into a cloud covering, and Otter flapped her giant wings, breaking through the fluffy white, then caught an air current and rode it upwards.

"There's the *Swale!*" Bran pointed out the pirate ship. But I shook my head.

"Take me in closer to one of those Ministry ships," I called.

"Are you *insane*?" she hollered back.

"Was that ever a question? Just do it!"

"No!"

"Trust me."

"I do," she yelled. "But I have to get you to the airship."

The moment the words were out of her mouth, a hulking Ministry ship rammed one of the larger passenger ships.

Bran scream in pain and fury. She didn't argue again. She banked and soared over a Ministry ship.

"There, that one."

"You sure about this?"

I stole a knife from her belt. "'Course not!"

As the eagle dove, then turned, I worked my hand free and let myself fall. For a moment, I was free of restraints. Air filled my lungs. It gave me that heady feeling of bliss, then I slammed onto the Ministry balloon. The nets were handy. But also made of steel barbs.

Muck!

Gloves would've been nice. Too late. The barbs tore into my skin as I gripped the wire. But the underside was free of it. I adjusted my bleeding hands and took care where I placed my feet. Now what?

I drew Bran's knife and stabbed into the balloon. A noxious gas blew in my face. This wasn't full of air, but something else. I peered into the tear. There was only a small empty space. I stabbed into the next layer. And then another, but it barely made a dent in the massive airship. The balloons were compartmentalized.

Right.

Sheathing my knife, I started to climb down and around the balloon, even as gypsy ships swarmed about firing cannons. Suddenly a burst of flame hit the ship I clung to. Where did that come from?

The *Swale*. Wil stood at the rail hurling his fire at anything that got close. Small wonder airship captains liked him.

The sky was full of aeroplanes and skyriders zipping like insects around the larger airships. It was a multi-tiered battle that I didn't entirely understand the dynamics of. But I didn't need to understand any of it. I just needed to cause a bit of chaos.

I spotted the gatling gun perched on top of the balloon. It was situated in a fortified turret and spun three hundred and sixty degrees. I'd seen a gatling gun before. Spring-loaded, hand-cranked, it was a multi-barrel rotary machine that was capable of laying an entire line of men flat in a matter of seconds. In this case, that meant eagles and their riders.

Keeping clear of the gun, I rounded the balloon until I spotted a hatch in the turret. It was locked from the inside. Of course. I crawled around to just under the gun, and waited for the gunners inside to reload, then used a leather hair tie to cinch one of the ten barrels to a support rod from underneath.

The gun clicked and the rotary barrels tried to turn, only my tie was jamming it. Snickering, I pressed my back against the turret, knife in hand. The hatch opened and the first man out got my blade in his back. He slumped and slid and got caught on the barbs. I rushed inside the turret, and made quick work of the next by the simple action of slashing the tube that attached his mask. With his air supply hissing madly into the sky, I tossed him out of the turret, then turned to inspect the gun.

There was a crank on the side. Parts of it were made of brass and iron, and a long rod stuck out of the top. Cartridges. Right then. I removed my hair tie, stuffed it in a pocket, and tested the range of the thing by swiveling it at a Ministry ship on our starboard.

I turned the crank and the machine spit out a line of bullets at the unsuspecting airship. The barrage ripped through the balloon and its layers like a knife through butter, and the airship tilted. Pirates joined the volley, and soon the great hulk was falling to earth.

I reloaded, and heaved the ten barrels off their support harness, then positioned it with the barrels pointing down. One ship down, one to go… I turned the crank.

The balloon under me sagged, then collapsed, and the voluminous sail began swallowing my turret. Muck, I hadn't thought that one through.

I threw myself out of the turret and grabbed onto the side of the balloon that was still afloat. Barbs cut my flesh, as the airship tilted towards the earth, lopsided with one side completely devastated by the rapid gun. I scrambled to the highest point and took a look at my options.

They were all bleak. Wind whipped at me, snatching at my hair. Then I saw a diving white eagle cutting through wind currents with an aeroplane on its tail.

Bran was coming for me, but the aeroplane was closing in on her, its propeller nearly chopping Otter's feathers. Bran was forced to bank sharply. Clinging to a falling airship as I was, I still shuddered with relief that she'd shaken her attacker.

A shadow blocked out the moonlight. I looked up to see the underside of an airship, with its propellers and dangling lines. I jumped, and for a moment I soared, then my fingers latched around a line. I climbed up and right over the railing to flop onto deck.

I lay there panting, wondering what madness I had been infected with.

"You'll turn my hair white!" Mordecai yelled down at me. He had his legs off, and the deck was heaving all over the place as he lowered himself from the railing beside me.

I leaned over and planted a kiss on his cheek. "The color will look great on you, Stubby."

I hopped to my feet, then grabbed the rail as the airship

shuddered beneath us. The ship keeled to port, nearly on its side, then rose sharply on an air current.

I grabbed Mordecai's collar. He was sandwiched on the bulwark, but I knew that'd change. As the ship righted itself, he started sliding across the deck. I held him fast.

Jacopo did slide across the deck, going to the low side of the ship. He came up and thrust a hand out as a rain of bullets flew at us. A Ministry ship was firing at us from below, but only a few bullets hit.

Metal was in the earth, I realized. Jacopo must be a Stone-tongue. But that realization was cut short—a second Ministry ship loomed above us. The battle was dizzying.

"Weight the air!" a voice boomed over the chaos. Wil stood at the helm, his hands moving confidently over the wheel. I felt a shift in the air that I couldn't explain, and then the *Swail* began to fall. I felt like heaving.

A barrage of cannon fire hit the underbelly of the Ministry ship, and Wil hurled a fireball along with it. The assault punched a hole in the hull.

"Brace yourselves!" Wil bellowed.

I did, keeping a hand on my father, as the entire airship banked sharply, turning nearly on its side, then swooped down through cloud cover.

"Thin the air!"

We came down on an aeroplane, slammed it to pieces, then leveled out right in front of the Ministry ship that had been below us. I held my breath as the ship adjusted course, making to ram us. Cannons burst, but our barrage barely dented the plated bow. The airship kept coming.

Wil's eyes smoldered at the helm. And when he saw me, the edge of his lip raised. A blink later a burning Ministry airship plunged from the cloud cover above and fell on top of the ship coming at us. With a rending of metal and explosions, both ships tangled together and dropped out of sight, leaving a trail of black smoke and the acrid taste of gunpowder in my throat.

The sounds of cannons, and guns, and the whirr of aeroplanes all stopped. The night turned silent.

"That man's going to turn *my* hair white," I muttered.

Mordecai had a death grip on a belaying pin. "I would like to return to the ground now."

29. HOPE

ASH FELL, TURNING EVERYTHING GRAY. IT WAS A COLOR I WAS used to, but not here. Trees burned, craters marred the isle, and fires had turned the sky black. The bombs had done their damage.

Most of the living had fled in airships, but a few returned to search for survivors among the dead.

I spotted Bran with Otter. She was fussing over some injury to the eagle's wing. The second I hit ground, she ran up to me and punched my arm. "You're the maddest Windwalker I've ever seen!"

"What's that?" I asked.

"Someone with no sense, that's who," she fumed up at me. Then pulled me into a fierce hug. I returned the gesture.

"That sounds like me."

Wil stalked past us, and I felt a wave of heat trail in his wake. I untangled myself from Bran and we followed his trail to the Queen.

"Find the living, gather our dead, and search for our children," Aoife called. "We need to fly. More will come."

"How did they find us?" someone called.

The gathered gypsies looked to Wil, then to me, and finally to Mordecai who was slowly making his way onto solid ground. There was suspicion in their eyes.

"We weren't followed," Wil said. "I made sure of it."

"I can vouch for that," Bran said. "I did the scouting."

That left me and Mordecai. I heard a shuddering breath, and I glanced over my shoulder at my father, then quickly took his arm as he swayed. He was as pale as a ghost.

"I think this may be my fault, Evie," he said.

Muck.

Aoife made a sharp gesture. "Go, hurry. Leave this to me. You all know what to do." Her face was streaked with blood and her white hair stained. I'd wager she'd been on one of those eagles.

The gypsies glared at Mordecai and me as they left to search for survivors.

A tent sagged nearby, half untouched, the other half flapping in the wind. Aoife took Mordecai's elbow and walked him in that direction. Wil rummaged through the wreckage and found two stools. Mordecai waited for Aoife to take a seat, before sitting down with a sigh.

"How?" Aoife asked.

Bran was there, too, a furrow between her brows.

Mordecai set down his walking stick. "A moment."

"We do not have time," Aoife said.

Mordecai began rolling up his right trouser leg, exposing the skinny round wood and the rubber and steel joints of his artificial leg. Aoife fell quiet as he turned a small valve on a vulcanized rubber socket at the top. A hiss of air escaped, and only then was he able to pull off his leg. His residual limb, or his stub as I called it, was wrapped tight in stockings and a sheath of rubber for padding.

His cheeks flushed at the attention as he fiddled with the socket and peeled back an outer layer of leather, revealing folded papers molded to the outside of the socket.

"You had it this whole time!" I said.

Mordecai gave me an apologetic look.

"You tricked us," Aoife's voice dripped with venom.

"No," Mordecai said. "The copy I made is correct, right down to the Sage King's seal. However," Mordecai unfolded the contract, "I think *this* seal may be traceable."

"How would that be possible?" she demanded.

"I don't know," he admitted. "But in the Below they use Sniffers, creatures who can sniff out…"

"We know what they are. Their range doesn't extend beyond the Gloom."

Wil took the original contract from Mordecai, and studied the seal. "It could be imbued with some kind of ferromagnetic ink…"

"It could be a lot of things," I said. "Including a spy among your people."

Aoife frowned at me, and Bran placed a hand on her aunt's shoulder. "They've found us before, aintín."

Aoife placed a hand over hers. "And they will find us again."

"Why keep this for yourself?" Wil asked Mordecai.

"I kept it so we could search for Gan."

"But you don't need this. You say you have the entire thing memorized," Wil pointed out.

"Yes, but you're not planning to use the contract for its original purpose."

"Which is?" Aoife asked.

"To sweep the air shafts of whatever that place is," Mordecai said. "It occurred to me that the Ministry might have a way to detect forgeries of the Sage King's official seal. Since you don't intend to get to the building from the Below, I didn't think it mattered. But perhaps I was wrong…"

Aoife held up a hand. "No, I was wrong. Life has stolen the trust from my bones." She looked to me. "But I watched you destroy two Ministry ships."

"Bran gave me a lift and Wil picked me up, which reminds me…" I started to unsheathe the knife I'd stolen, but Bran shook her head.

"Keep it."

Wil snapped his fingers, and a flame sparked on his fingertip. "So we burn the Seal away." The flame curled under the paper.

Mordecai grabbed Wil's wrist. "*Wait.*" He brought Wil's hands down to his level. To Wil's credit, he didn't resist, but knelt. Mordecai used the flame to run it under the paper at a safe distance. With heat, the seal faded away, revealing a time, date, and location that I recognized in the Below. It was a dock on the River Styx. As soon as Mordecai moved the flame away, the Sage King's seal reappeared.

"Oh, we're daft, we are," I said. "What use does a sweeper crew have for longitude and latitude?"

"Hmhmm," Mordecai was toying with his goatee, "the coordinates are just standard Ministry procedure." Then he looked to Aoife. "We need time. Give us a chance to find Gan and any whisper of your stolen children." It was the closest thing to a plea I'd ever heard from him.

Her eyes filled with sorrow. "Our sails are already full of wind. The clans have scattered. It's too late to trim them now."

"Then we'll outrun them," Wil said. "We have five days before the planned attack. At least let us *try*."

Aoife gave a curt nod. Will burned the seal, and exchanged the original for the copy. "May the Elements protect you," Aoife said.

And we were away.

30. SHROOM SMUGGLING

FIVE DAYS SOUNDED LIKE PLENTY OF TIME. IT WASN'T. NOT TO scout an operation of this scale. The tricky part was that the scheduled sweeper rendezvous at the dock was on the same day as the planned assault.

Muck.

But here's the real catch. We had no way of knowing if the Ministry had found another Sweeper for the job and rescheduled the date after the theft of the first contract. But since the Ministry liked to be punctual, Mordecai and I agreed that with their infinite egos, they'd assume the contract was destroyed in the battle and reissue it unchanged.

"The planned strike could give us an advantage," Mordecai whispered. We'd sailed at full speed to the Fringe, a floating trader's outpost that was an amalgam of airships, wicker platforms, and propellers lashed together to create a floating city. I didn't have time to gawk, or worry about the craftsmanship. Wil, Bran, Mordecai, and I disembarked from the *Swale*, and Wil hired a smuggling skiff to sneak us into Bedlam.

Fog swirled around us. Not the toxic pea soup, but thick, silver fog that smelled of crisp air. Our propellers were silent. We drifted by balloon sail, skimming the Gloom. I could see the difference easily enough. What troubled me was that our captain, an Airtalker, appeared to be having a shroom-induced journey of his own. He was tickled to death with the Gloom, and kept dipping his hull into it.

"How could being bombed while we're trying to break into a place be an advantage?" I asked. We were huddled in the bow of the skiff, gray coats wrapped snuggly around our shoulders. Wil was glaring daggers at the Airtalker, and Bran was using her Knack to make the fog thicker around us. She kept casting uneasy glances at the greenish Gloom under our hull.

I felt Mordecai's shoulder lift. "Distraction."

I thought of Wil and the distraction he'd provided for the HOOF operative. That had gone splendid. But I didn't say so. Mordecai was uneasy about me venturing to this unknown place. He'd argued that he should be the one to go.

I shot that down right quick. But I was guilty of the same thing. When Bran volunteered to come, I'd tried to talk her out of it and got a taste of my own stubborn nature. Needless to say, I'd lost that argument.

Great engines whirred overhead. Ministry ships and their giant propellers. I tried not to think of how many there might be, or how precarious our situation was in a rickety wicker skiff. Maybe a shroom or two *would* help. But we were the only cargo. Our smuggler was heading into the Below to pick up a shipment. Shrooms were a thing of the Below, and the Above paid well to be poisoned by the hallucinatory mushrooms. We in the Below *were* good for something.

Even the air currents looked like they were tripping. The

closer they got to the Gloom, the more erratic they behaved. The air looked drunk. And I'm not talking about the happy kind. But the angry drunks who liked to pick fights kind.

Not long after, our questionable skiff bumped into something solid in the fog. We unloaded ourselves onto a rotting dock jutting from a tower. I kept a firm hand on Mordecai as we hurried into an old servant's passage.

I stopped on the stairwell to listen. It was quiet. The air was stale, and the Gloom was only a foot below, shifting like a muddy pond. "Right, then, keep your masks on you at all times," I said to Bran and Wil. "Otherwise you'll choke on the fog and die an unpleasant death."

Wil grunted. He'd nearly done just that. And Bran kept casting uneasy glances at the Gloom lapping against the stairs. I grabbed her hand and held it. I was thinking she was wishing she hadn't come either.

"*Do not* give up your masks. Do not set them down. There are chains attached to them for a reason. Understood?"

Bran and Wil nodded.

"Wil, you stick with Mord, smash anyone who tries to snatch him. Catchers are always looking for a pretty face to sell in the slave markets."

Bran paled, and Mordecai gave me one of his "I'm not amused" looks. "I'm well past my prime for that," he said.

"And you'll stick with me, Bran." I gave her hand a squeeze.

Mordecai adjusted his cravat. He looked splendid in frock coat and a tall hat. Every bit a lord. Wil was passing as his bodyguard, and I was glad for it. Mordecai needed one, and I was sure Wil would take care of him. They were off to the Rook, to meet with Wil's lord-shagging operative.

"Right, then." I started off.

"Wait." Bran pulled on my hand. "Your mask."

I flicked my cowl up over my head. "I'm in my element here."

31. LOCAL

THE STAIRWELL SHOT US OUT INTO A DUMPY COURTYARD THAT was full of muck. I'd been in these old towers before. Abandoned by owners for different reasons: some lost their fortunes to shroom addiction, cards, or drink; others moved out when the rookeries started moving in; and still other lords disappeared after they crossed the Ministry.

I pointed to inky vines that were climbing up the stone walls. "Keep away from those."

"I can't see a thing," Bran whispered.

I glanced at her. Was the fog really that bad? We slopped across the courtyard to a rotting plank, then stepped onto a cobbled street that had more potholes than stones left.

I took a deep breath, and listened. A faint rattle of wagons, the distant drone of machinery, and an acrid taste to the fog. Factories. We were in Snettish. I had my bearings now.

Keeping Bran's hand in mine, I led her through alleys and lanes. A large, hulking man rolled past, driving a wagon pulled by a pair of cloaked servants. He yelled out a threat at me, and I answered in kind. Bran tensed, reaching for her short sword, but I made a calming gesture.

"What did we do?"

"It's a common greeting. There's lots of shadows in the murk. It's usually the friendly ones that'll get close enough to slit your throat. He was just warning us away, and I was warning him. No harm done."

"This isn't what I expected."

I was enjoying the stroll. It was nice to have a friend on my arm, and good to be home. But I did worry for her. I doubted Bran would survive a cycle in the Below.

"What did you expect?" I asked.

"It's so… close. I feel like I'm being crushed." Her voice was muffled by her respirator, but I could hear it shaking.

"Don't focus on what you can't see. Use your ears." I'd never realized how developed my other senses were. I moved mostly by feel.

"But I can't *feel* my element. I should be able to, the air is thick with water, but it's… cut off."

I was mucking bad at comforting someone. My life motto for myself was "deal with it." But even I recognized saying that might be a bit harsh. So I said nothing, awkwardly.

Then something brilliant popped in my head. "Mordecai can feel his legs still," I blurted out.

"I've heard others say that about their missing limbs."

"He can curl his toes and everything," I said.

"But he can't use his legs," she said. "That's how it feels. The water is there, but it's not."

"We'll just have to find you an artificial Knack."

She was wearing a full-hooded plague mask and the way she cocked her head made her look like a curious bird. "What in the sky would that be?"

"A pint."

BUT EVIE, YOU SAY, I THOUGHT YOU WERE IN A HURRY? THERE is always time for a pint in the Below. And I wanted to show Bran that the Below wasn't all bad.

We were soon settled in my local, sitting at a table in front of a glowing hearth. Some color had returned to her cheeks, and she watched the patrons with a curious eye as they laughed and ragged on each other.

"Is it different for you now? Knowing what's above?" she asked.

I took a sip of my bitter, and savored it a moment. Aggressive, bold, and filling. Our brew is in high demand in the Above. They say it's the hops or the barrels. But I say it's the muck that makes Below Bitter prized.

"Not really," I said. "For all its filth and misery, this is home. It's familiar." I smiled, and leaned closer to whisper. "And I like lurking about the fog. Makes me feel a proper burglar."

"I think you're much more than that, Evie."

I felt my cheeks heat. A rare thing. I was good at taking punches, but a compliment was another beast that always managed to catch me off guard. I was floundering for something clever to say, but nothing came to mind, so I just raised my pint to her.

"Re-e-ed!" a voice crooned. "Buy me a pint?" Mick was a familiar face. He had a bulbous nose that had been punched too many times, and was currently flushed with drink. His call brought others, and soon enough I was making fictitious introductions and buying a round for the table. Popular, I was.

"Brilliant tattoos you got there," Sally said, making herself comfortable next to the gypsy. Tomas sat on my other side to try his wiles on me. And Mick soon joined us, carefully managing five ales in two hands, and not spilling a drop.

"What I'd tell you lot?" Mick said. "Gone off for days on end and brings back a new friend."

Tomas sulked behind his pint while Sally waggled her brows. "There's always room for two more in my bed."

"'Cept when it's me," Mick grumbled.

"If you had two coils to rub together, maybe I'd consider it."

Mick cradled his mug lovingly. "That's a whole lotta pints I'd be missing, love."

We went back and forth in good-natured banter, while Bran tried to keep up with our quick tongues and low wit. I could tell she wasn't keen on the smell emanating from my mates. Muck was an acquired taste.

I eventually steered the conversation to matters of import: union talk. Most of it was piss and wind, but I garnered a few useful bits. And soon enough we were saying our goodbyes as I dragged Bran out of the pub.

She stumbled down the steps and I caught her. She was on the tipsy side. Oh, muck. I should've realized the bitter might affect her. I could tell by the way she was humming that she was at least enjoying herself.

"Home isn't far," I said. "Though every fiber of my being is wanting to put a blindfold on you," I admitted as we crossed a stone bridge, and headed to wider streets.

Bran leaned on my arm. "Would you, now?"

I glanced down, and grinned. "If you like."

"Well, I'm as good as blind already. I'm in your hands, Evie Scarrow."

Wasn't that the truth. I could feel every point of contact she was making with me through my coat. My senses were plenty alive down here.

Mordecai and Gan had a bolthole in every quarter, even in the Rook. My local pub we'd just left was in Huntsmorrow, which was mostly merchants and markets. Huntsmorrow wasn't as posh as the Rook, but it wasn't West Winch or Snettish, either.

Me and Bran strolled past barbers and haberdasheries, respirator crafters and the union shops. The bitter had left her more comfortable.

Everything was unionized in Bedlam. The Freeborn Mason's Society, the Honorable Society of Watchmakers, the Lamplighter Extraordinaire Empire of Radiance (leeries had their sense of humor), and the list went on into eternity.

I took Bran to bolthole number three, which was hidden in plain sight. *Scarrow and Co.* was situated in a stately building that rubbed shoulders with the leerie's union hall. Walking on stilts as the lamplighters did, they were tight with Scarrow and Co., who crafted exceptional artificial limbs. That name wasn't a coincidence. Mordecai was gifted. He did occasional work for the high-paying class, and more regular work for the unfortunates who couldn't pay.

He was in demand, and had a posh workshop where thief-takers didn't come knocking every day demanding protection money.

Once inside, I locked the seals on the door, then switched on the fans and waited for the toxic air we'd let in to clear out. We shed our dirty boots and coats, and I opened a second door into a cozy kitchen.

A large man with an expansive gut looked up from a stove. His eyes crinkled with joy. "Red, my dear, I gave you lot up for good."

"Close to it."

The smells made my mouth water. Mr. Devish was an artist of the culinary kind. And he didn't let his lack of arms get in his way. The man was stirring a soup with an arm that had a spoon on its end. He could swap out utensils as needed into a rubber socket on what should've been his elbow.

"This is Red," I said. We hadn't wanted to risk someone recognizing her name. The less Mr. Devish knew the better for him, and he was happy to live in ignorance of our ways.

"Two Reds? Oh, dear, we can't have that," he said. He extended his other arm, and Bran shook steel fingers. Working for Mordecai had its benefits.

Another door swung open. "What can't we have?" a feminine voice asked. Mrs. Devish was a cheerful woman in a starched apron and with a bosom you could set a pint on. She was also three feet tall.

"There's two Reds now. As if one wasn't bad enough."

"Oh stop it. Earl. She's too old to tease anymore." Mrs. Devish reached up, and I stooped down to give her a hug. "I know enough not to ask if you'll be staying, love."

"For a day or two. I need a watchful eye on Red here, while I duck out for a tick."

"Is Mordecai coming?" Mr. Devish asked. "I have a new idea for an arm."

"You collect arms like women collect roses," said his wife.

"I should arrange my arms into a bouquet for you…" Mr. Devish mused. His wife laughed, and I pulled Bran across the kitchen to the servant's stairwell.

"He'll be along. And bringing some company, too," I called as I pulled Bran up the stairs. She was smiling ear to ear, but I couldn't tell if that was from meeting the Devishes or the drinks. "This is lovely," she said. "It reminds me of one of our airships."

I started, surprised, then glanced at my room with new eyes. Thankfully it was clean. My decorating style was whatever caught my interest. There was no rhyme or reason to it. Most of it just things I'd pinched over the years, but some of it things I treasured, like a raven's feather or glass baubles I collected on a string.

The carpets were plush and the bedcovers warm. But I saw what she meant. There was so much color in my room. Crystals strung out to catch firelight, hanging silks and patchwork bedspreads.

"I suppose it is." I threw open my wardrobe, and started changing.

"So many scars," her voice at my back was closer than I expected, and I turned slightly in surprise. Her fingers, cool and light, trailed down my back, tracing the slashes and cuts, the burns and bullet holes that marked my body. I paused to take a steadying breath, then finished cinching the bind around my breasts.

When I turned to her, there was sadness in her eyes. I chalked it up to drink. Her fingers lightly caressed my arm, drifting along the tender side of my wrist, and finally swirling over my palm.

I wanted to taste her lips. "Are we friends, or… more?" I whispered.

"Definitely friends. I'm not sure about the rest."

I slipped a hand around her neck, and drew her closer. She melted into me, her body arched against mine, her lips parted, and she looked up at me in… a daze. I quickly drew back.

The sudden movement made her blink, and I saw hurt flash across those blue eyes. "You're tipsy, Bran," I said, my voice breathy in my own ears.

"Why does that matter?"

"I don't make a habit of kissing drunk women."

She frowned in confusion. "Is it because I'm a woman?"

"It's because you're drunk. And that's why I have to leave you here for a bit. Make yourself at home—"

"I'm coming with you."

"No, you're not."

Bran glared up at me. "I let you ride Otter into battle with me."

"*I* wasn't tipsy."

"Gypsy rum is just as potent."

"Look, Bran," I took her hands in mine. "It's dangerous out there. I can't be looking after you."

Her hands slipped from mine, and she crossed her arms. "I'm not some innocent flower, Evie," she said. "I don't need looking after."

I reached for a shirt. She had no idea; she really didn't. "I'm off to see some rough people. And I'll likely be mucking about a sewer."

She wrinkled her nose.

"Take some time to adjust to the Below. The Devish's are downstairs in case you need anything."

I finished dressing, grabbed my weapons, and shrugged on a battered coat. All the while Bran shot daggers at me. There was nothing for it. And there was no time to make things right.

32. THE WAIT

"Evie, you're pacing back and forth like you're itching to slaughter someone." Mordecai sat in his favorite chair in the great room. He'd shed his coat, but being the proper sort, retained his cravat and waistcoat.

Wil stood at the hearth, a hand on the mantel, staring into the fire that reflected in his eyes. Bran was still fuming at me. I'd come back to find her asleep in my bed. Being a proper gentlewoman (in some things), I took a blanket and slept on the rug. Whatever it was between me and her, it didn't feel like sport, and I suspected she was more innocent than she liked to admit.

"I searched all the docks in the area those charts of yours pointed to, and there was nothing. No Enforcers and no Ministry buildings. Just a crumbling embankment, muck, and rotting planks. Even rats and tramps steer clear of the area."

"You shouldn't have risked it," Bran said.

"I can handle things."

"You don't always have to go it alone."

I stopped and looked to her.

"Charlotte will find something," Wil said. He was certainly confident in her abilities.

"Well, she's late," I said. "And what if your charts differ from Ministry charts? Those latitude and longitude coordinates could be off."

Mordecai studied the three of us over his wine glass. "The charts may be correct and our bearings in the Below inaccurate."

"Have you ever known me to get lost?" I asked.

"No," he conceded.

Everything hinged on this unknown woman. I didn't like the idea of meeting with her at our legitimate shop, but for a woman of her class, coming here would raise fewer eyebrows.

I hated waiting. I disliked the tension and the buildup. I wanted to get on with it.

"Miss Wren, would you care for some wine?" Mordecai asked.

"No, thank you," she said. "I wouldn't want to get tipsy."

That was fine, but I needed a stout drink. I went over to the sideboard, and raised a glass to Wil, who gave a slight nod. I poured two brandies and handed one over to him. He took a sip, then a moment to savor it.

A bell interrupted me in the middle of a swallow. I heard Mr. Devish's ponderous footsteps, and the door opened. A pleasant voice drifted into the foyer. Greetings, introductions, and finally Mr. Devish appeared.

"There's a Miss Charlotte Holly to see you, Mr. Scarrow."

"Show her in, please," Mordecai set down his wine glass, and used the higher armrests to push himself into a standing position.

Charlotte Holly was regal in green satin, her golden hair piled in an elaborate arrangement. Her cheeks were flush with pink and her décolletage was low. Somehow she appeared more scandalous in that frock than when she'd pranced over to the union lord's safe.

"Miss Holly," Mordecai gave a slight bow.

She returned the gesture with a curtsy, then turned to Wil and held out her hand to him in greeting. He bowed over it and brushed her knuckles with his lips. I wasn't familiar with pirates, but I was fairly sure most of them didn't perform that maneuver with such practiced grace.

Mordecai made introductions. Charlotte's eyes flicked over me dismissively, then settled on Bran with interest.

"We've met before," I said, trying to distract her.

Charlotte arched a delicate brow. "Have we?"

Wil cleared his throat, loudly.

I bit back an impolite comment. "More or less," I said. "What do you have for us?"

We waited until she was seated to take our own seats.

"I have a name." We waited. "Have you heard of Mallard Pennyworth?"

"The richest Sweeper in Bedlam," Mordecai said.

"Oh, right. Yes." I'd burgled his tower, and my skin still crawled from rifling his drawers. "But word on the street was that one of his… toys castrated him, then slit his throat," I said. "How could he hold the contract?"

"For years, he held an exclusive contract with the Sage King. When he was killed, the unions went into a bidding frenzy. That's what started this whole affair. Eric Mayweather won the bid."

"Who's that?" I asked.

She gave me a puzzled look. "The man you stole the contract from."

"Ah." I never bothered with details. Why did I need to know names of people I stole from?

"Eric is dead." Charlotte's eyes flashed at the telling. She apparently relished details. "Rumor has it the Red Death sent an assassin. So as you can imagine, the next round of bidding wasn't so frenzied."

"So who has it now?" Bran asked.

"Jake Coil."

I started. "The Brute of Snettish?"

She nodded, distaste plain on her face. "He's not even a lord."

Oh well then, not being a lord just takes the cake. Never mind the heaps of slaves he buys and sells, and the work-houses of death he keeps.

Mordecai frowned, toying with his mustache. "I wonder what scared the other lords away."

"The risk of failure?" Wil asked.

I tilted my hand. "There's enough lords short on masques that they'd jump at the chance."

"Unless they know something we don't," Mordecai said.

"Which could cover an entire city," I pointed out.

"Hmm."

"Do you think it's a trap?" Bran asked.

Mordecai looked up. "It may be," he said with a sigh.

"Did you get a date?" I asked.

Charlotte shook her head. "I don't have any roads into Jake Coil's turf."

I clapped my hands together. "Right, then. Let's get to work."

"Evie…"

I cut Mordecai short. "It's either that or I pace myself right through this carpet into the Under Below. We don't have time to worry about a trap."

He opened his mouth to argue, but Gan's life was at stake. So I made sure he didn't have to choose between the two people he loved most in the world. "Chart me a route through the pipes. Leave the rest to me."

33. STEP ONE

A LARGE RED-EYED HORSE CLOMPED OVER THE COBBLESTONES. It was an old, tired thing, as tired as its driver. Animals had adapted better to the toxins, though their lives were as short and miserable as rats like me.

I leaned on a lamppost, chatting with a cheerful leerie, who was half-pissed but still on his stilts.

"…then she says to me, I always wanted a tall man, so she leads me home, and I hoist 'er up to her window all noble-like, and climb in right after. But once she see's me without me stilts, as bare as I was born, she says, 'I thought you'd be taller.'" He wheezed at his own joke.

And I laughed right along with him as a wagon passed. "Oi, got to fly," I said. I hopped on the back of the wagon, then moved along its bed as quiet as could be.

A figure stepped out of the fog and gave a call. "Got any carrots?" a deep voice asked.

"Not for sale," the driver said.

I came up from behind and clamped a hand over the driver's mouth. "We're renting your wagon for one cycle," I whispered. A boy sat next to the driver, his eyes wide. "The boy will be safe."

The figure from the fog reached up and hauled the driver down, then passed him off to two others waiting in the mouth of an alleyway. I plopped down on the seat and took up the reins. The boy beside me was shaking with fear, so I raised my goggles and winked at him. My red eyes always threw off denizens. No one ever expected a grown rat, let alone a sun-touched one. I clucked my tongue, and Wil hopped in the back and hid under a sack.

"Here's the deal," I held the reins with one hand and threaded a masque in another. "Your partner is safe."

"He's my dad," the boy squeaked.

"Well enough." I flicked the coin at him. "We're just borrowing this wagon."

The boy stared at the masque, turning it this way and that. Then he bit the coin.

"Like I said your dad will be fine," I said wryly.

"Sure."

Easy as that. We had a grocer's cart.

"Now there's one thing I need from you…"

34. TAKEOVER

JAKE COIL HOUSED HIS SWEEPER CREWS IN A SECURE CORRAL, only the fortifications were intended to keep people from escaping rather than keeping thieves out. No one wanted to steal a bunch of sickly sweeper rats.

A bored guard glanced at our approach from his gatehouse. He put up a halting hand, and the horse stopped out of habit.

"State your business."

"Grocery delivery," the boy on the bench said, far too cheerfully. The guard gave a bored wave, and the horse plodded forward. Well, that was easy.

"Easiest masque you'll ever make, aye?" I whispered.

"Don't get cocky," Wil said from under his sack.

"I'll stop being a cocky bastard when I'm dead," I tossed over my shoulder. The sack snorted.

The boy pointed out the grocer's entrance. I helped him unload while a hovering cook glared at us. "Rotten. They's all rotten."

The boy shrugged.

"Pay us better, why don't you," I said.

The cook glared. "It be rat feed."

His apron sagged on his sloped shoulders, and I doubted he tasted his own food. He grumbled his way back into the stew house.

Each crew had a separate barrack, with a corral for the rats, quarters for their handlers, and an attached carriage house for wagons. A crane sat in the center of the yard, where the handlers forced their crews to train.

It was a wretched life.

On cue the boy dropped a crate, and the cook came out to berate him. Wil handed up a sack that was vaguely human-shaped and propped it up in the driver's seat, while I sidled over to one of the corral cages.

"Psst," I called into the dark. I flashed my eyes, and heard a stir. "You'll fly if I win. Savvy?"

A figure edged forward. Covered in muck and smoke, the only distinguishing thing about the child was a pair of red eyes. Rags hung from their body. "What's the best lot of you?"

"Crew one," the rat whispered.

"Fancy the handlers?"

They shook their head.

"What I thought. What's his mug?"

"Fat on food and a chimney sucker."

"And the carriage taker?"

They nodded towards a building, holding up three fingers. I tipped my hat and passed a meat pie their way. They immediately started breaking it in pieces to hand out to their fellow kin. That tugged on me something fierce, and I swallowed down an urge to set them free. Muck the gypsy children, there were children here who needed homes.

At that thought another occurred, but I tucked it away for later chewing.

As the boy climbed back onto his seat with his 'father', Wil slipped through the shadows along buildings and joined me beside barrack number three. There was fierce competition between the handlers. Fights were common, and some handlers pitted their rats against each other for sport. Since it was common for handlers to sabotage the wagons of their rivals, the handlers slept in the same building as their caged wagons.

Pecking orders always made my jobs easier. It left room for people to muck up.

Wil pressed himself against stone, the gray of his clothing blending with the fog. For all his size, he was light and swift on his feet.

I climbed up the side of the building using uneven stones, and pulled myself onto the roof. In the thick fog below, the cook was chattering to the sack human. The boy grabbed the reins from his 'father' and gave a nervous laugh. "Dad's dead drunk."

"Lucky bastard," the cook muttered, and retreated back to his hole.

As the wagon rattled away, I opened the top grate to a chimney-like structure jutting from the roof. The whir of a fan drowned out all else, and I took a moment to study the rickety thing. Large, clunky, and three-bladed.

I climbed inside the hatch, braced myself against the walls of the shaft, and scrunched down to close the grate overhead. Then I watched the fan blades.

Whoosh, whoosh… I dropped like a cannon ball. Blade three scuffed my cowl back, but the blades weren't sharp. As soon as I was clear I threw out my hands and feet to stop my fall.

That sort of maneuver was a heap easier when I was shorter.

I took a moment to listen, then moved swiftly through the

air shafts. When I came to a good-sized grate, I opened it, and slipped down into a hallway.

Voices sounded from below. Two men playing cards from the sound of it. I crept down the stairs, taking care of creaking floorboards. Then stopped halfway down, and waited.

Wil's knock came right on time. Both men looked to the door. I flew down the stairs and gave one of them a quick, hard smack on the back of the head. The second man fell off his chair in surprise, and I was on him in a blink. I clamped his mouth shut and drove a knife into his heart.

His death wasn't instant, and I stared straight into his fading eyes while he died. I wanted him to know a rat had done him in.

The door soon opened to Wil's picks, and before the pair could bleed all over the place we dragged them out back to a sewer hatch. After a good search and divestment of anything useful, down they went. It'd be the same place they dumped sickly rats and dead ones, so no one would notice the smell.

"That was easy enough," Wil muttered when we were safe inside.

"No one cares or even thinks about rats," I said. "We're disposable. Kept as long as we're useful."

Wil eyed me as he stooped to set right the table and chairs. "Is that what Mordecai and Gan did? Kept you?"

I gave a start. "No," I said. "Not at all. They're different. We're a proper family. As proper as can be in the Below, at any rate."

"I'm glad for that. For your sake. Now what?"

"Now we wait," I said. "But first, let's get acquainted with our crew."

35. THE CREW

WHEN I OPENED THE CAGE DOOR, TEN RATS CLIMBED ONE OVER
another to cower in the farthest corner. Blending in and the
bottom of the pile were the only defenses left to them.

The shadows writhed with rags, limbs, and arms. Not a
one standing out from the rest. Wil had on a respirator, and it
was a good thing, because he'd likely have retched at the
smell. At least one in the crew was leaking pus.

It was easy to surmise that Crew One was driven by sheer
terror.

The look of panic in the handler's eyes as I drove my
blade into his heart warmed me. I stepped inside the corral
and lowered my cowl. Then I lifted my goggles. Wide eyes
rolled in filthy heads. Slowly the pack unwound, curiosity
replacing fear. No one expected a sun-touched rat.

"That's right," I whispered. "I'm your new handler." I
gave them a wink, and tossed down a satchel of food. Meat
pies, fresh bread, jerky, and fruit. And water. *Clean* water. Not
the filtered muck this lot was given. "Things will be different
around here from now on," I said. "But you got one more job
to do. Savvy?"

Small hands reached for the food, tucking it in close. I left them to mull that over. It pained me to close the cage door, but I needed them and I knew they'd run off if I left it open.

Wil was cracking his knuckles in the main room. The air was heavy with sweat and smelled reused. "You can remove your respirator," I said. "But you may not want to."

He did, and took a few tentative breaths. When he didn't start choking on toxins, he let the mask dangle from its chain. I turned to the desk and searched through the contract tickets. All rubbish jobs.

I gave a look around the room.

Wil kicked aside a ragged rug. "Here." He bent to pry up a loose floorboard, and sure enough there was a strongbox underneath it. I let him have a go at the lock. He wasn't as deft as Mordecai, or quick as me, but he got the job done. Wil left the searching to me. A few masques, a load of snips, and one prized sweeper's ticket—a work order sent from the higher-ups complete with time, date, and location. The same cycle as before, and only a few hours earlier than the gypsies' planned attack. Muck. Why couldn't my life be free of explosions? Was that too much to ask?

Wil bent over my shoulder to read it. "For all their might and finery, the Ministry still needs their pipes cleaned," he noted.

"It takes climbing skill," I said. "And small, disposable bodies."

"At least give them proper food and clothing. A clean bath—"

"Why?" I asked.

Anger flashed in his eyes. "*Why?*" he growled. "It's barbaric the way those children are treated."

I rolled my eyes at him. "'Course it is, but you're not

thinking like a lord. It's easy enough to get a new batch of rats."

"Not all lords are despicable," Wil said.

"And I'm not entirely full of muck."

He offered a hand, and I accepted. The moment our hands touched, I was fully aware of the man. Of the strength in his grip, the gentleness of his fingers, and the heat of his skin. For a moment, I felt like I was falling, the breath stolen right out of me. He pulled me up easily, and we stood nearly at eye level, the air between us charged as he held my gaze with his own.

I couldn't seem to find my tongue. Here was a complicated mess of a man, and all I could focus on was our naked palms pressed together. What would all of him feel like?

Wil let go of my hand. The contact was broken, and I cast around for something to say. So I went on the attack. It was always my best defense.

"What do you know of lords?" I asked. "You surprised me with that bow of yours to Miss Holly."

A shadow passed over his eyes. "I was born a lord's son."

My brows shot up. "Another sad story?" I asked.

He lifted a shoulder. "Not really." He took a seat, the weight of his physique testing the wooden chair. I took the other, and waited.

"I don't want to talk about me. My story is… common enough."

"Common? A lord?" I snorted. "You're talking to a rat here."

"I did notice. Your eyes are distinctive."

"Like you're one to talk."

He showed me his teeth. "Comes with my Knack. Fitting, I suppose. But really, how did you end up on the streets?"

"How'd you end up a pirate?" I shot back. I didn't like talking about myself either. There were too many gaps. Too many holes. Things about me that never added up. My birth for one, my death for another, and my rebirth for a beginning. How could I tell him what I didn't know?

36. INTO THE BELLY

OUR SWEEPER CREW WAS WILLING, EVEN EAGER ONCE I'D filled their bellies and explained the deal. They were mostly rats, with a few normal-eyed children in the mix who'd had the unfortunate luck to be born to shroom fiends or drunkards. They clutched junk respirators (likely the ones they were sold with) and every breath was a wheeze as they fought for air in the toxic fog.

If anyone else had come into their corral offering promises of freedom and wild plans, they'd have sneered behind their muck-covered faces. But I was one of them—a rat. Full kin. A verified red-eyed muck-born. And a sun-touched at that.

I spent most the cycle seeing to their wounds. Muck, coupled with sweat and lack of bathing, caused all types of skin infections. I'd watched Gan treat sweeper children before. Groin rot was the worst of it. Testicles fell right off. It wasn't a pretty end. I did what I could do for this lot. They were better off than most, considering their top spot in the pecking order. All of them had shaved heads. No handler wanted to deal with lice.

They didn't even flinch when I turned the hose on them.

Wil rifled through lockers and found clean but threadbare shirts and overalls for the lot. No one wanted filthy rats in their air shafts either.

Three of the sweepers had names: Tim, a quiet boy with open sores, who boasted he could climb a burning crane. Ena, a girl whose voice had been damaged by a noose put around her neck, and Crumb, a painfully small child who made runt sound like a tall word. The three of them had been sold by their kin. The other seven were nameless rats. Wil and I tended to them all.

I could hear his teeth grinding through the whole ordeal. He didn't like what was done to them any more than me. But his hands were gentle, and he kept his voice soft when he spoke to them.

Our time came, per contract, and with a nod to Wil I tucked the work order under the handler's greatcoat and donned the smelliest plague mask I hoped to never wear again. Handlers weren't keen on personal hygiene.

With whip in hand, I motioned the crew into a caged wagon, while Wil hitched up the horse. Then off we rolled, right past the gate guard.

"This is too easy," Wil muttered.

"No one pays any mind to rats," I reminded.

"Maybe, but I went through plenty of trouble to get information on that original contract." He took up over half the wagon bench and I was pressed up against his shoulder. I could feel his frustration. "It doesn't make sense that they'd just... hand over information like that to a second-rate Sweeper."

"Really, you did all the work?" I asked. "'Cause I can attest to the fact, by the bumping on my head, that Miss Holly did all the hard work."

He glanced at me. And I shrugged a brow.

"We paid for it," he said.

"You didn't see the lord she had to shag."

He was quiet as I navigated the streets. I took a detour, not a long one, but a needed one. I pulled the horse short at the mouth of a lane. A tall cloaked figure stepped out, followed by a smaller one wearing rags and a respirator designed to look worn. Mordecai and Bran. I didn't like this part of the plan. But Crumb, the little runt, had been wheezing so badly he could barely stand, and a sweeper crew, per union law, always needed ten cleaners and two handlers.

I handed off the reins to Wil and jumped down. "Psst, you, Crumb."

The boy cowered.

"Come on now."

Bran hopped into the wagon cage and picked the boy up. He was too weak to put up much fight. She handed him down, and I set him beside Mordecai. "This is my dad, here. He's got no legs and he needs help. Got it?"

Crumb wheezed.

I caught Bran's eyes behind her mask, and hesitated at the back of the wagon. There was nothing for it. I closed the cage door, then turned to Mordecai.

He pressed a silk pouch into my hands. "What's this?" I asked, even though I knew what it was. I just didn't know why he was giving it to me.

"In case you need a power source, or… things go badly."

I stared into the eyes of his mask. I wanted to say everything to him, but words got stuck in my throat. He lifted his respirator with his breath held and pressed his lips to my cheek. The mask popped back down before I had time to worry.

"Don't take any risks," he said, his voice muffled and hoarse.

Ah, muck it. There was a lump in my throat, and I couldn't even come back with something witty. I jumped back into the driver's seat and clucked the horse forward. I spared one look over my shoulder at the tall figure resting his hand on the shoulder of a little wheezing boy.

37. THE FERRYMAN

WE NAVIGATED THE LANES AND WAYS, AND FINALLY PULLED UP
to the designated dock. As before, when I'd scouted, there was
nothing but fog and the lap of water. The back of the wagon
was dead silent.

"The air feels… heavy," Wil muttered at my side.

"It's thick, it is." Visibility was low, a bare three feet even
to my eyes. The horse suddenly reared with a cry. I kept a
tight hand on the reins, but he danced and strained against
the bit. I set the brake, handed off the reins, and hopped
down to grab the reins under his chin. My presence seemed to
calm him, but he still danced nervously.

For all I knew we could be surrounded by a regiment of
Enforcers. This could be a trap. And I'd just rolled right into
it. We didn't have an exit plan. We didn't have a way out. We
didn't even know where we were going.

This was suicidal.

I stopped my wild thoughts before fear got a hold of me.
What was an answer worth? Answers were worth everything.
Without one Mordecai would die of a broken heart. And I

didn't think I could lose him, too. Closure was worth dying over.

The horse stamped uneasily, even with blinders on. I felt it too. Whatever *it* was. Cold fingers walking down your spine. Something dark brushing up against your foot in murky water. The crawl of tiny legs over your cheek. That's what it was— the unknown.

I pulled my collar close and stuck my eyes on the dense fogline. The rats in the back were quiet as could be.

Then I heard it, faintly at first. A creak, a groan, bone on bone, moving water. The horse reared, and I was nearly pulled off my feet.

"Shush, fellow. Calm down now," I urged.

A large, low shadow moved out of the fog along the water. It clunked against the dock, and a ramp crashed down.

I jumped back with the horse. A light bobbing in the murk illuminated sturdy planks spaced perfectly for a set of wagon wheels. It was a barge.

We waited for some seconds, but no one called us forward. I glanced back to Wil, but he was lost in the fog.

"Might as well," I muttered. I pulled on the horse's reins, but he didn't want to budge. Could you blame him? But I knew the crew wouldn't get on that barge if we uncaged them. They'd fly for sure.

Wil flicked the reins, and slowly, with my urging, the horse danced nervously forward. When I got to the far side of the barge, I pulled him to a stop and Wil set the brake.

Water lapped against the barge. Luminescent eels picked at its wood, and something large splashed beyond the fogline.

Have I mentioned my dislike for water?

Our terrified crew rushed to the far side of their cage, pressing against the wall closest to the driver's seat. I heard

Bran's urgent whisper to Wil, but couldn't make out her words.

The ramp clanked back in its place.

Who was behind us?

The barge lurched forward with a splash.

Wil turned in his seat, one hand straying to the knife on his belt. I kept a calming hand on the horse, hoping he wouldn't decide to leap in the water. Then I started edging around the wagon. It was a tight fit and there was no rail on the barge. No safety. Just the planks for the wagon wheels set right next to a short two foot plunge into crystal clear water. As I edged along the side, I tried to ignore a certain large glowing fish with spiky fins and a predator's confidence.

The rats were still crammed against the forward cage wall. Bran had her back to them, crouched in a protective stance with her eyes on the stern. She glanced at me, and though the mask hid her face, I could sense fear. "Careful," she hissed. "It's a greater elemental."

Muck. Now I had to look. I kept moving, drawn to the stern. And when I got there, I wished I'd stayed in the driver's seat. A massive, tentacled creature had wrapped itself around the stern of the barge. It glowed with a gentle, pulsing light as it pushed the barge across the Styx. Its luminous light drove the fog back, giving me a look at its handler.

A skiff followed alongside. A tall figure, cloaked in inky mist, stood in the boat. Its hands were chained to an oar. My feet slipped off the barge, but I caught myself on the wagon. At the splash of my feet, the tall figure lifted its head to look at me. A deep blackness dwelt beneath its cowl.

Mouth dry, I hurried back and scrambled onto the driver's seat. My hands were shaking.

"What is it?" Wil asked.

I was shivering so badly my teeth chattered behind the

respirator. I tore the thing off and gulped in air. The fog was fresh here, but so cold it stung my lungs.

Charon wasn't a myth.

But then I already knew that, didn't I? Those dark places of my mind were dark for a reason. I'd seen the Ferryman before.

BEFORE

I HIT THE WATER, AND FELT NO MORE. EVERY BONE CRUNCHED in my malnourished body. I drifted, weightless, as luminescent creatures wrapped around me.

I was still falling when something tugged me upwards, towards the dark. I remember pain.

I remember agony.

I remember a cowl of mist, and a face of nothing. An arm cradling me, and an ethereal hand passing over my lips. A figure leaned close, and a cold wind filled my lungs.

Savior.

AFTER

Yes. Death was my savior. He'd fished me right out of the Styx.

"Are you all right?" a voice was asking me.

I swallowed down memories, and hugged the smelly greatcloak to me. "I'm just peachy," I lied. "We're being pushed across the Styx by a sea monster and escorted by the Ferryman. Why wouldn't I be all right?"

Wil stared at me for a time. Then very deliberately faced forward. "That explains the lack of guards." It was said so matter-of-fact that I started shaking with quiet laughter.

We'd gone mad, you see. I was sure of it.

40. THE UNKNOWN

The barge clunked against a shore. Stone pillars marked a gateway, with torches flickering in front. Runes were etched into the stone. Though I'd never seen their like before, I could read the inscription.

Stop! This is the Empire of Death.

That's what Gan used to say about the state of my room.

Considering the drama of our journey, I was not expecting the empire of death to be a clock tower. There were fires fed by some unnatural means spewing from pipes jutting from the barren ground. The red flames burned back the fog. If you could call it fog. It was more like red mist twining around pools of light. The air felt heavy, and smelled faintly of rotten eggs. Sulfur.

And yet the pipes of red flame did illuminate a clock tower. It was tall and topped by a bizarre clock. A latticework of webs crisscrossed its face and red mist seeped from its sides.

"A star-taker," Wil whispered. "We use them to navigate the skies."

Navigation would have been nice about then. But no one came to give us direction. I looked for the Ferryman, but he had disappeared in the murk along with his sea monster. Why did I get the feeling that our sweeper crew wasn't meant to return? It would make sense. With enough masques as compensation, a sweeper lord wouldn't bat an eye over a dead crew.

Our horse eagerly crossed onto shore, and we set out along a pathway lit by burning torches. The outside of the clock tower was striated stone, a foreboding obsidian with deep vertical grooves. All slick stone, I knew, and solid. The tower could likely take a direct hit from a barrel bomb and only come away with a scorch mark.

"Why is red mist leaking from the star-taker?" Bran whispered at our backs.

I didn't know. But the cold coupled with the mist reminded me of the Ghostmakers. Muck. I didn't tell them that.

"I expected Enforcers," Wil whispered. "Not this."

We entered a circle of torches that marked the end of the 'road'. Wil pulled on the reins and the horse danced nervously, but there wasn't anywhere to go. I stepped down, and waited. The earth was frozen. The mist was frigid. Everything about the place felt *wrong*.

Beyond the torches shadows shifted in the mist, but nothing materialized inside the ring of fire. I shivered as I opened the cage door.

"You lot ready?" I asked.

They shook their heads.

"Come on now," Bran whispered. To set an example she stepped down from the wagon. But the rats held their ground, shivering something fierce. From cold, but mostly with terror.

I hated what I was about to do. I brandished the handler's whip. "Come on, out with you!" I needed to keep up appearances.

The crack of a whip in the air sent them scrambling. When my crew was huddled on the ground, I checked my pocket watch. Two hours. We had two hours before the Gypsies and Devils unleashed hell. Or died trying. I clicked it closed.

"You've been through worse than this, rats," I said. "Keep your chins up."

Bracing myself, I stepped out of the circle of torches towards the tower. Shadows shifted away. I touched the obsidian. Cool as ice. The rats gathered around me, bristling with their cleaning brushes and poles, and our hidden weapons. A door opened in the side of the tower.

"You're late." A plump, brown-haired woman with her hair pulled into a tight bun stood in the doorway. She wore a housekeeper's dress, and held a heavy ring of keys that could double as a murder weapon. She wore a half respirator.

"First time 'ere," I grunted. "Horse didn't like the barge."

She waved us to the grocer's entrance with a huff. Why wouldn't the *Empire of Death* need a grocery delivery every once in awhile? Maybe some boots repaired, or a hat or two delivered from the milliner?

The floors gleamed, the washbasin shone, and the soft light of lanterns contrasted with the angry flames outside.

The woman gave us a once over, and wrinkled her nose. "Don't touch anything. I'll show you to the shafts."

She led the way, then paused. I could see her counting us. Two handlers, ten rats to the crew. I held my breath, hoping she wouldn't spot something amiss with Bran.

To distract the housekeeper I asked, "What is this place?"

"You're not paid to ask questions," she snapped.

I shut my trap.

"Show me your ticket."

I did. The housekeeper took it from my hand, and with

barely a glance, led us to a hallway off the kitchen with an access hatch. She opened it up.

Fresh air blew from the air shaft. She checked her chain watch. "The fans will be shut off in a tick. You'll have an hour to sweep. No more." She turned on her heel and clicked away.

I waited for her steps to fade. "Right, you lot. We're not cleaning. We're searching. Savvy?"

The crew nodded.

41. THE WORST KIND

slick, the air stale, fans creaked and cobwebs grew in corners.
These air shafts hadn't been cleaned in years.

Mordecai had mapped our route, and as I stood staring
into the dark hole I realized he'd been right. The air shafts did
lead down.

I glanced at Bran and Wil. We'd talked it through before-
hand, and being the more experienced in tower burglaries, I'd
told them this was our best bet. But I was uneasy.

There was nothing for it. I climbed into the shaft.

Sweat cooled on my back as I braced to open the final
grate. It swung outward with a clang and I nearly bit my
tongue. A foot of water pooled far below, but it was clear and
there was stone underneath.

We'd passed no other grates. All paths led to this room,
deep under the clock tower. It felt like climbing into a

dungeon, and that gave me hope. If Gan was here, wouldn't he be kept in a dungeon?

The grate looked solid, so I hooked my toes on it and used it as a foothold, then a handhold. As I lowered myself down, my breath caught. An immense cavern stretched into shadow. Water dripped from stalactites, drops audible in the silence, and it wasn't a pleasant sound; it set me on edge like a fork running across a plate.

Below, rectangular blocks of obsidian were spaced at precise intervals on the cavern floor. I cinched a rope, and let the coil fall. After another search of the shadows, I slid down the line to land on one of the raised platforms. Eels swam around the obsidian blocks and I frowned at the thing. It was a sarcophagus—an ancient word that I happened to know the meaning of: Flesh Eater.

Without thought I hopped into the water. The rope wiggled as Wil started making his way down. I held up a hand, but he was too busy climbing to notice. Eels converged around my feet. I could feel them moving around my ankles. One latched its stickies in me but quickly let go, and they all moved away in a swarm. Why didn't their poison work on me anymore?

"Don't touch the water," I whispered, but the cavern took my voice and tossed it about in echoes.

"They should leave me be." His own deep voice joined my echo. He hopped down, and sure enough the eels fled. "Water elementals don't like Firestarters."

Together we pushed at the lid of the sarcophagus. It took our combined strength to budge it. Red mist seeped from the lid as it opened, and in the blue light of the eels we stared down into the face of a child.

42. FLESH EATER

Wil staggered back against a neighboring sarcophagus as if he'd been struck. A tattoo, a gypsy mark, was inked on the boy's arm.

I gripped Wil's shoulder. More for my own support than his. The child lay in a cradle of glass tubes and copper coils. Red mist swirled about him. There were needles stuck in the child's wrist and jugular, and tubes up his nose and in his mouth. Blood passed through tubing then over a blue flame, where vapor rose and gathered in a vial with a steady drip.

I knew enough of laboratory equipment to know what was going on. I'd seen a similar setup in Mordecai's workshop when he purified metals to get to the essence of a thing. His voice echoed in my mind. *"When you distill something, you boil it down to its essence. A distilled part is the most powerful."*

Poe had done it with rumor. Mordecai had distilled lightning. Why not distill sun-touched for their Knack? Because it was beyond evil. That's bloody why.

"They're harvesting gypsy children," I realized in horror.

The cavern seemed endless. How many thousands were here?

"He's still alive," Wil said.

Barely. Somehow that was worse. Better to be dead in that thing than half-alive. Wil started tugging at tubes, ripping them out of the child. I couldn't watch. I doubted the boy would survive.

We needed a way out of here. Where was the water coming from? There had to be an entrance. There had to be an exit.

I picked a direction and started walking, heading towards the far side of the cavern. But that was a mistake. My respirator didn't quite block out the stench. I moved it aside and sniffed, then gagged. Bile rose in my throat. I swallowed it down and put my respirator back in place. Quickening my pace, heedless of the splashing, I waded through rows of sarcophagi towards the stench.

I came across a lichen-covered gate at the far end. It was chained shut. I picked the lock in ten seconds flat. As I walked through, I knew what I'd find. The stench was unmistakable.

I took out a vial from a pocket, and shook it alive. Blue light came to life in the glass, illuminating walls built of child-sized skulls staring from the dark. A maze of them. How long had this been going on?

I moved farther into the maze. The skulls were larger. Older. I followed the smell until I came to a far chamber with another lichen-covered gate. Only this one was different. A pile of rotting gypsy children lay in front of the gate.

I wrenched off my respirator, and retched my guts out.

43. NIGHTMARE

A NOISE CAME FROM THE LARGE TUNNEL. A SHUFFLING SOUND.

I rushed to the second gate, and shoved my arm through the massive bars. My light pushed at darkness. There, just beyond, a shadow moved in the tunnel.

"Who are you!" I called. My voice echoed, but I didn't care. I was fuming and itching for a fight. "What do you know of these children?"

The thing moved away. I noticed a loose bar off to the side. It wasn't even attached. I gave it a yank, then slipped through and raced down the tunnel, my light illuminating metal train rails under the murk.

The shadow lumbered, hunched, and with a pronounced gimp, but it kept moving just outside the range of my light. Anger propelled me, and I launched myself at the thing. I tackled it, and we went down in the water. But the figure wasn't as solid as I imagined. It was frail, maybe human, and wearing a tattered, muck-stained cloak.

I put my knife to the thing's throat. My vial was bobbing in the water, and it illuminated the twisted face of a woman. Her hair was braided and gray. The wrinkles in her face were so defined that they nearly swallowed her milky eyes. Her lips rolled over toothless gums.

"Who are you?" I demanded.

"Please. Please," she begged, her voice a wisp of sound.

She didn't seem to be able to breathe, so I got off her and moved my blade away from her throat. She blindly searched the water, until her frail hands found a basket. She clutched it to her breast, cowering against the tunnel wall.

"The dead children…" The words burned in my throat. "Why are you here?"

She cocked her head and sniffed the air. It sounded like a Sniffer. "I know your scent," she whispered. "It's faint, but it's still there."

"What do you have to do with this hell?" I shouted.

She patted the air, until she found me. But when her fingers circled my arm she was no longer frail. Her fingers were claws, long and reaching. I tried to back away, but her grip was steel.

She brought up her right hand and opened it. An eye blinked at me from the middle of her palm. I tore my arm free, earning a rip of claws and a low cackle.

"I'm born of dark dreams," she said with a click of sharp teeth. "I lurk in shadows, in filth, in forbidden thoughts. I am *Nightmare.*"

With every word, she grew in size, the shadows gathering to her like a cloak. I edged backwards. She towered over me, her head brushing the tunnel ceiling.

Then I stopped and held my ground, my jaw firm. "I have no nightmares," I said. "Life is plenty enough for me."

The shadow dimmed in size, and she wheezed out a laugh. "True, true enough, child. This place is such. I prefer Mara, by the way." Her lips peeled back, revealing rows of fangs.

I'd drawn my knife at some point, and now I tightened my

grip. "Those children. Do you have something to do with them?"

"I could never." Mara shook her head. "It's worse than anyone could dream, isn't it?" she whispered.

"I'll make whoever did this pay," I vowed.

"Some survive," she said, and took a step towards me, but she was small and frail again, so I held my ground. She seemed to feed off fear.

"You mean the children?" I asked.

She brought up a clawed hand, and hesitated. "If I may?"

Since she asked so politely, I nodded. Her hand turned, and the claws opened, so she might study me with that eye in her palm.

A claw caressed my arm. "*You* survived," she whispered.

I swallowed. It couldn't be.

"They dump children in the cave. I come every day to search for survivors."

I glanced back towards the pile of rotting carcasses. "What do you do with the survivors?" But I knew, already, didn't I? In my heart, I knew.

"He drains them of their essence. Takes the glow right out of them. I carry them off and lay them in the muck along the Styx." She tapped my goggles. I nudged them up, and stared her in the eye. "Rats, they call them. Red eyes. But they've been drained of spirit, so they never live long."

44. BREATHE

LET'S TAKE A BREATH. I FEEL THIS KIND OF DISCOVERY NEEDS A moment to settle. To truly sink in and appreciate what was done to us rats. What was taken from us.

Now. Are you angry?

You bloody should be.

I SHOOK WITH FURY. "DO YOU CUT MARKS OFF THEIR BODIES?"

"The mark he gives them. Yes."

She didn't know. Mara thought the butcher marked the children, like a slave brand.

I rubbed at the raw patch of skin on my upper arm. "Why don't I remember?"

Mara inclined her head down the tunnel, towards the pile of dead. "Would you want to remember that?"

No. No I wouldn't. And I wished I could scrub that room from my mind. "Why don't you *do* something? Tell someone?"

She snapped her hand closed, and wheezed, her breath a noxious mix of garlic and oranges. "Nightmare has no power over Evil."

"What else is in the Clocktower?"

"The Red Death," Mara whispered. "Beware. He pollutes everything he touches." She started to shuffle away.

"*Wait.*"

But she kept shuffling.

"Help me get the children out of here!"

Mara stopped.

"This whole place will be bombed soon," I said.

Mara tilted her head. "Better to die, isn't it?"

"No!" I hissed. "No, it's not. I'm thankful you saved me. You gave me a chance. That's all I'm asking for those children. No matter how small a chance it is."

Mara turned to face me. "You survived. But you're dead now, child."

Her words hit me like a gut punch.

"And yet… you're alive."

"What the muck does that mean?" I demanded.

"You walk the realm of life and death; of earth and air; of fire and water. You stand at the Crossroads."

"Where's that?"

"*Between.*"

Why did I think I'd get a straight answer from a nightmare? "What am I, then?"

"You are the Fifth—the binding element."

"What does that mean?" I asked urgently.

"That you should not be."

I growled. I was tired of hearing that. "And yet I am."

"Such is Bedlam," she admitted. "Bring the children here."

"Swear it?"

"My word is enough."

I had no choice. I raced back down the tunnel to find most of our crew standing stunned on a few sarcophagi. The red-eyed among them looked haunted, and I wondered if a part of them knew they'd been here before.

Bran was prying open a lid with a sweeper pole, tears leaking from her mask, while Wil was shoulders deep in a sarcophagus. He looked up at my approach. "They're drugged, or… I don't know. They keep *dying* when I unhook them!" His voice was raw.

"There's a woman in the tunnels...past the dead. She'll help us get out."

"We can't leave them!" Wil snapped.

There were too many children. We were too powerless. There wasn't enough time. Unless… I leapt on top of an unopened sarcophagus, and ran full speed over their tops, jumping from one to another, until I spotted an iron stairway that led up to a door. I hit the stairs and up I went, but the iron door at the top was barred. Of course it was. They were never planning on letting the sweeper crew leave.

Worse yet, I heard the fans knock, and air started flowing out from the vents with a rattle. There'd be no climbing back up through the air shafts now.

Muck.

And then my day got even worse—red mist began seeping under the cracks in the door.

"*Ghostmakers!*" I yelled.

46. GHOSTMAKER

I BACKED DOWN THE STAIRS AS A BAR SCRAPED ON THE OTHER side. There was no use drawing my weapons. I knew what they did to air.

The iron door creaked open and a being of mist and shadow filled the doorway. Blood-red tendrils dripped from its fingers, coiling outwards like a nest of snakes.

"We have no need of you anymore," the thing hissed, drifting fully into the cavern. Bran fired her pistol, but the lead passed right through, dinging the stone at its back. Wil and Bran were helpless in the Below without their Knacks.

"Run to the tunnel!" I shouted.

For a split second, my sweeper crew looked about to bolt, but then they converged on the open sarcophagi, hoisting what children they could between them.

"You cannot run," the Ghostmaker said. Like a breath, red mist spilled down the stairway. My lungs burned with cold, as ice formed and spread, cracking over the water.

A warm draft of air tickled my ears. I glanced back. Air streamed from an air shaft. Its current ran strong, spiraling downwards, pushed by the fans, so that bloody housekeeper could tend the children. That's why they needed air here.

I ripped off my goggles and respirator, and inhaled. Air filled my lungs. It filled me to the tips of my toes.

The Ghostmaker drew back. "The impossible."

"What did you do with my friend, eh?"

Its round black eyes fixed on me. Mist swirled, and formed a curving smile in the blackness under its cowl. "Feassting." Whipping coils lashed outward. Wil yelled a warning, hurrying to my defense, but I answered with an attack of my own. Air slammed into the whip, and pushed it back.

I gathered the air to me, and leapt. I was light as a feather, and swift as wind. I crashed into the thing with all my fury. The red mist dispersed in a poof. Then reformed in a hallway beyond the open door.

Wind swirled around me, my hair a wild mess of curls, as power infused my bones. The Ghostmaker threw itself at me. I was knocked back, and my wind scattered. A cold shadow descended, sucking the breath from my lungs, tugging at some inner part of me.

The red mist pushed its way into my nostrils and climb down my throat. I choked on the air. But I was a rat. I'd grown up on this muck.

Death himself had breathed life into me.

I took a deep, willing breath, and sensed the moment the Ghostmaker realized its mistake. I searched for that something —the source that made him *be*. Then I reached out, my hand swirling with dark light, and crushed it.

The mist evaporated.

I lay on my back gasping for air. My whole body trembled with exhaustion. I felt drained and limp as a dead fish.

"Evie?" Bran's face hovered above me, her hands hot on

my cheeks. I was too cold to shiver. "Evie? What did you do?" she whispered.

I gulped in air like it was medicine.

Wil was standing over us, sword in hand. *"Listen,"* he hissed.

I heard it, faintly.

Bran helped me to my feet, while Wil moved towards the distant sound. Down the hallway and up another stairwell. I tried to follow but staggered, so Bran put her shoulder under my weight. Together, we shuffled down the hallway.

Wil kicked down a door. I heard pistol shots. The housekeeper came running down the hall, her keys rattling. "You're not supposed to be here!" she screeched.

Wil came back out of the doorway. He grabbed the woman by the throat and slammed her against the wall. "Are there others?" he demanded.

She fumbled for a knife at her belt. He ripped it from her hand and tossed it down the hallway. There was movement at the end of it, as a uniformed Ministry guard rounded a corner. Wil put a bullet between his eyes.

"Answer me!"

"No others," the housekeeper croaked. "This is the only nursery."

A nursery. Of course. The Ministry took infants, too. They had to wait for the children to be strong enough to survive the distilling process.

"Who do you serve?" he hissed.

"I... I ... the children."

"Then why do you let them *die?*" he demanded.

Bran left me to rush into the nursery. I braced myself against a wall, then forced myself to move. The door to the nursery was open. Toddlers sat on caged beds. They were clean, well fed, but wide-eyed with terror, while infants wailed in cradles. There were more than I knew what to do with.

Three bodies lay dead on the floor. One woman, two men. They wore crisp Ministry uniforms.

"Are there any more of you?" Wil demanded.

"Yes, of course. The nurses."

Wil nodded to Bran, who took off down the hallway in search of nurses. I chased after, following blasts of pistol fire, the smell of black powder, and the sound of ringing swords. I found Bran plunging a dagger in a Ministry man's throat.

Somewhere high above an alarm sounded. Muck. We needed to leave. Now. But I had to find Gan first. The thought of him brought back all my training.

I planted my feet in horse stance, and focused my mind. Deep breath in, slow breath out like a crashing wave. Air invigorated my muscles, and my breath stoked a fire deep inside my core. Opening my eyes, I plucked up a guard's sword and stalked forward as the first explosion rattled the sky.

The gypsies had begun their assault.

47. UP

BETWEEN BRAN AND ME, WE ROUNDED UP ANOTHER FOUR nursemaids, and marched them past a hallway of dead guards.

"Don't wait for me," I told her.

She stopped, started to argue, but looked into my eyes. Her respirator hung from its strap around her neck. Quick as could be, she stood on her toes to kiss my lips. "Best come back."

"Don't ever doubt it," I said.

A thunder of boots sounded from a stairwell. I darted for the door and threw my weight against it. A quick turn of a crank, and the locks clicked into place. Right, now what?

"Oi!" I yelled down the hallway. "Housekeeper."

Bran dragged the pale woman into the hallway. "Where would I find the adult prisoners here?"

"There aren't any," she said.

"There has to be!" I hissed.

"Perhaps…" She faltered, her eyes rolling towards the ceiling in what I feared was a swoon. "We don't go to the upper levels," she whispered.

Bran yanked her back into the nursery as I pondered my next move.

Enforcers on the stairwell. Right. I walked into what looked like a sitting room, and kicked out a stained glass window. There was only one way to go.

48. SHOWDOWN

I DID WHAT I DO BEST: CLIMBED. THE STRIATIONS ON THE clock tower made a nice corner for me to brace against. I pushed my arms and legs outwards against opposing faces to support my weight. It was all about pressure and balance, like standing on a wall, but this obsidian was slick and dangerous.

Maybe this wasn't my brightest idea.

Distant explosions seemed a lifetime away as I made my way up, always keeping three points of contact with the wall. The gypsies and pirates were throwing their might against the Ministry. A suicidal diversion. One that I was thankful for at the moment.

Red mist pushed down on me from above, but I'd taken the air currents with me. Don't ask me how. I just did. Wind swirled around me. Not in a playful way, but in agitation. Nervousness? No. It was anger.

Questions chattered in my mind. A dangerous thing when you're off the ground. Did I have a Knack for air? But then how had I survived a sarcophagus with my Knack intact? And how was I using it now, in the Below?

There was something else I didn't know: had my eyes

glowed before that day Mordecai and Gan found me? The day I woke up in a bone orchard. There was no use for it. And no answers up here. Only impossibilities.

I bashed through the first stained glass window I came across. Then crouched on the sill, looking into a stone corridor. The air was frigid, and the hallway nearly empty. Mist coated everything. Mist and moss. Save for two drag marks on the floor.

I hopped inside, crunching on glass, and crept forward, passing a whole row of stained glass windows. Between the windows, pools of shadow gathered. Those pools didn't seem natural, so I kept my steps in red light. A door at the end of the hallway beckoned.

I itched to draw my knives, but what good would steel do against Ghostmakers? Instead I took in a deep breath, and blew it out. Wind snatched at my hair and swirled around me like a cloak.

I stalked to the end of the corridor, and nudged one of the double doors open. The chamber beyond held the faces of four massive star-takers, one on each side of the tower's square top. Staircases climbed and joined under each clock face below rafters that stretched above them into shadow.

Giant hands ticked, gears caught gears, their teeth grinding. Bells hanging overhead were silent for now. Steam hissed along a maze of pipes and tubing. The clock chamber reminded me of a giant-sized version of Mordecai's workshop.

Red mist seeped out from the star-taker faces to blanket the floor and roil with a life of its own. Everything centered around a man chained in the middle of the floor. He was pale, thin, and young, weighed down by chains and with tubes and coils spilling from him like a cloak of horrors. But my gaze flitted past the chained man to fix on another. A second man was suspended by a chain from a rafter, his toes barely touching the floor and his arms stretched painfully above him. Blood dripped down his familiar features. His ribs were stark against bruised skin and his every breath a battle.

Gan was alive. Barely.

I wanted to run to him, but I was no fool. Shadows surrounded him. Feasting. On what, I didn't know. I slipped into the room, and took cover behind a stone pillar. But any hope of stealth was shattered when a voice echoed in the chamber.

"Brilliant, isn't it?" the voice said. Male and confident, he leaned on a topmost railing peering down at his masterpiece. He wore a mask of white with black eyes, and a gentleman's suit and coat. His gloved hands rested on a long staff with a stylized serpent coiled up its length.

The Ghostmakers drifted away from Gan. Four in all. They spread out, moving silently along the walls. I braced myself between two pillars and climbed.

Flashes of light flickered beyond the star-taker faces. The figure turned towards them. "It took the natives long enough to work up the nerve, didn't it?"

"You ever get lonely talking to yourself?" I asked, reaching up and around to pull myself onto a lip of decoration.

"I have my inventions to keep me company." He had a cultured, high-class accent that hinted he thought highly of himself. "And I have guests often enough, such as your friend here. Muunokhoi Ganbataar. Roughly translated into proper as 'Vicious Dog, Steel Hero.' Lovely isn't it? That I should be so honored to host a hornless dragon from Song Mountain."

Song Mountain? Those titles meant nothing to me. I paused at the transition from pillar to rafter to glance down at Gan. He raised his eyes to me. One was swollen completely shut, the other full of blood. He gave a small shake of his head.

Muck him, I thought. I'd fallen for Gan's 'Run!' routine before, and I wasn't about to fall for that again. What did he think? That I'd come all the way up here to tell myself, "Oh, this looks tricky. Might as well go home now."

The Ghostmakers were milling about on the floor, their tendrils of mist twining upward in the four corners of the chamber.

"Sorry to disappoint you, but my name isn't so grand. What's yours?"

"How rude of me." His mask turned towards me. "General Thomas Black."

"I'm fairly sure the proper translation for that is scum."

"So shortsighted." He considered me as I walked across the rafters. This high up, the bells obscured my view of Gan and the Ghostmakers. "I see you don't appreciate what I've accomplished."

I frowned at a grouping of copper tubes that were caked in ice; other pipes hissed with steam. Everything seemed connected to the man in the center of the room. "What is this? Some type of giant fog machine?" I asked.

"Something like that," he drawled. "Why don't you come into the light where I can see you."

I walked across a rafter, so I could look down at the General. "Here I am."

Although fixed, the movement of his mask seemed to change his expression from disapproval to consideration. He gestured at the chamber. "All of this was made with purpose. But you… you're serendipity."

I wrinkled my nose. "I don't like that word," I said casually strolling along the rafters, drifting closer. The Ghostmakers' tendrils were climbing. How far could they reach?

"What would you use?" Black asked.

"Dumb luck?" I waggled my brows down at him. I couldn't see his eyes, but I could see his shoulders stiffen.

"You're a curiosity, to be sure. You shouldn't *be*."

"That's what your minions down there said."

"I will enjoy studying you," he said.

"No foreplay? Just straight to the dirty bits?"

"Would you trust any offer I made?"

"No."

The mask smiled. A trick of the light. A tilt of the head, I don't know, but I swear it did. "So you're making a bunch of fog and killing children. Why pat yourself on the back for that?"

He spread his hands. "The natives of An Aisling proved… disagreeable. Bedlam, especially. I spent years quashing uprisings, until I made a discovery—a mineral that suppresses the troublesome elemental powers of the natives. Llyr here," he gestured to the man chained to the floor, "has an exceptional Knack for water. He keeps the fog thick—my delivery system for the Red Death. It keeps everyone in their place."

"And then you started distilling their essence," I said. I leapt ten feet to another set of rafters, directly above the platform where Black stood. "So you could do… what? Conquer the rest of An Aisling?"

Black laughed. "I could crush this land and bring it to heel as surely as I've brought Bedlam under my foot."

I pointed at the flashes of cannon fire outside a clock face. "Doesn't look like you have the natives crushed to me."

The General clucked his tongue. "The battle makes an excellent exercise for my men. They grow restless without something to fight. You're nothing more than cattle let out to pasture. We need you to reproduce, so we can harvest your Knack."

"And then what?" It took effort to keep my voice even.

The General tilted his head towards the Ghostmakers. "I create unstoppable soldiers."

"If you can crush us already, *why* do you need unstoppable warriors?"

"There are greater wars on greater fronts."

"Huh. So here you are stuck on some backwater mining gig. Did you fall out of favor with your Sage King?"

The General slammed his staff down on the platform. The red mist changed course, their tendrils retracted and all four Ghostmakers converged on Gan.

"*Stop!*" I shouted. Wind caught my hair and swirled around me, ready to leap at the creatures.

"Come down here."

Gan was lost to me in red and shadow, but the chain he hung from quivered. He was convulsing. Without a moment's thought, I leapt down onto the general's platform, drew my pistol and fired. My bullet hit him in the heart. But he didn't fall. He remained upright, red mist seeping from the hole in his suit.

The General started laughing. Red mist began seeping from his mask, from the sleeves of his dark coat, and from the edges of his collar. "As I said, I will enjoy studying you." Tendrils lashed out at me. I dropped my pistol and thrust out my hands. Wind slammed into mist, cutting through his attack. I launched myself at the man, drew my knives, and went on the attack. I was a dervish of steel and air, wind moving with me, driving me, making me light as a feather.

His mask cracked under my blade.

And then the cold came. Four shadows converged on me at once, and their poison climbed into my throat. The wind around me died. When the first Ghostmaker reached inside of me, I thrust out a hand and dark light flared. I crushed its presence. Then another. But the air was still and so cold. There was no wind to draw upon, and what breath I had was freezing in my lungs.

I fell to my knees with a raspy cry, and struck out blindly.

"Don't kill her," the General said. His voice was so assured, so self-important. What was I but an annoying rat?

Every bone in my body ached with agony. I shivered so badly, I feared my teeth would crack against each other. Gasping on the ground, I fumbled for the case at my belt. My numb fingers curled around a glass tube.

"Here's death for you," I hissed with the last of my breath, then slammed the tube onto the stone. It bounced without breaking.

Muck!

I watched it, dumbstruck, through a fading tunnel of red as it rolled right to the edge of the platform and dropped off the side.

A faint *tink*, and the essence of lightning burst into the clock tower.

49. LAST RESORT

White hot light streaked outwards. The star-takers exploded with a rain of glass, pipes burst, ice cracked, and the red mist vaporized in a flash of searing light. A bolt hit me straight on, rattled my bones, decided it didn't care for me, and shot right out into the fogline.

Everything hurt. I smelled fire, too. I rolled over to suffocate the flames on my coat, then dragged myself forward. I was dazed and numb, as I watched lightning crackling across the fogline. With every charge, the fog thinned, then lifted, exposing a night sky.

Airships fought and burned. Aeroplanes buzzed and eagles swooped. It was a slaughter. The Ministry was winning. A great maze of buildings and canals, of rivers and lakes stretched as far as I could see under the moon. I watched it all flat on my stomach with my chin on the edge of the stone platform, as wind whipped through the shattered clock faces.

Gan.

What had I done? I rolled to the side, groaning, and came face to face with the shards of a white mask and a pile of clothes dumped on the platform. I reached for the wind, and it came, swirling around me in defense.

I searched the darkness but if it held any shadow, I couldn't tell. Using a remnant of railing still standing, I pulled myself up. The chamber was in ruins. Half the roof had caved in, bringing down a mountain of rafters, bells, and stones. A bell had landed beside Llyr, falling timbers had got caught on the brass before they could crush him. He was weakly pulling tubes from his veins.

Off to the side, buried in smoldering wreckage, I spotted a body. Gan. I ran to the stairs and nearly fell, half slid, half stumbled, till I collapsed on top of him. Burns marred his back. He wasn't moving.

"You can't die," I breathed. Panic clutched at my heart. I made myself stop, and took a deep, calming breath, then rolled him over. He wan't breathing. I put an ear to his chest. Nothing.

I screamed with rage, and slammed my fists on his chest. "No!" Again. "You mucking bastard!" I yelled, hitting him again. "Not like this. Not now." Again, I hit him. "Breathe!"

In answer to my plea, the wind around me stirred, then pushed into his slack-jawcd mouth. His chest rose. Once. "*Breathe*," I begged. I brought my fists down on his chest, over his heart.

Another gasping breath.

I put an ear to his chest again. *Thump. Thump. Thump.* A thready whisper of a beat. "Breathe," I whispered through tears. His chest rose, then he gasped and jerked awake.

I looked down into his one good eye. It rolled with confusion, until he finally focused on me. My tears dripped onto his skin, and I held his hand like a lifeline. "Muunokhoi Ganbataar?" I asked. "I'm happy as muck you didn't name me."

Gan coughed out a bloody laugh.

50. A BEGINNING

WHAT CAN I SAY ABOUT THE REST? WE TOOK OUR BATTERED
selves from that clock tower, the wounded supporting the near
dead. We limped along, hoping Luck himself would keep us
upright through that long, abandoned tunnel.

Those children big enough to carry infants did, though
they themselves should've been carried. We adults managed
the rest, while Gan and Llyr dragged themselves forward with
sheer determination.

We emerged on the banks of the Styx with near to a
hundred children. The rats gawked, but those we rescued—
the Lost—they just stood silent and stared at nothing.

Wil and Bran turned their eyes towards the stars, but they
weren't looking with amazement. It was dread. The sky
burned with airships.

Gan glanced heavenward, his face grim. "You've done it
now, Evie."

I had, hadn't I? The Above was laid bare to the denizens
Below. All the towers, the airships and sky isles, and the bright,
searing sun.

What would become of us now?

That, my friend, is another story.

But even as I pen this one, Mordecai is standing over my shoulder reading. He says my grammar could use improvement and my penmanship leaves something to be desired.

This is *my* story. And I'll tell it as I wish, so…

MUCK OFF

AFTERWORD

If you enjoyed Windwalker and would like to read more of the series, *please* show your support by leaving a review.

Reviews help authors keep writing stories you love. Without support from readers, authors are forced to move on, and sequels are never written.

Want to stay up to date on new releases and announcements? Sign up to my mailing list at www.sabrinaflynn.com/news

ACKNOWLEDGMENTS

A huge thank you to the usual suspects who helped polish my latest creative adventure.

To Erin Bright for her creative advice and helping me with A/C duct work and airflow systems.

Merrily Taylor for her developmental critique and constant support. What would I do without you? And to Alice Wright for her "super-fan" support!

To Lyn Brinkley-Adams, who for some reason will take the time to read anything I write. I owe you double thanks, because I forgot to mention you in my last book!

Rich Lovin for his honesty and sharp eyes. To Jinny and Vivien for their hair care tips. And finally, but not least, Tom Welch, who had a time arguing with Evie over her grammar choices. (I don't know what I'd do without my line editor!)

And of course I'd like to thank the aliens that designed the cool chapter headers. I'm not joking. My cover designer, Merrybookround, had to check on the copyright legality of using a symbol purportedly created by aliens. Hopefully they won't come angrily knocking…

ABOUT THE AUTHOR

Sabrina Flynn is the author of the bestselling ***Ravenwood Mysteries*** set in Victorian San Francisco. When she's not exploring the seedy alleyways of the Barbary Coast, she dabbles in fantasy and steampunk, and has a habit of throwing herself into wild oceans and gator-infested lakes.

Although she's currently lost in South Carolina, she's lived the majority of her life in perpetual fog and sunshine with a rock troll and two crazy imps. She spent her youth trailing after insanity, jumping off bridges, climbing towers, and riding down waterfalls in barrels. After spending fifteen years wrestling giant hounds and battling pint-sized tigers, she now travels everywhere via watery portals leading to anywhere.

You can connect with her at any of the social media platforms below or at www.sabrinaflynn.com